Praise for Lee Harris's Manhattan Mysteries

"Lee Harris . . . gives us a new detective and a grittier neighborhood in *Murder in Hell's Kitchen,* but her storytelling skill remains top quality."

—TONY HILLERMAN

"Lee Harris is a good writer and she has a winner here."

—*Mysterious Women*

"Harris knows a lot about cops and a lot about women and she knows how to plot a good mystery. *Murder in Hell's Kitchen* is so believable I kept expecting to read more about the case in the morning papers."

—STEPHEN GREENLEAF

"If you enjoy police procedurals, look no further than *Murder in Hell's Kitchen.* An absolute knockout of a novel about law enforcement officers as human beings."

—JEREMIAH HEALY

Praise for Lee Harris's Christine Bennett Mysteries

"Harris's holiday series . . . [is] a strong example of the suburban cozy."

—*Ellery Queen's Mystery Magazine*

"Inventive plotting and sharp, telling characterization make the Lee Harris novels a pure pleasure."

—ROBERT BARNARD

"A not-to-miss series."

—*Mystery Scene*

By Lee Harris

The Manhattan Mysteries

Murder in Hell's Kitchen
Murder in Alphabet City

The Christine Bennett Mysteries

The Good Friday Murder
The Yom Kippur Murder
The Christening Day Murder
The St. Patrick's Day Murder
The Christmas Night Murder
The Thanksgiving Day Murder
The Passover Murder
The Valentine's Day Murder
The New Year's Eve Murder
The Labor Day Murder
The Father's Day Murder
The Mother's Day Murder
The April Fools' Day Murder
The Happy Birthday Murder
The Bar Mitzvah Murder

MURDER IN ALPHABET CITY

LEE HARRIS

BALLANTINE BOOKS • NEW YORK

Murder in Alphabet City is a work of fiction. Names, characters, places, and incidents are the products of the author's imagination or are used fictitiously. Any resemblance to actual events, locales, or persons, living or dead, is entirely coincidental.

A Fawcett Book
Published by The Random House Publishing Group

www.ballantinebooks.com

ISBN 0-449-00735-9

Manufactured in the United States of America

First Edition: January 2005

OPM 9 8 7 6 5 4 3 2 1

For Jim Wegman,
my friend and co-conspirator

ACKNOWLEDGMENTS

My deepest thanks to James L.V. Wegman for the enormous amount of work he put into this book and every mystery I have written. Special thanks to my friend Lora Roberts for sharing her knowledge about beads, to my friend Jonnie Jacobs for a great three-letter word, and to my friend Carol Walsh for saying "Do it!" Thanks to my editor, Pat Peters, for all her hard work. Thanks also to my New York City research team: retired police officer Luis Liendo, a veteran of the Nine; and to Allyson Wegman and Bob Koleba, students of the city and its history.

LEE HARRIS

Required in every good lover . . . the whole alphabet . . .
Agreeable, Bountiful, Constant, Dutiful . . .

—Miguel de Cervantes, *Don Quixote*

1

ONE GOOD THING about working on cold cases was that no one dragged your ass out of bed at three in the morning to look at a still-warm body. The only warm bodies in cold cases were the investigators', and occasionally there was some reasonable doubt about that. Today everybody was cold, but that was due to the weather, which wasn't likely to change anytime soon. The sky over Manhattan was dull gray, thick, and impermeable. The air held so much moisture, her skin felt wet as she walked to 137 Centre Street from the subway.

The police surgeon had given Jane Bauer, forty years old and newly promoted to detective first grade, the OK to return to work from sick report after the holidays. He suggested workouts at the gym and walking to work to get the muscles back into condition, but it was too cold to follow the second directive. She had returned last week to a desk full of paperwork and an office almost crackling with incipient spasms of electricity. Her partners disliked each other—she smiled at her understatement of the situation—and she was actually relieved to find them both alive and sniping when she first set foot in the office.

"Morning, Detective," Annie, the police administrative aide, said, brushing past her on the run.

"Morning."

Gordon Defino was hanging his coat on the hook when she entered the office. "New case this morning," he said.

"About time. Another day of paper pushing and I might ask for a transfer."

Sean MacHovec, as expected, crossed the threshold at exactly eight forty-five, the start of the 9×5 tour, nine to five in ordinary speech. How the hell does he do it? Jane wondered. They exchanged good mornings.

"Annie says we get a new case today. Old enough to smell bad. Coffee?"

Defino grunted. Jane articulated a syllable. MacHovec, happy to have an excuse to leave the office, departed.

"Nothing changes," Defino said.

Jane laughed.

Defino gave a grudging grin. "Sharpens your sense of humor."

MacHovec with coffee and Annie with nothing in hand arrived simultaneously.

"You're wanted in the whip's office pronto," Annie said. She looked at all of them but let her eyes rest on MacHovec, whom she hated. MacHovec returned her message and stare with a grin that told her he outranked her and she served him, regardless.

They took their Styrofoam cups and ambled over to Captain Graves's office. He leaned over the desk to shake Jane's hand.

"How're you feeling?"

"I'm fine, thanks. But I think I'm scarred for life." She said it lightly, although it bothered her whenever she looked in a mirror. A faint discoloration marred her right cheekbone, proof of the beating the rest of her body had recovered from.

"A little plastic surgery'll take care of that. I can give you a name if you'd like."

"I'll think about it." She wondered if the handsome Graves knew from personal experience.

"This isn't exactly a cold case, Detectives." He laid a palm on a thick file sitting on his desk. "A schizophrenic man in his thirties, Anderson Stratton, lived over near Tompkins Square Park—Alphabet City. He was known in the neighborhood, apparently liked, usually approachable, although he had his down times, spent some time in hospitals. Bottom line: He was found dead in his room, emaciated, apparently having starved to death."

"Autopsy?" MacHovec asked.

"Yes. Other things turned up—he didn't take very good care of himself—but nothing that could have caused his death."

Jane waited. Something was coming. Homicide detectives, especially from a special assignment squad, didn't spend their time looking for a killer in a case of starvation.

"Stratton came from a high-profile family. The parents didn't live in New York, but the power extended up to the governor. And there's a sister." He paused and let the obvious sink in. She didn't believe her brother had died of starvation. "She's been pushing this as a homicide without success since the day the body was found."

"So this is a PR job," MacHovec said in his usual blunt manner.

"Now we're getting heat from One PP. What's new is that she's a friend of the commissioner. We'd like to put the case to rest. I'm asking you to do a stroke job," Graves admitted.

MacHovec groaned, one of his unendearing little habits. Jane tensed. This was not the venue to vent one's feelings.

Graves went on as though he hadn't heard. "There's a lot of paper in the file. I'm asking you to rustle it around and add another pound of Fives to the pile."

"Are the parents still alive?" Jane asked.

"The mother is but she's not well and not involved. The sister is Flavia Constantine." That was the punch line he had held back.

"Gregory Constantine's wife?" MacHovec asked, a hint of awe in his voice.

"Ex. But you got the connection. See if you can make her happy. I'm asking you to stroke this thing and put it back in the file. Reopen the autopsy report. See if there are any neighbors still living in the building who remember him.

"And there's something else." Graves pulled a sheet of paper from beneath the file. "Mrs. Constantine hired a private investigator to look into the death, guy who was on the job, name's Wally Shreiber. He said, interview the super; the name's here. You can interview Shreiber too, if you want. He's not a dope and he didn't come up with anything."

"How long you want us to work on this?" Defino asked. A practical man, he was looking forward to the next real case, the sooner the better.

"Enough time that it looks like you did a thorough job. Talk to the sister first. Her number's clipped to the file jacket. Be nice to her. You know what I'm saying? She's not doing this to make a buck. She cares."

MacHovec looked ready to get up and go. His coffee cup was empty.

But Graves wasn't finished. "This originated as an aided case. Some neighbors called the police. They're all in the Fives." He tapped the file. "Any questions?"

There weren't any. That was it. MacHovec grabbed the file and his coffee cup and led the way out of the whip's office and over to theirs. "Babysit a fucking socialite," he grumbled as Defino closed the door. He dropped the file loudly on Jane's desk.

The note paper-clipped on top was in Graves's handwriting on six-by-nine notepaper. "This is her private number," Jane said.

"Maybe she'll send a private car for us," Defino said. "She can afford it. When did Stratton die?"

Jane opened the folder. "Eight years ago last November."

"If you think she'll take us to lunch, I'll come along," MacHovec offered. He was the desk man. His partners were the ones who wore out shoe leather.

"You making the call or shall I?" Jane held the notepaper out.

"Queen Flavia'll probably be impressed by a male voice." He snatched the paper out of her hand and picked up the phone. "Mrs. Constantine, please. Oh, yes, Mrs.

Constantine. This is Detective Sean MacHovec, New York Police Department. I—" It was obvious he had been cut off. He sat nodding and rolling his eyes. "Yes, ma'am. We have reopened the case of your brother's death. When will our team be able to speak to you?"

Jane sipped her coffee and pulled the latest flyers out of her in-box, dropping them one by one into the wastebasket as she finished reading them.

MacHovec hung up. "Flavia can't wait to talk to you. But she has this very important luncheon engagement"—he articulated the words with a sneer—"so the soonest she can see you is two-thirty if that fits in with your busy schedules."

"Fits in with mine," Defino said. "Gives us time to go through the file."

"Right. You coming, Sean?"

"Forget it. I'll keep my seat warm."

Homicide files are always thick. This wasn't a homicide file, but it looked like a four-pounder. The usual aided case, a case of illness or death from natural causes, could be closed quickly. This one might never be considered closed by the sister, but officially it was a dead end.

Jane and Defino huddled at his desk, turning pages in the file, making notes. On a cold November day a call had come anonymously from someone identified as a neighbor. Two sector cops drove over, had the super open the door, and found the emaciated body of Anderson Stratton sitting in a chair facing the window of his third-floor walk-up. He had been dead for some time. The photographs were enough to turn the most experienced stomach.

On the floor, visible in two of the pictures, were pizza cartons from a local pizzeria. A Five early in the file was an interview with the manager of the store. Andy Stratton ordered regularly but hadn't called for about a month at the time his body was found.

The super knew the sister by name. She dropped in to see her brother once in a while, even took him for a walk sometimes. She paid for the apartment through an accounting firm. The checks were always on time.

Neighbors had varying opinions of the deceased. Some were very fond of him, brought him meals from time to time. Others who had seen him, or heard him, during his bouts of illness were fearful of him. "A raging bull," one of them commented. "Should've been in a straitjacket," another said.

A woman who sometimes cooked for him wept during the interview. She had meant to look in on him, but hadn't gotten around to it. She felt guilty that Andy had died, especially because he had gone hungry.

No one in the neighborhood knew any of Andy's friends, if such people existed, who lived elsewhere. Few of them recalled when he moved into the apartment; he had just appeared, become part of the community, and then vanished. It was not an unusual scenario. The people who had a roof over their heads were the lucky ones, however undependable the roof might be. Alphabet City was full of homeless people, many of whom may have had afflictions as bad as Stratton's and may have come to the end of their lives with the help of alcohol, narcotics, or worse, but they either lacked caring relatives or managed to avoid them.

"Want to call this guy Shreiber?" Defino said, looking up from the file.

"We can see him tomorrow. Sean?"

"Got it." He was off the phone in a few minutes. "Ten tomorrow morning. But he can't tell you much."

"It's another Five," Jane said. That would be the justification for nearly every interview; it would add to the file a DD5—the Detective Division form for recording interviews and other information.

They continued through the early part of the file, the discovery of the body and the first interviews. No one suspected any cause of death except a natural one. "He was real tired last time I saw him," a woman in a small produce market said. "I gave him an apple and told him to eat it, but he just held on to it and walked around, looking at everything like he'd never seen grapefruits and oranges before. When he went out, he put the apple back. I felt sorry for him."

"He paid cash, always cash," a man in a coffee shop said. "He'd put his hand in his pocket and pull out a bunch of bills, big ones, little ones. He'd peel off a couple and put 'em on the table. He never caused any trouble."

It became a familiar refrain: He didn't make trouble. He wasn't any trouble. He never bothered anyone.

The autopsy indicated he hadn't eaten for a long time. Nor had he ingested any water. A bottle half full of water lay on the floor within reach if he had bent over. It was capped and the contents were not contaminated.

Why had he stopped eating and drinking? No one in the building recalled seeing anyone enter or leave Stratton's apartment in the weeks before the body was found. No one heard unusual noises from the apartment. His medication was in the bathroom. Some pills had been removed but the ME had not found any traces of the drugs in his system. He had stopped taking them when he had stopped eating.

"Looks like the guy gave up on life," Defino said, pushing his chair back. "Depressing."

"You see this about his clothes?"

"Yeah. Sharp dresser for a guy one step away from being homeless."

"She must have bought it all for him."

"So she tried. She was well-meaning, but she couldn't beat the problem. Doesn't mean someone killed him."

"I guess we'll get an earful," Jane said.

"Let's have lunch."

2

THEY TOOK THE Lex to Seventy-seventh Street, walked a block west to Park Avenue, and then south. One of New York's finest residential streets, Park Avenue was a world away from its origins. Through most of the nineteenth century, there was no street at all. Trains traveling to and from New York moved on tracks in a depression far below street level. It was only after the tracks were covered that a street was created. The filth and stench of smoke were replaced by fresher air and the most expensive apartments in Manhattan.

The divider was kept clean and well-planted, uniformed doormen graced every entrance, and yellow taxis outnumbered private cars on the roadway. Even on a raw day, one sensed the elegance and opulence of the area.

At the entrance to the massive apartment house where Flavia Constantine lived, they showed their shields and photos to a uniformed man at a desk who was obviously expecting them.

"First right. Take the elevator up to nine."

"This is gonna be something," Defino said as they rode up.

It was. The elevator opened into a small foyer with one door opposite the elevator. Jane rang. Mrs. Constantine herself opened the door.

"Please come in. Marian, take their coats."

Marian was a maid in a black-and-white uniform out

of an old movie. She said nothing, took the coats, and hung them in a closet. Mrs. Constantine led them across the marble floor of the entry to the living room.

Windows looked out on Park Avenue, but it wasn't the view that was breathtaking; it was the paintings on the walls. Jane was hardly a connoisseur, but she had taken an art appreciation course in college and she was sure the largest painting was a Picasso. It was the first time she had seen one outside a museum.

"Make yourselves comfortable, please. If you'd like coffee or anything else, I'll be glad to get it for you."

It was the first time Defino hadn't asked for anything. "No thanks," he said, and Jane shook her head.

"I'm Flavia Constantine," the regal woman on the sofa said. She was dressed in a pewter-colored silk dress that rustled. A diamond pin displayed tiny flashes of color when she moved. Her makeup was perfect. It made Jane wonder if she had remembered to renew her lipstick before they left Centre Street.

"I'm Detective Jane Bauer. This is Detective Gordon Defino. We're part of a squad that investigates open homicide cases."

"It's about time," Mrs. Constantine said. "I've waited eight years for the police department to recognize that my brother's death was no accident."

"We're investigating the possibility that it's a homicide," Defino said.

"I understand. I will do whatever I can to assist you. Andy was not suicidal. He was sometimes confused and muddled, but I never heard him suggest he wanted his life to end."

"Would you like to tell us about him?" Jane asked.

Mrs. Constantine sat erect on the sofa. Her ringed hands rested on her lap, but she moved them occasionally as she spoke. She was a slim, handsome woman about fifty with dark, perfectly arranged hair, slender legs wearing shoes whose cost Jane could only estimate. There was nothing smiling or warm about her. She was as cool and stiff as her silk dress.

"My brother was a poet," she said. "He wrote magnificent poetry. The words sang as you read them. He wrote with passion and intensity. All the things he could not articulate in speech found their way into his writing. He had a great mind, too great, perhaps, the mind of a philosopher, and his brilliance emerged in his poems. My brother lived in two worlds, a bad one and a worse one, and somehow he found a way to write about both of them with feeling and clarity."

"Was he writing anything in the time before he died?" Defino asked.

"There were papers lying on the floor and on the table next to him, but nothing was intelligible. Most of it wasn't even legible. If you're thinking he might have left clues to his death, I can assure you there weren't any. I have every piece of paper that was in the apartment when he was found."

"Did your brother work at all outside his apartment?" Jane asked.

"He volunteered sometimes at a homeless shelter. Not very often. He had difficulty keeping to a schedule. If the spirit moved him, he would go down and help out for an hour or two, serving meals or reading to the children. He liked children, but they frightened him. They were unpredictable." For the first time, she smiled. "He wrote a wonderful children's story and he read that to them. I've read it to my granddaughter. It's a remarkable story, full of allegory and symbolism. My brother was a brilliant man but he was afflicted, through no fault of his own. I have often wondered how God chooses those who will suffer."

There was an uncomfortable silence. "I'm sorry for your loss, Mrs. Constantine," Jane said. "Can you tell us what makes you think that your brother's death was a homicide?"

"I've given you one reason, that he was never suicidal. He hated the bad times, but no one ever heard him say he wanted to die. There are other reasons. He was looking forward to coming here for Christmas. When I spoke to him the last few times, he mentioned it. He had been working on a play and he thought he might get a group of local amateurs to produce it. He was very excited about that; he said it would make him credible, give him a leg up. Off-Broadway might be next. In a circumstance like that, you don't sit down in a chair and stop eating and drinking."

"I don't mean any disrespect, Mrs. Constantine," Defino said, "but the medical examiner said it took at least two weeks for him to die. I gather you weren't in contact with him during that time."

"No, I wasn't. I was away for almost a month. I talked to him a few days before I left. He was in good spirits. Then I called him the night before my trip. He didn't answer. That wasn't unusual. Sometimes he was out. Sometimes he didn't want to be bothered and he didn't answer the phone. It was late and I couldn't go down to check on him. I sent him a postcard from France. It was in his mailbox when the police found him."

"There were pizza boxes in the apartment when the police came. Is that what he ate mostly, takeout?"

"Andy didn't cook. He heated things up, he ordered out, he went out and ate in one of the local places. Often he didn't have a clear concept of time or he just didn't care what time it was. He slept when he felt like it, he ate when he was hungry, he changed his clothes when he decided he was tired of what he was wearing."

"But he ate when he was hungry," Jane said. "And he had the money to pay for it."

"He always had the money and yes, he ate. He didn't eat much, just enough to fill himself up. He was like a newborn that way. You know how they push the bottle away when they're done eating? That was Andy. At one moment he decided he'd had enough and he didn't take another bite." She moved her eyes from one to the other, talking to both of them equally.

"Did he have a girlfriend?" Jane asked.

She didn't answer. She rubbed her hands together and a diamond ring caught the light. Then she said, "Andy shared much of his life with me. But I was not intrusive. He wasn't a child and I couldn't ask about personal things, sexual things. I saw to it that he had clothes to wear and money to spend. If there was a woman in his life, or women, he kept that to himself. I'm sure he was capable of that kind of love."

"Who might know if he had a relationship?"

"The police claim to have interviewed everyone in the apartment house, all the people in the neighborhood who might have known him, waitresses, the super. Nothing like that turned up. And I hired a private detective. You're welcome to talk to him. He didn't find anything either."

"What do you think happened to your brother, Mrs. Constantine?"

"I think that someone who pretended to be his friend prevented Andy from leaving the apartment, from eating, from drinking. I think Andy became too weak to resist, and eventually he died."

"Why would someone do that?"

"Perhaps they thought I might arrive and they could extort money from me. I know you find this hard to believe. I see the skepticism in your faces. You think my brother became tired of life, he was weak, and his mind was racked with pain, he lacked the energy to call for a meal and it was just easier to sit in the chair and fade away than keep himself alive. There was someone in that room with him, Detective Defino, Detective Bauer." The eyes moved. "Someone prevented him from living, and that's murder."

"Is there anyone in particular that you suspect?" Jane asked.

"It's not someone who lived in the building. I think it's one of the homeless people who imposed himself on Andy. Andy sometimes let people come into the apartment, maybe even stay overnight if it was cold. I think it was one of those people, someone who ingratiated himself with Andy, who saw him take money out of his pocket and sensed there was a source for the cash. But the police got there before I did and that person disappeared."

"Well, we'll explore that idea as far as we can," Defino said. He was edgy; he wanted to go.

"There's something else. After they took Andy away, I went through the apartment myself. It was quite messy and it hadn't been cleaned for some time. The crime scene people took a number of things from the apartment and they dusted for fingerprints. I'm not criticizing the job they did, but I found something on the floor." She reached for a small leather pouch that had lain on the end table near where she sat. It was a few inches long and wide and zipped shut. She handed it to Jane. "Look inside. Be careful."

Jane unzipped it. Inside were perhaps twenty tiny beads. She took one out between her fingers, looked at it, and passed the pouch to Defino.

"I had them checked by a jeweler," Flavia Constantine said. "They're not seed pearls as I thought they might be. They're ordinary commercial beads and they're not worth anything."

"They were strung on a necklace," Jane said. A tiny hole had been drilled through the bead in her hand.

"Andy didn't wear jewelry, nothing. He had a watch but he refused to wear it. It was on his night table and the battery had died. With a digital watch, you can't tell when it stopped. But he had no rings, no necklaces, no bracelets. He never wore anything around his neck. In fact, he liked loose collars. Someone else wore those beads. The string broke and they fell to the floor. The floor was slanted—it's a very old building—and when they hit the floor, they rolled into one corner of the room. I found them behind a bookcase."

"Did you show them to the detective working the case?" Defino asked.

"I showed it to Mr. Shreiber. I gave him one. He said essentially what the jeweler told me, that it couldn't be determined where they came from. Nor did he know who had worn them. But there had to be more than the beads

I put in that pouch. There's barely enough there for a small bracelet. And the police assured me there was no string with more beads on it."

"So it looks like the string broke, the wearer grabbed what was left, and let the others go."

"Yes." She smiled. Defino had told her what she had figured out herself. "The person wearing the necklace took the rest of them with her. Him. Whatever."

"We'll certainly try to track down the owner," Defino said, giving Mrs. Constantine hope, fulfilling their mission of the afternoon.

"Take a few with you. Do you need a bag for them?"

"I've got one." Jane pulled a plastic sandwich bag out of her bag, part of the equipment she regularly carried.

"Thank you," Mrs. Constantine said. Her eyes had become bright. "I've waited so long for someone to take this seriously."

"We're taking it very seriously, Mrs. Constantine. What can you tell us about Wally Shreiber?"

"The detective? He seemed competent. He was well recommended. He did all the right things but he turned up nothing. I don't blame him. I just think that people with a new perspective may be more successful."

"We'll give it our best shot." Defino handed the pouch to her.

"And you'll keep me informed."

"Every step of the way."

Mrs. Constantine stood and Defino leaped to his feet. Jane hoped it wasn't as apparent to Mrs. Constantine as it was to her how much he wanted to get out of there.

Jane walked over to the large painting and found the signature. It was a Picasso. Something like a chill passed through her. She owned little besides her clothes and the contents of her apartment. Here was a woman who owned a world treasure.

"It's a Picasso," the voice of their hostess said behind her.

"Yes. I thought so. It must be a great joy to have it here."

Mrs. Constantine blinked. "It is. It's a wonderful piece. I'm glad you like it."

They walked to the foyer and were given their coats. The maid went outside and pressed the button for the elevator. Jane assured Mrs. Constantine that they would report whatever they learned. The door closed before the elevator arrived.

Defino lit the cigarette between his fingers as soon as they were on the sidewalk. He inhaled as though it were air and he had been suffocating. "We get back to Centre Street, I'm putting in my papers."

Jane tried not to laugh, then stopped trying.

"That's funny? We're a couple of babysitters making nice to a kid on the verge of a tantrum. Except the kid is in her fifties and lives in a museum and if we're not good to her, she'll go crying to the governor."

The characterization wasn't unfair. "Let's give it two weeks, Gordon. One more pound of paper. We'll find a couple of new sources. We'll tie it up with a red ribbon and hand it to Graves."

"Find a homeless guy who hung out at Tompkins Square Park eight years ago and kept Stratton from eating. Shit, she might as well have asked us to locate a dog. And the fucking love beads."

"Maybe it's a lead."

He looked at her with raised eyebrows, took a last drag on the butt, stepped on it, and started down the stairs to the Lex.

"You two don't look like you just had tea on Park Avenue," MacHovec said cheerfully as they walked into the office.

"We didn't." Defino took his coat off and hung it on a hook.

"Well I've been busy. Made some calls about this Stratton guy. He spent some time in a loony bin."

"You would too if you had Constantine for a sister."

"Why'd they let him out?" Jane asked, sifting through her messages.

"He wanted out and they felt he wouldn't be a danger to himself."

"He supposed to see a shrink while he was out?"

"Yeah." MacHovec pulled out a sheet of paper and tapped it with his pencil. "But Stratton didn't keep appointments."

"What about meds?"

"He was on 'em but who knows if he took 'em."

"He didn't," Jane said. "The autopsy said there weren't any in his system."

"So he didn't see his shrink, didn't take his pills, didn't call out for food. What does his sister want you to dig up?"

"Somebody wearing love beads," Defino growled.

"Wasn't that the sixties down in the Village?"

"Who fucking knows?"

"Well, kiddies, you're both in such a good mood I'll leave you to entertain each other. You coming in tomorrow before you see the PI?"

They both said yes. MacHovec got his coat and left.

"He's in rare form," Defino said.

"So are you. Why don't you take off? If Graves wants a report, I'll give it to him."

"You don't have to ask me twice."

When she was alone, she called her father, made sure he was OK, and walked out to where she could see Graves's office. No one was at the desk. She took the hint.

3

HOME WAS THE apartment Jane had moved into a few months ago, a building in the West Village where the familiar grid of Manhattan streets dissolves into chaos. Here you almost needed a compass to determine directions. For tourists it was confusing; for Jane it was charm. The building was solid, prewar, and her apartment had a fireplace. She dropped the case file on the sofa, hung up her coat, secured her weapon, and checked the answering machine. Not a single message. Good. She could do justice to the file tonight in preparation for the morning meeting with Wally Shreiber.

Then she started a fire. She had become accustomed to sitting in front of the fire while she ate dinner, a pleasure she had not anticipated until after her fortieth birthday. Home was now where the fire was.

In jeans and a sweatshirt she ate stew she had cooked over the weekend, drinking a beer with it, feeling the warmth of the fire. It didn't get much better than this.

Except for the case. Defino was acting out the way she felt too, annoyance at having been chosen to hold a hand, waste time, get nowhere. MacHovec didn't much care. He sat at his desk five days a week and dug up information without regard to its usefulness. As long as they paid him, he would go along with it.

Jane pushed the dish and glass aside and pulled over the file. A color photo of a healthy-looking Anderson

Stratton was in the envelope along with pictures taken after his death. It required a good imagination to find a resemblance. Emaciated was an understatement. Why does a guy stop eating and drinking? In one photo the telephone was clearly visible on the table beside his chair. If he had lost the strength to hold it in his hand, to push the buttons, why had he allowed himself to wait so long? Had the demons of his disease so clouded his mind that he was unable to recognize hunger and thirst and to respond to them?

He had been a good-looking guy. Something about his face reminded Jane of Flavia Constantine's face, but the features went better on a man. She was a plain woman even with all the makeup and hairstyling.

Assuming Constantine was on the right track for a killer, even she could come up with only a weak motive, that Constantine and her bucks would show up at some point, the money ripe for the taking. Weak was an understatement.

Andy Stratton had survived thirty-six years of life without having broken any bones or requiring any surgery. Nothing affected his digestive system adversely and there were no drugs, good or bad, in his system. Some old burns scarred his hands and a small cut on his left hand had nearly healed, most likely from trying to cut something with his right. A rotten apple core in the garbage was a possible explanation. So at some point he had eaten an apple.

Jane got up and added two logs to the fire, waiting in front of the screen till they caught. The file, open, lay on the coffee table. She found the sketch of the apartment, then the larger sketch of the room where the body was found. Stratton was facing a wall with two windows. To the left of the window on the left, a tall bookcase covered the wall to the corner of the room. On the adjoining wall was a desk. It was in that corner, where the left-hand side of the bookcase ended, and against that wall that Mrs. C. had found the beads. It was truly a find, Jane acknowledged. The crime scene people had not moved the bookcase. In the photos it was nearly full, thus too heavy to move easily unless the books were removed.

One photo, taken from behind the chair, showed the windows and bookcase. If Stratton were sitting in the chair wearing a necklace that broke, the beads might easily roll to that corner if they hit the floor. Jane estimated he would have to be leaning forward for that to happen. Otherwise the beads might well have settled in the chair itself, finding their way under the cushion, perhaps even into the innards. She wondered if the chair still existed.

What was more likely was that he was standing when the string broke—or another person wearing the necklace was standing. The beads were tiny. They seemed better suited to a woman, even to a girl, than to a tall man in his thirties.

She kept reading till ten, the interviews on the Fives blurring in monotony. "I saw him sometimes in the street but I didn't know him." "He's dead? What happened? I haven't seen him for a long time." "He was a quiet neighbor. Most of the time. I don't even know his name." "Andy? Yeah. He had a real gift. He wrote great poetry. I wondered what happened to him. I haven't seen him in a month or more."

They went on and on. The pizza deliverer knew more about him than most of his neighbors. "Nice guy, real nice. When I delivered, I never saw him, you understand. He left an envelope outside the door with money in it. I pushed the bell, left the pizza, took the envelope, and went downstairs. He was real generous. Once I went halfway down to the next floor and I waited to see him open the door, just to make sure, you know? He didn't come for a long time, like five minutes. Then I heard the door open. I tried to get a look but I couldn't see his face. It was crazy. But he was a nice guy."

Find a killer in those interviews. She returned everything to the file, rubber-banded it, and put it near her handbag. The facts and opinions of the case, the dialogue of the interviews, would interfere with her sleep tonight. It was unavoidable. Even believing that this was not a homicide, even smarting from having been asked to undertake a lost cause, she couldn't help internalizing what she had read and seen in the file.

In her bedroom, she stopped in front of the dresser and smiled at the snapshots stuck in the mirror frame and the framed photo on the dresser. Lisa Angelino smiled back at her, the baby she had given up twenty years ago and whom she had seen for the first time just before Christmas. That smile was the biggest bonus in her life.

Lisa had contacted her in the fall, and in December, when Jane had recovered sufficiently from the beating at the end of the last case, she had flown to Kansas for a few days to meet her daughter and her parents. The Angelinos had greeted her at the airport as though she were a visiting celebrity and had gradually warmed to her as they realized she was not competing for the love of their daughter.

They had walked and talked, inspected the tiny town the Angelinos lived in, driven to visit their relatives and friends, and stayed up late every night talking and talking; there seemed no end to what they could tell each other. Before leaving, Jane promised to fly Lisa to New York in the summer, where she would meet Jane's father, who suddenly saw himself as a grandfather, a miracle he had never expected.

The smile in the snapshots told her the bonus went both ways.

They met at Centre Street on Tuesday morning. Annie came by to say that Captain Graves wanted to see them right away. Coffee in hand, they trooped into his office.

"Mrs. Constantine is very impressed with you two," he began. "She made a phone call after you left and it filtered down to me. She add anything new?"

Jane told him about the beads. Although Shreiber, the private investigator, had known about them, the police hadn't and they weren't mentioned in the file. They would generate a few more questions to ask in the new round of interviews.

"See what you can do with it," Graves said, not exhibiting any enthusiasm. At least he was a realist. "What's on for today?"

"The PI," MacHovec said. "Ten o'clock."

Graves looked at his watch. "Better get going."

They were a few minutes late but Wally Shreiber didn't mind. He had an office with a shared secretary who stayed out of the way. They all shook hands, introduced themselves, and sat down with coffee.

"You're working on the Stratton case," Wally Shreiber said. A file lay in front of him on his desk. "She still at it?"

"She'll be at it forever," Defino said.

"You're right there. She's not letting go. I thought maybe she had something when she hired me, but I gave it my best and I came up with zilch."

"We're two weeks away from that."

"We've read most of the file," Jane said. "What did you do that the police didn't?"

"I talked to every drunk, every whacked-out guy, every petty thief in Tompkins Square Park. A lot of them knew Stratton. Stratton would go over there when he was feeling good, talk to the guys, maybe even give them money. Most of them didn't know where he lived, but it's not impossible that someone followed him home. His building's right on Tenth Street, across from the north end of the park. Still, most of those guys were too out of it to have the motivation to follow someone home and kill him."

"And he might be seen," Jane said.

"Right. There were old-timers in that building, people who'd lived there since the big war. They see a filthy homeless guy come into their building, they take a look, maybe they call the police."

"What about a girl who's wearing a necklace of little beads?"

"OK, you got me there. You really think a girl went in and kept Andy from eating or drinking for a couple of weeks? Those beads could've been dropped a year before Andy died. You think of that?"

Jane had. "You're right. We don't know how long they were there, whether they were coated with dust when Mrs. C. found them."

"Exactly."

"You said something in a note about seeing the super."

"Yeah, you should talk to him. He's a white guy, young, or he was eight years ago, and I think he's a writer or musician. The super job gives him a free apartment and some walking around money. He knows what's going on in the building and the neighborhood. He didn't like me very much, didn't like the cops either, but maybe you can sweet-talk him. It's happened before."

"What shape is the building in?" Defino asked.

"I forgot to tell you. They renovated it about a year after Stratton died, gutted it completely. Gentrification. It's happening all over the area. So the apartments are gone and so are the people. You may still find some of them; the super might know where they went. Some of the older tenants moved into other old buildings just to keep their rent down."

"But the super's still there?"

"Yeah. He liked the lifestyle, although he bitched a lot about the kind of people that were moving in. Their jeans were Lauren, not Levi's. Makes a difference." Shreiber grinned.

"What impression did you get about Stratton's mental condition?" Jane asked.

"It depended. If he took his medication, he could be OK. I gather he was very bright. I talked to people who had discussed pretty highbrow stuff with him, politics, world affairs, philosophy. He read a lot. He didn't make it through college because he broke down and had to leave, but he educated himself."

"Any record of suicide attempts?"

"None I could find. I talked to his psychiatrist. He hadn't seen Stratton for a long time, at least a year, because Stratton wouldn't go, even when Constantine sent a car to take him. But he had access to the records in the institution and Stratton never tried to hurt himself. I have to tell you, he had to be encouraged to eat sometimes. Eating wasn't high on his list of priorities."

"So he may have just sat down in his chair and read books and not bothered eating," Jane said, feeling discouraged.

"This could be one of those cases that looks like what it is, an accidental death."

"What's your impression of Mrs. Constantine?" Defino asked.

"She's an interesting woman. She's as rich as God. You see that apartment? I saw that Picasso, I couldn't catch my breath. She was still married to Constantine when I worked for her, but I only saw him once for a minute. Not the communicative type. I don't know why she bothered to get divorced. She could've stayed married to him and not known he was around. Maybe she wanted the money in her bank account, not his.

"I think she grew up protecting this brother from the world. It was like a personal affront when she couldn't save him. She comes across as a tough broad, but I don't think she has a nasty bone in her body except where Constantine was concerned. She also hired me to look into that, whether he had something on the side."

Defino raised his eyebrows. "And?"

"What do you think? A guy with that much money has what he wants. Probably didn't mean much to him, just a little diversion like horse racing or baccarat. Although he married a cute little piece of ass after the divorce. It was in the papers. I was out of it by then."

"So Mrs. C. kept the art and the apartment and Mr. C. moved on."

"There was enough there, no one got cheated. Believe me."

"What you're telling us is that you believe Stratton died of natural causes, probably brought on by his mental condition," Jane said. They weren't getting anywhere. They might as well wrap this up.

"You expect me to say anything else?"

That seemed to do it. They both stood at the same moment. Wally helped Jane on with her coat.

"You have any specific questions, give me a ring. I know why you're doing this. The pressure comes from high up. Maybe you can put it to rest this time."

Wally had a warm, firm handshake. He walked them to the door and said it had been nice meeting them.

"The apartment's not there, the tenants have moved, and we have to put in two weeks trying to make like it's the old neighborhood."

"You have a way with words, Gordon."

"Yeah, like Stratton. Ready to visit the crime scene?"

"The nonexistent scene of the nonexistent crime. Why not? But let's have lunch first. I could use something hot."

The day was blustery. Hot sounded like a good idea. They found a place that had soup on the menu for Jane and some kind of pasta for Defino. After they ordered, Defino called in for both of them. Graves was big on making rings.

4

ANDERSON STRATTON HAD died in an old building that looked out on Tompkins Square Park in the bulge of Manhattan on the east side below Fourteenth Street. Here, First Avenue, which stretched to upper Manhattan, no longer ran at the eastern edge of the island as it did farther north. Four avenues, A through D, ran north to south in the area east of First between Fourteenth Street on the north and East Houston Street on the south.

The bulge included part of the Lower East Side south of Houston, home to waves of immigrants that changed every generation or two. West of Alphabet City the area was called the East Village as it lay due east of the Village or the West Village. As every New Yorker knew, Fifth Avenue was Manhattan's east-west dividing line.

Tompkins Square Park, lying between Avenues A and B and from Seventh Street to Tenth Street, had a long and often colorful history. In the sixties and seventies it was a haven for flower children, drug dealers, and, of course, users. It was a real problem for the NYPD; no matter what the cops did, a sizable number of vocal people condemned them for it. The park and the streets surrounding it were part of the Ninth Precinct. The Nine had one of the highest Line of Duty death rates and one of the highest Medal of Honor rates, too many of them awarded posthumously. Not all the people who hung out in the park were strangers to the Nine.

They changed to the Fourteenth Street–Canarsie local and got off at First Avenue, the last stop in Manhattan. From there the subway went to Brooklyn, crossing the East River through a tunnel.

"Haven't been here in a while," Defino said, pulling his coat collar up as they reached the sidewalk. "Freezing cold."

"Gets worse near the river."

"You work the Nine?"

"No, but I worked Chinatown. It's almost as bad."

"And lived to talk about it."

"In the end it'll be the weather that kills me. Let's walk down to Tenth."

It was too cold to talk. They walked briskly, Jane wishing she had brought a scarf for her head. Defino had pulled a small, wool visored cap out of his pocket and put it on, the first time she had seen it. By the time they reached Stratton's building, her ears were burning with cold.

The building had several outside stairs up to the first floor. They went inside the small lobby and stood there for a moment to warm up. Jane was almost shivering. Defino folded the hat and stuck it in his pocket. The super, it turned out, was in the apartment under the stairs, so they went back out again and rang the bell next to his door.

No one answered. "There's a note here," Defino said. " 'One to four, emergencies only.' "

"Ring again."

The door opened. The man staring at them was tall and lanky, wearing jeans and a flannel shirt. His hair might once have been light brown but now it was a faded non-color, brushed straight back from his face. His cheekbones were prominent, his nose a little too large, and his mouth firmly set. There would be no sweet-talking this one.

"There are no vacancies," he said. "No one's lease is expiring. I am very busy. Good day."

Defino's foot was ready and the door remained open. Two shields were thrust in front of the super's face.

"What is this?" he asked. "There's no one here to bust. I live a clean life."

"We'd like to talk to you," Jane said. "May we come inside?"

He wanted desperately to turn them away. She could sense his outrage. They had disturbed him during his work or meditation or whatever it was that kept him going. But he wasn't stupid. He opened the door and let them in.

It was the neatest super's apartment Jane had ever seen. Not only was it clean and orderly, but the furniture was attractive, some of it made to order for the space. They sat on a firm modern sofa, the super sitting opposite on an upholstered high-back chair.

"Your name?" Defino said. The case and the weather seemed to have hardened him.

"Larry Vale." He looked a little rattled.

"You were the super here when Anderson Stratton lived in this building?"

"Yes."

"Did you know him?"

"Yes."

"Did he go out every day on a regular basis?"

Larry Vale sighed as though he had been through these questions so many times he could not imagine why anyone would ask them again. "Sometimes."

"You want to be more specific?"

"When he felt like it, when he was up to it, when the weather permitted, when he wasn't wrapped up in his work, he usually went out in the afternoon. If I had to guess, I would say he worked into the night and slept late in the mornings. He wasn't a morning person."

"Did you have a friendly relationship with him?" Jane asked.

"Yes."

"You go up to his place sometimes for a chat?"

"More often he came here. He'd be coming back from wherever he went and he'd ring my bell and come inside and we'd talk."

"About what?"

Vale looked disdainful. "About poetry and music and philosophy." He sounded as though there weren't a chance in the world that either detective would know what the words meant.

"And it didn't strike you as strange that Mr. Stratton didn't show up at your door for a month?"

"I didn't think about it. It wasn't a regular thing. I took care of the building, not the tenants. What is this about anyway? Andy died six or seven years ago."

"Eight," Defino said.

"We're reinvestigating the circumstances of Mr. Stratton's death," Jane said.

"The guy starved to death. What circumstances are you talking about?"

"How many people do you know with a pocket full of cash who starve to death?"

"I don't know people with pockets full of cash."

"But you knew he paid his rent on time and you knew he had money to live on."

"I knew that, but even if it crossed my mind that I hadn't seen him for a week or two, it didn't make me think he was sick or dying."

"Who visited him?" Defino asked.

"He had friends in the neighborhood. Maybe some of them went up to see him."

"You see people go up there?"

"Not often. I'm below street level here. I can't see the tops of people without bending over and looking up. I tend to mind my business, strange as that may seem to you. I would see the pizza guy sometimes at night. Oh, and there was the little girl."

"What little girl?"

"Some little Chinese girl, maybe from the laundry, but maybe not." He screwed up his face as he finished speaking.

"Where's the laundry?" Defino asked.

"They were on Avenue A. I think they're still there."

"She have a name?"

"I'm sure she must, Detective, but she never told me."

"How old was she?"

"I'm not a good judge of children's ages. She could have been eight or ten."

"Did he ever mention her to you?" Jane asked.

"As I said, we talked about—"

"Yeah, I know," Defino interrupted. "Music and philosophy. Just answer our questions."

"No, he never mentioned the Chinese girl."

"Did you ever meet Mr. Stratton's sister?" Jane asked.

"Once or twice."

"Did she give you any gifts of money to keep your eye on her brother?"

"No, she did not." His pale face had reddened.

"Did she ask you to look out for him?"

"In a way."

"In what way, Mr. Vale?" Jane asked, her own irritation nearing Defino's.

"If he seemed ill, I was to call her."

"Then you had her phone number."

"Yes."

"What else?"

"That's it. I didn't see him ill. I never called her."

"Was she generous at Christmas?"

He took two long breaths before he answered. "Yes."

"But you never knocked on his door when you hadn't seen him for a month."

"What do you people want? A man died in his apartment. Nobody hurt him; nobody killed him. I was not his keeper just because his sister handed me a Christmas envelope."

Defino stood. "OK, Mr. Vale. If you think of anyone else who visited Stratton, you can call us at that number." He handed Vale his card.

Vale stood. His face had lost some of its ruddy color. "Can you tell me why you're asking these questions? Andy died alone in his apartment. What are you looking for?"

"We're investigating his death," Jane said. "There are unanswered questions. Can you show us where his apartment was?"

"All the apartments have been changed," Vale said. "I don't have a key to the one that replaced Andy's, but I can show you approximately where it was."

"Let's do that."

Vale left the room and came back wearing a heavy jacket. They followed him outside and up to the street where he pointed to the third floor. "The windows are all new but those on the left are more or less where his were."

"So he could see the park from them."

"Yes. And he had his chair set so he faced outside. It made him feel good, he said, to see the trees and the grass and the people walking around."

"Thank you, Mr. Vale," Jane said. "If we have any other questions, we'll be back."

THEY SAT IN a coffee shop a block away, warming their hands on mugs of coffee.

"You were in rare form," Jane said.

"He ticked me off."

"No kidding."

"So we find the laundry?"

"It's another Five."

"I love this case," Defino said bitterly. "It's another Five and another Five."

"Drink up."

"At least it'll be hot in the laundry."

An old grandmother sat in a corner of the small store, doing nothing except watching what went on. A moment after they entered, a woman one generation younger came from the steamy back to stand behind the counter.

"You do shirts here?" Jane asked.

"Shirts, yes. You got shirts?"

"Not right now but maybe tomorrow. What time do you open?"

"Open seven. See?" The woman pointed to a schedule hanging on the wall.

"And how much are shirts?"

"One dollar fifteen."

"That sounds great. How long does it take to get them back?"

"Four day."

"Is your daughter here?"

"Wha?"

"Your daughter. You have a daughter, don't you?"

"No unnerstand."

"Your daughter doesn't work here?"

The old woman in the corner growled a few syllables.

"No unnerstand. You got shirts?"

"We'll be back."

They walked outside. "What do you think?" Jane said.

"The usual. She understands what she wants to. Let's come back with a translator."

That had been the plan, to size up the woman's command of English or her willingness to admit she understood it. Jane had worked in the Five, the Chinatown Precinct, and could call on a bilingual detective she knew, but they would follow procedure and report to Graves. He might want to go through channels to show Mrs. C. they had done it the official way.

They walked over to Avenue C, a block east of the park, and then south to the station house, which was between Tenth and Ninth Streets. The wind was fierce, the East River only two blocks east at that point. The river was the eastern limit of the Nine.

Inside the house, the desk sergeant was yakking with a uniform but turned around when he heard voices. Jane introduced herself.

"Sergeant Wayne Cooley," he responded. "Jane Bauer, Jane Bauer. Do I know that face? Yeah, it was splashed all over the papers a while ago. Nice to meet you."

"Glad to be alive. This is Detective Gordon Defino. We're looking into a cold case from the Nine."

The men shook hands.

"Cold? We got lots of them. What's yours?"

"Something that began as an aided case eight years ago and will probably end as one in a couple of weeks, but we have to dig up whatever there is on it." Jane shook his hand as they were talking.

"Well, you came at a good time. This is the first lull we've had in twenty-two years. I don't expect it to last." As he spoke, the door opened and two uniforms hauled in a handcuffed black man with long filthy hair, clothes out of someone's trash, and an attitude. "What'd I tell you?" He turned to the cops. "Hang on a minute. So, Detectives, who you lookin' for?"

"P.O. Barry Ford was first on the scene. This was eight years ago."

"Ford, yeah. I'll radio a ten-two; he'll be here in five." He radioed Patrol Officer Ford. Ten-two meant "come to the station house."

Five minutes later, when Ford arrived, the unruly suspect had disappeared and temporary peace was restored. Tall, black, and well-built, Ford was still driving a sector car. Like other sector cops, he would have learned every nook and cranny of his sector, every back door, every fire escape. Jane thought he probably knew every inch of the park as well. He would be a good person to ride a car or walk the streets with.

Introductions made, they sat in an interview room to talk. Jane explained the situation and Ford excused himself to find the aided case forms on Stratton to refresh his memory.

Returning with the paperwork, he resumed his seat. "That was the rich guy," he said after scowling over the paper. "Starved to death in his living room."

"That's the one."

"What're you looking for?"

"Don't laugh. Maybe it was a homicide."

"Yeah, there was a relative that bothered us. I remember. A sister, right?"

"Right."

"Drove the captain nuts till he agreed to reopen the investigation. There was nothing there. The guy starved to death."

"You remember anything we can put on paper?"

"I've seen a lot of DOAs in my time on the job. I used to work up in the Two-six." Harlem. "But this one was a little odd. I thought the guy was kinda young for a heart attack and he didn't look like a junkie to me, so I figured something medical. I saw a lot of ODs uptown. This apartment was OK, not a crash pad for druggies, nothing outta place, no burglary. Bed was made, or at least the cover was up. Dirty clothes on the floor or maybe in the closet, clean clothes in the dresser. But there were roaches. They were crawling over everything. Empty pizza box. Maybe not so empty. He looked like he was asleep. Sat in a chair facing the window like he was lookin' out at the park. Bottle of water on the floor near his foot.

"Guy had all his clothes on so there was no weirdness going on. The apartment was empty. Door was locked. We had to get the super to open up. Just your ordinary dead guy."

Defino had been writing furiously, taking down every word. "Any sign someone had been there?"

"Nah. Just the pizza box. Coulda been there a month. I called the desk, made the notification, gave the info back to Central, told them we would be outta service at the location and about what we found, and called for a supervisor to respond. You know the drill."

"Right," Defino said.

"The squad finally arrived; the ME showed up and the guy was gone to the ME's place by Bellevue by the end of the tour. I had the super lock up before we sealed the door. I don't remember his name."

"Vale," Jane and Defino said together.

"Yeah, Vale. Guy with something up his ass. I remember him. You know they rehabed that whole building since then? Looks pretty good now."

"We were just there," Defino said.

"So what else do you need? I got my meal comin' up soon."

A cop would walk through fire to ensure that he didn't miss a meal.

"That's it," Jane said. "Thanks. You've been a lot of help. Just one more thing. The Chinese laundry on Avenue A? We heard a little Chinese girl delivered Stratton's laundry. You know her?"

He thought a minute. "Yeah. I know the place. They got a daughter maybe eighteen or nineteen, pretty girl. Works in the back sometimes. She goes to school, I don't know where. They won't talk to you. No speaka da English."

"We're coming back with a translator," Jane said.

"You guys really think something went down in that apartment?"

"We have to make like we do." Defino tapped his pencil on the table.

Ford shrugged. "Good luck."

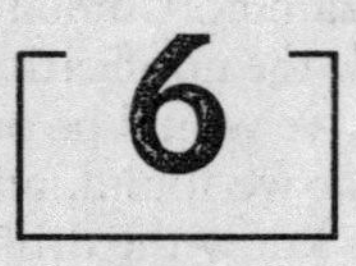

BACK AT CENTRE Street, Captain Graves agreed to request an interpreter from the deputy commissioner of community affairs. Mrs. Constantine would be reading a report at some point and the less she had to criticize, the happier everyone would be. He put in the call to the DCCA himself, and before the day was over, Police Officer Roberta Chen called to say she was available tomorrow. She was a liaison to the Chinese community and language skills officer assigned to One Police Plaza, near enough to the Chinese community that she could respond if there was a need for her face and language skills. Jane gave her a time and place and a little background.

"They'll talk to me," Chen said, "but they may not say much."

"Anything they tell you is more than they told us."

Defino sat at the typewriter and tapped out his Fives.

"I checked up on your super," MacHovec said over the din. "He's clean. The Chinese laundry's had their problems. Lotta complaints against them a few years ago—the usual, lost shirts, damaged sheets—but nothing much recently."

"Thanks, Sean."

"And I called the owner of the building." He pulled out a page of notes. "The renovation was on paper before Stratton died, but no one had been informed yet. It took them a while to clear the building, no surprise there, and then it was over a year till it was livable. I've got the names and new addresses of a couple of the old tenants." He passed the sheet to Jane. "The one on top, Komiskey, I don't know if he's still alive. Landlord said he was pretty old when he moved."

"We'll take a look. Thanks."

"Least I could do while you were freezing your asses out there today."

"That's what we were doing." She read the list, written in MacHovec's large dark print. There were only three names. "Where'd the others go?"

"He thinks Florida for one, living with a daughter for another. This was all he had."

"We can do it tomorrow. That and the laundry."

"Then what?" MacHovec said.

"I don't know. Maybe we try prayer."

Before they got that far, they would have to walk through the park with Stratton's photo and talk to the people there. Gentrification had brought young couples and families, most of whom hadn't been there when Stratton died. But there was always a chance that someone sitting in the park or jogging or taking a walk would remember him. Beyond remembering him, there was probably nothing, but it counted as a Five.

MacHovec left, Defino finished his angry typing and ripped the last Five out of the machine.

"Jeez, they don't weigh much."

"A few more tomorrow." She repeated her conversation with the interpreter and showed him MacHovec's list of tenants who had moved. "They're all right there."

"Too bad. I thought maybe this time I'd get a trip to Florida."

"You can have it. I'm going home and making a fire."

"See you tomorrow."

The fire roared and crackled. She had picked this apartment because of the fireplace. It was in the Sixth Precinct, where Jane had worked for ten years. An NYPD rule prohibited cops from living and working in the same precinct, so she knew her days at the Six were over. With that fireplace, she would never leave. Changed into a sweatsuit, she scanned her mail, tossing most of it without opening it.

After dinner she sat in the living room facing the fire and the TV. Nothing appealed to her on the screen so she shut it off, grabbed her book and a beer, and began to read. The phone rang soon after and she took it over to her seat.

"Jane? How the hell are you?"

"Flora, hi. I'm doing fine. Sitting in front of a real fire."

"Don't rub it in. I take it you're back on the job."

"I went back last week. I was getting antsy at home. You know me. And the police surgeon OK'd it."

Inspector Flora Hamburg knew her better than almost anyone else on the job. "You staying with the cold cases?"

"Yeah."

"You get tired of it, let me know. I still have a little power around here and I get a kick out of throwing it around. All your bruises gone?"

"I feel fine. I've been checked out from head to toe."

"Just looking after you. How's your love life?"

"That's an unusual question coming from you."

"I decided that, after twenty years of nonstop policing, maybe you should give a thought to something a little sexier."

"Let's just say I'm between relationships. No one at One Thirty-seven Centre is even mildly seductive."

"Seductive. I wouldn't think so. I hope they get their shoes on straight, that crowd. Except for Graves, but he's not available."

"I don't go out with men who aren't available."

"I'm glad to hear it. You feel like dinner next week?"

"Sure."

"Put me in for Wednesday. I'll call you the night before."

If anyone on the job was Jane's mentor, it was Flora Hamburg. Homely, brash, overweight, her weapon always flapping against her hip, Flora was dedicated to the betterment of women in the department. She had steered Jane in every right direction since they had met early in Jane's career. And Jane remembered clearly the day Flora had said she would never inquire about personal relationships. "Just don't fuck where you work," she had said, her words, as always, ringing with the sound of a command.

What had made her ask that unnerving question tonight? Jane drank the beer slowly. She couldn't possibly know. When Jane had begun her affair with Hack ten years ago, they were together so often someone might have gotten wind of what was going on, but no one had. Hack had been super careful, occasionally canceling a date when it would be better to continue an impromptu night out with the boys. Now, with the relationship far less active, the chance of anyone learning anything was significantly lower. Hack was married and Jane had stopped him from leaving his wife. It was the reverse of the old story, the married man with a million excuses for staying married. It was this unmarried woman who didn't want to break up the marriage, what was left of it, who wasn't sure she wanted to commit to a permanent union.

But it was so hard not to see him. She got up and rinsed

out the beer bottle. If Flora knew, if anyone knew, it would be the end of two careers. Neither of them wanted that. But it would be so nice to talk to him tonight. It was a cold night and he was the warmest man she had ever known.

"Think about the case, Janey," she said aloud. If only there were a case.

MacHovec didn't care. As long as he sat in a warm office with a telephone nearby, as long as the checks came in regularly, he could be counting computers in a warehouse. Defino wanted to clear cases. Wasted hours and days ate at him.

And there's me, Jane thought. She was like Defino, but she kept it to herself. She had fallen into the role of peacemaker between the two men on the team. She could tolerate MacHovec's sloppy appearance and his bending of rules because he did his part of the job well. And she genuinely liked Defino. They hadn't been together long, only since last fall, but she sensed she could count on him the way she had always counted on Marty Hoagland, her longtime partner in the Six.

On her lap was a chunk of the Stratton file. At the moment, it was doing nothing more than keeping her lap warm. She opened it from the bottom and started flipping pages from the moment the call came in eight years ago. It was all so routine except that people don't sit looking out the window when they're hungry. They reach for the phone, they put something in the microwave, they open a can. They call their sister for help. Why hadn't Stratton done any of those things?

She wrote down the name of the psychiatrist. Like everyone else in this crazy case, he was worth a Five.

Officer Roberta Chen was waiting for them on the corner of Tenth and Avenue A. Medium height, halfway through her twenties, dark-eyed and gorgeous, she shook hands with the detectives and said, "Hi, I'm Police Officer Roberta Chen. Call me Bobby; everyone does. We thought it would be better if I didn't wear a uniform."

"Good thinking," Defino said. "These folks didn't want to give us the time of day when we started asking questions."

"I grew up in that kind of family. I can handle it."

They walked to the laundry. A woman with a stroller was just coming out, cooing to her baby. No one else was inside.

"Jane, you come with me. Three people will be too threatening."

Defino put his coat collar up, grinned, and waved them in.

Inside, Bobby Chen began speaking fluent Chinese. She addressed the old woman in the corner and the younger woman behind the counter. Even not knowing the language, Jane could see how deferential she was being.

After a short conversation, Bobby turned to Jane. "It's the daughter you want to speak to, right?"

"Right."

Another conversation with comments from the grandmother. The woman behind the counter shook her head. A man came out of the back room and added his voice. He sounded annoyed. A customer came in and all conversation ended till she left. Then Bobby began again.

Jane became aware that the man, who had returned to the back room, was talking to someone. The second voice was faint but definitely female. She wished Defino had gone around the back. Stores often had back exits, perhaps leading to an alley behind the store. She moved toward the door and stopped when she heard a clear female voice.

"Can I help you, Officer?" The person behind the voice was taller than either of her parents. She wore black pants, a white shirt with the sleeves rolled up, glasses, and a short haircut. She was slim and pretty and spoke like a New Yorker.

"We'd like to talk to you," Bobby said in English.

"This is an inconvenient time. May I meet you in half an hour? In the coffee shop around the corner?"

Bobby looked at Jane.

"We'll be waiting."

"I thought you'd never come out," Defino said as they walked to the coffee shop. "My hands are like ice."

"I'm sweating," Jane said. "How do they do it in the summer?"

"They need the money," Bobby Chen said.

"Did you get the girl's name?"

"She calls herself Rose in English. I don't think you'll have any trouble, but I can stick around if you'd like."

"Stick," Defino said. "You've done OK so far."

The girl walked in exactly as promised and sat at the white Formica-topped table with them. "My parents didn't understand," she said. "I heard you say 'Stratton' and I realized you were talking about the man who died several years ago."

"We were told you went to visit him sometimes in his apartment," Jane said.

"I didn't really visit. I brought him his laundry. Usually, he took it in himself. Sometimes he picked it up. But most of the time he wanted it delivered."

"How did it work?" Jane asked. "Did you leave it outside the door or did he open up for you?"

"At first he left an envelope with the money. It wasn't always the right amount but my mother straightened it out when she saw him. And there was always a quarter for me. I felt very rich." She smiled. "Then I came one day and there was no envelope. I rang the bell the way I always did and started down the stairs when I heard the door open. Mr. Stratton was there and he called me. I went back upstairs and inside the apartment."

"What happened?" Jane asked, feeling a little queasy.

"Nothing bad," Rose said with her beautiful smile. "He was very nice. He gave me a chair to sit down in and asked if I wanted a Coke or something else to drink. He pulled money out of his pocket and gave some to me for the laundry. Then he asked me how I liked school."

"You stayed and talked?" Defino asked.

"Yes. For maybe fifteen minutes. Then I got nervous and asked if I could call my mother. He gave me the phone and I told her I was on my way. She was very strict and she knew just how long it took for me to get there and back so she was already worried when I called."

"So you talked about school and then you left," Jane said. "What happened the next time?"

"The same thing. I went in, he gave me a glass of Coke and sat me down on the chair. He asked me what I had learned in school, what I was reading, what kind of music I listened to. I didn't understand who he was and why he was asking me these things. I thought maybe he was a teacher and he was testing me. It was very confusing. But I liked it. I liked being there. I liked him. And I learned a lot from him."

"What do you mean?"

"He told me I had to work hard in school and go to college. He said you had to go to college to be a success. I'm probably not quoting him exactly, but the message got through to me, however he put it."

"How long did this go on?"

"I don't know. Until he died, I guess."

"How did you find out he had died?"

"My parents told me. I don't know how they knew. They were my parents and they knew everything." She said it seriously, as though she still believed it to be true.

Jane took out the plastic bag with the tiny beads in it. She laid it on the table in front of Rose. "Do you recognize these?"

Rose picked it up and poured a few beads onto her palm. She shook her head. "They look almost like pearls but I don't think I ever had any this small."

"They were found in Mr. Stratton's apartment after he died. We wondered who had worn them. Did he ever wear jewelry?"

She thought about it, sipping a cup of tea. "I don't think so. He was very plain. His clothes were casual. I don't remember ever seeing a chain or a bracelet or a ring on him."

"A watch?" Defino asked.

"I'm not sure."

"Wasn't the laundry heavy?" Jane asked. "You were just a little girl."

"I didn't think about it. My mother asked me to take it to him and I did."

"Was anyone ever visiting Mr. Stratton when you got there?"

"Just his lady friend, but she wasn't always there."

"Stratton had a girlfriend?" Jane failed to keep the surprise out of her voice.

"I suppose you could call her that. They seemed to know each other well."

Defino flipped a page in his notebook. "Do you know what her name was?"

"He called her . . . I think it was Bee-Bee. I thought it was a funny name."

"Did she talk to you?"

"Just to say hello. I think I bored her. She would sit and read while Mr. Stratton and I talked or she would go into another room. She wasn't always there when I left."

"You think you could help an artist make a sketch?" Defino asked. "We could get someone to work with you at the station house on Avenue C."

"I could try. I remember what she looked like. She had dark hair, long, and kind of a narrow face."

"Where can we reach you?"

She wrote a number on his notebook page. "It's my phone. If I don't answer, leave a message. It's the number my friends at school call. My parents don't answer it."

"Could she have worn the little beads?" Jane asked.

"She wore a lot of beads," Rose said. "Some of them were silver, some were colored glass or stones. I don't recognize these especially, but maybe they were hers."

"We'll set up an appointment with an artist and one of us will call you," Defino said. "Any time good for you?"

"I have no classes on Friday afternoon."

"Sounds good." Defino was suddenly upbeat.

"I have to go now. Are we finished?"

"Thanks for coming," Jane said. "We really appreciate it."

Rose buttoned her coat and said good-bye to each of them. Roberta Chen had said nothing. Now she spoke a few syllables of Chinese. Rose smiled and responded. Then she left the restaurant.

BOBBY CHEN TOOK off for the subway and Jane and Defino went back to talk to Larry Vale, the super.

"You see anything in the file about this Bee-Bee?" Defino asked as they walked.

"Nothing, and nothing about Rose either. I've been turning pages and there are damn few names besides the super, the pizza place, and the other tenants. Mrs. C. didn't rule out a girlfriend, but she didn't know one existed."

"I remember."

They rang Larry Vale's bell. It was still morning so he might be less annoyed at being disturbed.

The door opened. "It's you. What is it now?"

"A couple of questions," Defino said, irritation back in his voice. He didn't like this guy and he let it show.

Vale let them in. "I'm listening."

"Did Stratton have a girlfriend?"

"I wouldn't know. We didn't talk about women."

"You ever see a dark-haired woman go up to his apartment?"

"I told you yesterday: I didn't see people go up to apartments. And I don't remember any dark-haired women."

"Does the name Bee-Bee ring a bell?" Jane asked.

"No."

"We think she may have been living with Stratton." She left it open.

"Could be. He never mentioned it."

"Give it some thought," Jane said, making it sound like an order. She didn't like him any more than Defino did.

"I'll do that, Detective. Are we done?"

"For now," Defino said. Everything that came out of Defino's mouth sounded like a warning.

MacHovec had called the psychiatrist. "He'll see you at noon tomorrow but don't expect much. Stratton saw him once or twice and never came back. It's so long ago, he had to dig out the file to figure out who I was talking about."

"It's a Five," Defino said.

"You sound like a broken record."

"I feel like one."

MacHovec passed the sheet with the name and address on it to Jane. "He'll be eating his lunch."

"Sean, take a look through the names of the tenants and see if there's a woman whose name could be Bee-Bee."

"I've got them all here. No one's name even starts with *B*."

"Maybe someone they interviewed in the park." She turned pages in the file till she came to those interviews. "There was a Barbara, but she had two children, not a likely girlfriend."

"You really think a guy like that had a girlfriend?"

"She was in the apartment. The Chinese girl saw her. Whoever she was, she had some kind of relationship with Stratton."

"Maybe she was Social Services."

She didn't think so, but it gave Sean something to do.

Bee-Bee, she thought. BiBi. B.B. She picked up her phone and dialed Mrs. Constantine's number.

"Hello," she said, as though she were expecting a call.

"Mrs. Constantine, this is Detective Jane Bauer."

"Detective Bauer, yes. Do you have something for me?"

"I have a question. We think your brother may have had a woman friend whose first name was Bee-Bee. Does that ring a bell?"

"Bee-Bee. No, I can't say it does. What do you mean by a woman friend?"

"She was sometimes in the apartment with your brother. During the day."

"Hm."

"She had dark hair and often wore beads."

"The little beads. Were the beads hers?" A hint of excitement crossed the wire.

"We don't know."

"Bee-Bee. Dark hair."

"We're going to get a sketch on Friday. Maybe that will help. I just wondered if the name meant anything to you."

"Nothing, I'm afraid. But I'm glad to hear you've learned something new."

"I'll call when we have a sketch."

Defino was looking at her. Jane shook her head. "I'm thinking she may have been a groupie in the park or in one of the buildings they were tearing down. She may have liked the idea of taking care of a man who couldn't quite take care of himself."

"Happens."

"And after he died, she decided to grow up, give up the love beads, and have an establishment life."

"Let's hope the picture helps."

"You sound as if you're starting to believe."

"I'll believe when it's a fact." He sat down at the typewriter and started banging out his Fives.

MacHovec set up an appointment for Friday afternoon with the artist, who agreed to meet Rose in the Nine. Jane called Rose's private phone and left a message on the machine. It was such a long shot, that an eighteen-year-old could remember a face she had seen as a ten-year-old, it hardly seemed worth it, but it was all they had. Maybe this bright young woman had a photographic memory that would activate someone else's imagination.

Jane went through the list of former tenants at Stratton's building and began making calls to their new addresses. The first to answer was an old man who didn't remember Stratton and probably didn't remember what day it was. The second was an old woman who remembered Stratton but hadn't known him well. She had heard of his death from her neighbor on the fourth floor. It was a long time ago and that was all she could say about it.

The next phone call was to Irma Bender, who had lived next door to Stratton and had called the police because of the smell.

"Mrs. Bender, this is Detective Jane Bauer of the police department. I'd like to ask you some questions about your former neighbor on Tenth Street."

"The one who died?"

"Yes, Mr. Stratton. How well did you know him?"

"I knew him pretty good. I used to knock on his door sometimes and see how he was."

"Why did you do that?"

"He seemed a nice young man, but he didn't get out much and he lived alone and I worried about him. My son was living alone around that time and I always hoped someone would be looking in on him too."

"You said he didn't get out much."

"He didn't have a job. He told me once he had problems and sometimes at night . . ."

"Yes?"

"I would hear him. I couldn't tell if he was laughing or crying, but it didn't sound right. It made me feel, I don't know, crawly. You know what I mean?"

"I do, yes. Tell me, Mrs. Bender, did you notice if he had visitors?"

"Oh sure. He had food delivered sometimes, but he

never opened the door till they were gone. And now and then his friends would come."

"Did you see a little Chinese girl come to deliver his laundry?"

Silence. "I wasn't home all the time and if she was very quiet, I wouldn't hear. My hearing isn't what it used to be."

Which might be why she never told the police or Wally Shreiber about Rose. Jane had an image of the woman cracking the door when she heard footsteps on the stairs. Nosy people made good informants. "Do you remember any of those friends?"

"It's a long time. There was a long-haired man who always wore jeans. And a couple of girls."

"Did you ever hear any names?"

"No."

"Did you know where they lived?"

"How could I know that?"

"You might have seen them around the neighborhood."

"Well, I don't think so." She sounded offended.

"Thank you for your time, Mrs. Bender."

"Can I ask why you're interested in this?"

"We're just reinvestigating his death."

"You mean it wasn't natural causes?"

"We aren't sure. Do you have any reason to believe that someone might have killed him?"

Another silence. "How could I know that? It wasn't my food that killed him, I'll tell you that. Everything I gave him I ate myself."

"I'm sure it was great," Jane said. She marked the name on her list. If they needed to beef up the file, they could go over and talk to Irma Bender.

None of the other names yielded anything. She sat looking over the names and her notes. "Sean," she said.

"Yeah."

"Can you find out if Stratton had a relationship with Social Services?"

"I can try. It'll probably take them a month to dig out a file that old. But I can go down there."

"Thanks."

That was the only kind of legwork MacHovec could tolerate. He even knew how to charm the people over at Motor Vehicles, generally considered uncharmable. And when records from One PP were needed, he somehow managed to extract them from their drawers and boxes in less time than anyone else Jane knew.

He was on the phone now, sweet-talking someone who would as soon eat him alive as give him the time of day. "Mrs. Hartwell," she heard him croon, "this is Detective Sean MacHovec at One Thirty-seven Centre Street. I wonder if . . ."

Jane smiled and went out for a cup of coffee, stopping to chat with Lieutenant Ellis McElroy, the second whip. He was up to speed on the case although he hadn't participated in any discussions. Built like a tank, McElroy lacked Graves's natural good looks and appeal, but he was a straight shooter.

When she got back to the office, MacHovec was putting down the phone with a grin. "She'll do a rush job and let me know in three weeks."

Defino laughed.

"So I guess I'll take a look myself tomorrow morning."

Remembering a past incident, Jane said, "Let Annie know, OK?"

"Would I go anywhere without telling Annie?"

It didn't deserve an answer.

Steak, baked potato, salad, half a pink Florida grapefruit to start with. It was good eating and little work, a winning combination. After dinner, she called two numbers that hadn't answered this afternoon, people who lived near Stratton. Neither answered tonight. Where did old people go at night in the winter? Maybe to church. Maybe to the hospital. Maybe to Florida.

When she hung up, the phone rang almost immediately. "Hello?" She drew her legs up onto the sofa.

"Jane."

Her heart flipped. "Hi." It was a voice she would know in a coma.

"Just thinking about you. I can't see you tonight."

"How are you?"

"Bored. Working my tail off. You're on the Stratton case?"

"The Stratton death by starvation case. Only a sister could see a homicide here."

"She's made a lot of trouble for us. Give her a pound of paper."

"That's what Graves wants."

"You think there's a chance she's right?"

"No."

"You can't end up a hero every time."

"Don't want to. Flora Hamburg called, Hack. She asked me about my love life."

"What's eating her?"

"I don't know. We're having dinner next Wednesday. Maybe she'll say something. I won't."

"She doesn't know anything. She's just putting out feelers. I miss you like crazy."

"Me too."

"Maybe I'll see you after your dinner. I'm staying overnight in the city. Got a meeting at dawn on Thursday."

"I'll skip dessert."

"We'll have it together."

"I'm glad you called."

The nature of the relationship had changed in the last couple of months. It had been on for ten years and then Jane had turned it off, partly because Hack's daughter had started asking questions. It had been resurrected by circumstances and now had a sporadic quality. Meetings were less frequent and less planned, more volatile when they happened. She wondered sometimes what she would do if Hack's wife decided to leave him. There it would be, the golden opportunity, but would she take it? It was a question she never answered. She smiled thinking how good it would be to see him next week.

It was later on, while she was getting ready for bed, that a different question posed itself. She had been rummaging through the Stratton file since talking to Hack, nothing leaping out at her. Now, as she settled under the comforter, just the lamp beside her bed lighting the room, something about the super, Larry Vale, set off a silent alarm. He had seen the little Chinese girl delivering Stratton's laundry. From his front window, he had a view of the sidewalk and he could see at least the bottom half of anyone who arrived at the outside stairs. How did he know she was taking the laundry to Stratton?

She recalled that after he mentioned it to them, he had screwed up his face as though a flicker of pain had passed through him. He hadn't told the police or Wally Shreiber about Rose even though he knew about her. Maybe he had made a slip. Maybe he had told her and Defino something he had intended to keep to himself.

IN THE MORNING she called Wally Shreiber, the PI Mrs. C. had hired. "Good morning," she said. "Jane Bauer here. I have two questions."

"Just two?"

"At the moment. Do you know anything about the little Chinese girl from the laundry who delivered Stratton's clean clothes?"

The silence was her answer. "A Chinese laundry?" he said finally.

"A couple of blocks from Stratton's apartment. He dropped off his dirty clothes and they sent them back clean. Their daughter, who was only nine or ten at the time, carried it up to him."

"Where'd you hear about this?" he asked, as though it were more important for him to learn where he had failed than to follow up a lead.

"Vale, the super, mentioned it. We interviewed the girl's parents with a translator yesterday and then talked to the girl separately. Stratton invited her into his apartment."

"He didn't let the pizza guy in."

"That's what makes it interesting. He liked her, sat and talked with her, gave her a quarter tip."

"I never heard anything about it. What's it telling you?"

"Nothing at the moment. I just wondered if you knew about it."

"Sorry."

"And a woman named Bee-Bee who was sometimes with Stratton when the laundry came."

"Doesn't ring a bell. Hold on." There was a rustling of paper. "She's not on my list. Who told you about her?"

"The Chinese girl. She's about eighteen now, goes to college. She works in the store when she's not in class."

"Well, you found something I missed. I hope it leads somewhere. What did you think of the super?"

"Arrogant."

"That's the guy."

"Well, thanks anyway."

"Keep me informed."

She promised she would.

MacHovec wasn't at his desk and she remembered he was going to try to find out if Stratton had been under the wing of Social Services. Sean would probably stretch out his research to encompass the whole morning, so she didn't expect to see him till much later. At noon they had an appointment with the psychiatrist.

"Gordon, I had a thought last night."

The typing stopped. Defino was dressing up the Fives so they used a lot of paper. "More'n I had."

"How did Larry Vale know that the Chinese girl was delivering laundry to Stratton? He couldn't see where she was going."

"Hm."

She picked up the phone and dialed Vale's number. It rang three times and his machine came on. "This creep doesn't want to work too hard," she said, hanging up. "In the afternoon you can't disturb him and in the morning he doesn't take calls."

"Let's go down and shake him up."

Vale was there and not happy to see them again. "Was this trip necessary?" he asked as he opened the door.

Standing in the small foyer, Jane said, "How did you know the little Chinese girl was delivering laundry to Stratton?"

"What do you mean? I saw her come with a brown paper package."

"How did you know she was taking it to Stratton, not someone else?" Defino said. "You follow her up the stairs?"

Vale didn't look happy. "No, I—" He thought a moment. "I asked her," he said. "I saw her coming to the building once—I was outside, coming home myself—and I asked her where she was going. She said she was going to Mr. Stratton's apartment to give him his clean clothes."

"She told you that," Jane said.

"Yes. So when I saw her again, I just assumed." He shrugged.

Jane walked into his living room, uninvited. The windows were about street level, the floor below that. She could see a dog, a leash, and finally a woman passing from left to right. You had to bend a little to see the woman's face, but the girl would have been much smaller, maybe only waist high. Jane sat in the chair she had taken two days ago. From the lower perspective she could see heads as well as feet.

Back in the foyer, she thanked Vale.

"You came all the way up here to ask me that?"

"Looks like it," Defino said.

Out on the street, he said, "That guy brings out more hostility in me than my daughter does."

Jane laughed. His daughter was a teenager and gave her parents periodic agony. "That's why he does it. We've still got some time left before the psychiatrist. Want to walk through the park?"

"You like living on the edge."

"It's not as bad as it used to be."

"That's not saying much."

The most recent trouble in the park had been in the late eighties. The park had been taken over by street people and anyone who survived the muggers could buy almost any drug in existence. In the surrounding area, squatters had occupied empty buildings, and when asked to leave, refused vehemently. They claimed the buildings as their own since they considered themselves residents who improved the property by living there. As far as they were concerned, the legal owners had abandoned them. They managed to steal utilities from nearby buildings so they had gas and electricity that they didn't pay for. After several violent confrontations between the police and the activists, the buildings were cleared of squatters and the park emptied in a hats-and-bats operation—helmets and nightsticks.

The park still wasn't the kind of place where you sat on a bench in the sunshine and read the paper, but at least one didn't sense the nearness of an incipient riot. Jane had slipped her Glock into her coat pocket before they set foot on the grass and she noticed that Defino touched his chest, where his holster rested.

They didn't stay long. If she had thought she might find a local who would remember Stratton, she was wrong. They walked out near the Avenue B corner and continued north to Fourteenth Street to catch the subway to the psychiatrist's office.

"I'm Dr. Handelman." Graying and bespectacled, his image projected warmth. "Sit where you're comfortable."

They both avoided the couch, choosing instead heavy wooden chairs that faced the desk. The doctor was in his fifties, a tall man in a brown suit and a blue shirt.

"I'm afraid I must eat my lunch while we talk. I have a patient at one."

"That's fine," Jane said. "We're here about Anderson Stratton."

"I've reviewed his file and there's very little I can tell you. He moved to New York about ten years ago from a private clinic and took up residence in what they call Alphabet City these days, Avenues A and B down on the east side. His sister, Mrs. Constantine, looked out for him. I can't call her a caregiver as she didn't live with him, and he refused to have anyone come in and see him, check up on him, give him his medications. He was very firm about living independently.

"I had an extensive talk with Mrs. Constantine before her brother was released. She promised she would see to it that he kept his appointments. I believe she sent a car for him. He came twice, then didn't come for a few weeks, then came again. That was the last time I saw him."

"Did you think he was a danger to himself?" Jane asked.

"There was no record of his ever harming himself or attempting suicide. The clinic sent me his records and I reviewed them before his first visit. However," he paused and bit into his sandwich, "he didn't keep his appointments and that might be construed as self-destructive."

"Do you think he could have simply stopped eating because it became too difficult to order food?"

"It's possible although not likely. His death occurred almost two years after the last time I saw him. I don't know whether his condition was the same or had deteriorated. I don't know if he kept up with his medication. I'm aware that his sister didn't believe he died a natural death or a self-inflicted death, but I understand there was no evidence of anything else. May I ask why you're investigating his death so many years later?"

Jane and Defino exchanged a glance. "Why we're investigating is because Mrs. Constantine has put pressure on the police department to find a killer. Why it's so long after his death is that she's been trying for years to reopen the case, and apparently she succeeded recently."

"It sounds as though you consider this a wild-goose chase."

"We've been assigned the case, Doctor. We're pursuing it."

"I see. Well,"—he paused to take a sip of coffee—"not having seen Mr. Stratton for nearly two years at the time of his death, I can't say anything definitive. Yes, he could have become despondent, especially if he stopped taking his medication, and he may have gradually stopped eating. This is pure speculation, you understand."

"His sister told us he was a poet."

"That's in my notes. He considered himself a writer, a thinker, a philosopher if you will. He hoped to teach one day." He looked down at the paper in the thin file. "There isn't much I can tell you."

"What's your opinion of Mrs. Constantine?" Defino asked.

"Devoted, concerned, willful, opinionated. The Stratton family has a lot of money and paid handsomely for the clinic Anderson had been in. She was willing to do whatever it took to give her brother a normal life."

"Thanks, Doctor."

He rose and shook their hands. As they turned to leave, he reached for the *New York Times* and pulled it over near his coffee.

They had lunch and took the subway back to Centre Street. MacHovec was at his desk, back from his morning of digging in the files at Social Services.

"Got something?" Jane asked, taking off her coat.

"Social Services had Stratton under their wing. He wasn't always nice to them, from what I saw in the file. He pissed them off so they kept transferring his case from one social worker to another. Most of the time he wouldn't let them in, but I gather he was a loner."

"What are you leading up to?" Jane asked, sensing a kicker in all this.

"Well, looks like they sent a supervisor over and she worked her way into the apartment and maybe into his heart."

"She have a name?"

"Erica Rinzler."

"Not a *B* anywhere."

"And she's gone. Want to guess when she left?"

"When Stratton died."

"You got it."

"Ellis tells me you've got something." The whip stood in the doorway. An hour earlier, Jane had spoken to Lieutenant McElroy about the missing Social Services supervisor, whose name appeared on no local phone lists including suburbs of New York, New Jersey, and Connecticut.

"Something very thin, Captain Sean?"

MacHovec cleared his throat. "They went through a bunch of caseworkers that Stratton either ignored or tossed out on their ear. So they tried a supervisor, Erica Rinzler, and that seemed to work. She documented visits on a regular basis and said he was doing OK. She left the department sometime after Stratton's body was discovered."

"When was her last visit?"

"About two weeks before the body was found."

"And he was dead for a while when the call came in." Graves took the sheet of notes from MacHovec. "Looks like she visited every two weeks. That would mean he was alive two weeks before his body was found. We have any way of determining whether the laundry was delivered at the same time Rinzler made her visit?"

"I doubt it," Jane said. "We'll talk to Rose tomorrow when she meets with the artist at the Nine, but I expect her mother handed her a package and told her to deliver it, and whether it was a Tuesday or a Wednesday wouldn't stick in a kid's mind. And it was eight years ago."

"Ask her anyway. And you better start bothering Social Services for information on Rinzler. Get a warrant if you need one."

"It's possible she visited more often than she reported," Defino said.

"Right. And stayed longer. And maybe found him dead and kept quiet about it." He put the sheet on MacHovec's desk. "Find her," he said.

It gave them all a lift. To be wasting time on a noncase was depressing. To be working on a possible homicide was what they lived for.

"OK," Defino said jauntily, "what's her last address?"

MacHovec read it off, an apartment in the Murray Hill section of Manhattan, the East Thirties. "I already tried the phone number and it was reassigned. I got a call in to the phone company to see what the forwarding number was. Probably hear tomorrow."

"Want to look into this in the morning?" Defino swiveled toward Jane.

"Sure. Then we can be at the Nine to talk to Rose in the afternoon. She'll be there at one."

"Let's meet at the apartment house first and come here after."

"Suits me." She turned to MacHovec. "How 'bout some names of coworkers?"

"Right here. Her boss, another supervisor, and someone under her. Some of them are still there."

"Lots of Fives, Gordon."

"Yeah, but do we have a case?"

Maybe tomorrow they would have a better idea.

9

THE APARTMENT HOUSE was on East Thirty-sixth between Madison Avenue and Park, about in the center of Murray Hill, which ran from the high Twenties to Forty-second Street. Owned in the days of the Revolutionary War by Robert Murray, who built a country home around Thirty-seventh Street and Park Avenue, the land was eventually divided into building lots. In the early nineteenth century wealthy Americans built mansions on their estates there, most of which are long gone.

Today the area was a mixture of structures built in the first half of the twentieth century and their replacements in the second half. New York buildings often lasted no more than a generation, something that pained Jane's father. He felt that a building he had seen rise from a hole in the ground should remain through his lifetime. He moaned often about the demise of the Coliseum at Columbus Circle.

Defino was smoking on the street in front of the apartment house, one of those built later rather than earlier. "Morning."

"Hi. Little milder today."

"Better for tramping around. What's this guy's name?"

"Mike Willis." They showed their shields and photo IDs to the doorman and went to the super's door on the lobby floor.

The man who opened the door was startled by the shields and took a step back. "What's up?"

"We just want to ask you about an old tenant," Jane said.

"Oh. Sure. Come on in." He was in his forties, a little overweight, and losing his hair. His wife peeked around a doorway, smiled, and retreated. "Sit down. What can I do for you?"

"Erica Rinzler," Jane said. "Lived here about eight or ten years ago."

"That's a long time. I think I know the name but let me get the book." He came back a minute later, turning pages. "Yeah. She lived here for six years, moved in before I came, moved out, like you said, about eight years ago. Had a one bedroom on the third floor."

"Forwarding address?"

"Nothing here."

"Where'd you send the security?" In New York, a month's security or even two were automatic.

"No idea. Maybe she came back and got it. No, wait a minute. I know who that was, kinda dark-haired gal, wore a lot of beads. Nice smile. She didn't get her mail here. She had a box at the post office."

"Got the number?"

"This must be it." He read it off.

"What do you remember about her?"

"Not much. She didn't bother me like some of them do, so I didn't get to know her. And it's a long time ago."

"Any complaints about her?"

He shrugged.

"You know where she worked?"

He checked another part of the book. "Worked for the city."

"OK."

Defino handed him his card. "If you remember anything about her, anything at all, give us a call. You've been very helpful."

"What did she do?" Willis asked.

"Nothing," Defino said. "We just need to talk to her." A familiar tag line.

Willis looked at the card. "OK. I'll think about it."

It was all they could ask.

They decided to leave the post office for MacHovec. He had a connection in the post office system and he knew how to exploit it. They took the subway down to Centre Street where MacHovec had already heard from his contact at the phone company.

"No forwarding number," he said. "Guess she wanted to cut her ties. She didn't have a deposit—she'd had that phone for several years—so there's no address after Thirty-sixth Street. Looks like the lady made herself a dead end."

"Maybe there's a case," Defino said.

"You check to see if she had a record?" Jane asked.

"I'm doing that as we speak. Nothing yet. She doesn't own a car in New York, doesn't have a license. Maybe she liked the weather better in California."

"Keep at it."

He kept his eyes on the screen, keying from time to time. Then he looked up. "I checked out your super guy, Vale, at the Nine. He was picked up during one of the riots in the eighties, but charges were dropped."

"Most of them were dropped," Defino said bitterly.

"There wasn't anything else." He looked back at the screen, muttering "Rinzler" as he scanned it.

Jane turned to Defino and spoke quietly, giving MacHovec the atmosphere he needed to do his research. "What did Rinzler get from Stratton? Money is the only thing I can think of."

"Sex. Maybe she fell in love with him."

"I'm assuming she killed him, Gordon."

"Then she couldn't have been after his money."

"Unless she'd gotten all he had or all she thought she could reasonably get away with." She picked up the phone and dialed Mrs. Constantine. It rang several times, then the answering machine came on. She left her name and number and hung up. "I'll ask her what the financial arrangement was," she said to Defino. "He kept bills in his pocket and he got them from somewhere. I don't know if this guy was together enough to go to a bank and cash a check. If not, his sister must have gotten the money to him in some way. Maybe Rinzler learned how to intercept the delivery."

"So why does she kill him?"

"He figured out what she was doing and said he'd tell his sister. Or Larry Vale. He sat and talked to Vale, remember?"

"I wouldn't trust that son of a bitch with a nickel."

"But Stratton liked him. They talked about music."

"This isn't about music."

"OK, partners," MacHovec said, turning away from his screen. "I don't find where this woman is, but she isn't wanted anywhere I looked. And she doesn't seem to be in the prison system. So she's managed to cover her tracks, which means she's hiding something."

"Let's get lunch," Defino said, "and go up to the Nine."

It was a little early, but Jane agreed. As soon as they had the drawing of Rinzler, they could show it to Vale and the tenants who had moved into nearby buildings.

10

ROSE TSAO HAD arrived punctually at the station house and was already sitting with the artist when they arrived.

"Oh hi," she said as they entered the room. "Was I supposed to wait for you?"

Jane smiled. "Not at all. Don't let us interrupt. Will it bother you if we hang around?"

"Of course not." Rose turned back to the face-in-the-making. "A little too thin," she said. "That makes her old."

The artist, a sergeant named Giordano, made the face slightly fuller.

"I'll be back," Defino said and left the room.

Jane took her coat off and sat where Rose couldn't see her. She had watched similar sessions a few times and enjoyed seeing a face materialize from one person's memory and another's artistic talent. They worked for about an hour. Rose was a perfectionist and kept making small changes. The hair wasn't quite right, the eyes were too close together, the cheekbones—should they be so prominent?

Finally, she sat back, looking exhausted. "I think that's all I can do," she said apologetically. "It's not perfect but it's not wrong either. It needs a little more life in the eyes. She was a vibrant woman. She smiled a lot. And you know what? She needs beads around her neck."

"What kind of beads?" Giordano asked.

"Just beads. Colorful beads, blue, silver. She had some of those crystal beads that change color when you move. Prisms, I think they're called. I remember being fascinated by them."

"A grown-up flower child," Giordano said, sketching some blue beads along the side of the neck.

"Yes. Like that."

"You can go whenever you want," Jane said. "We're very grateful you took the time to do this."

"My mother always warned me about the park," she said as she put her coat on. "But there were a couple of people, park people, who would say hello as I came by. Sometimes they gave me a piece of candy or gum. I never had the fear that other people did. I thought they were pretty nice, even if they didn't have a real place to live."

"I'm sure you were a very sweet little girl," Jane said, thinking that that hadn't changed.

She found Defino talking to a detective in the squad room. He was an old friend from early in Defino's career and they were having a good time when she got there. Defino got up quickly, said his good-byes, and he and Jane went to collect copies of the sketch.

"His partner's on medical leave," Defino said. "He was attacked by a wild man with a knife six inches long."

"He coming back?"

"Looks like it. He doesn't have twenty years yet and he has kids ready for college."

"That'll keep you on the job."

The sketches of Rinzler were still warm. They took twenty copies, hoping to hand them out to anyone who would take them.

"Let's see if we can find Irma Bender. I talked to her on the phone and it sounded like she cracked the door every time she heard a footstep."

"Sounds like my mother-in-law. I don't know when she has time to watch all the TV in her life."

The building Irma Bender was living in now was on East Ninth Street, east of Avenue C, a short distance from the station house. As they walked east, they could see the Jacob Riis Houses at the edge of Manhattan and just south of them the Lillian Wald Houses. Named for two early movers and shakers in social work, the buildings were home to low-income New Yorkers. On the eastern face these complexes offered their occupants a splendid view of the East River and Brooklyn and Queens on the other side, the three old bridges that spanned the river, and, Jane had always thought, magnificent sunrises.

Defino must have been thinking the same thing because he said, "The poor always get the best views. Have you noticed?"

"It's free."

"Not on the Upper East Side."

That was true. There, a view east could cost thousands a month. Mrs. Bender lived on the fourth floor of an old, dilapidated walk-up. Her name was on the mailbox but there was no response to the bell. Not that it mattered; the inner door was unlocked. They climbed the stairs and rang the doorbell, which sounded loudly.

"Who's there?" The voice was loud and somewhat fearful.

"Detective Bauer, Mrs. Bender. We spoke on the phone the other day."

The door was unlocked immediately. "Oh. Who are you?"

"Detective Defino." He held up his ID as Jane was doing.

"Come in and sit down. I can feel safe awhile. I'm not sure I remember how it feels."

The apartment was shedding paint and cracks lined the walls, but Irma Bender kept it clean and her furniture made it look almost upscale. They sat in the living room and Jane handed the woman the sketch.

"Oh yeah," she said before she was asked. "I remember her. Tall, nice-looking girl. She was there all the time in Andy's apartment."

"You mean she lived there?" Jane asked.

"No, I mean she came a lot. There was hanky-panky going on, if you know what I mean."

"I don't know what you mean, Mrs. Bender," Defino said. "Could you spell it out for us?"

"I think they had a, you know, a relationship."

"Do you remember when she started coming around?"

"Not right away when he moved in. Maybe the last year he lived there. You know what? She started coming around the time his health got worse."

"Tell me about that. How did his health change?"

"He didn't look so good. I brought him food, you know, a little of this, a little of that. I didn't want the poor thing to waste away. I would see the pizza box in front of his door. What kind of a diet is that, pizza all the time? You need some red meat if you're gonna make it in this world."

"Did he stop going out?" Jane asked.

"Maybe he didn't go out as much. I wasn't there all the time, so I don't know what he did every minute of the day."

"Did they go out together?"

She shrugged. "Not that I saw. You folks want a little coffee? I can make it in five minutes."

Jane looked at Defino. He was the big coffee drinker.

"No thanks," he said.

"So how do you like this dump I live in? I had such a nice apartment over on Tenth Street. The landlord said he was renovating, I nearly died. I had a lifetime of stuff to move and I knew I'd never find anything as good for that price. Even this place, as bad as it is, costs more than Tenth Street. They let those landlords get away with murder."

"You remember the super on Tenth Street?" Jane asked, steering her back to the relevant topic.

"Larry? Yeah. I remember him. He's OK. He doesn't like to be bothered if it's not an emergency, but who does?"

"Was he friendly with Andy Stratton?"

"Could be. But I didn't see Larry in Andy's apartment too often."

"Did you ever talk to this woman?" Jane asked, pointing to the sketch.

"I don't know. Maybe I said hello on the stairs."

"Did you know her name?"

"How would I know that?"

Typically, the brash New York answer was a question. "Mrs. Bender, you said you brought food to Andy. Did you try to give him anything or just talk to him before he died?"

"Sure. I knocked on the door, I called, he didn't answer. Once—I remember now you asked—I left a little something wrapped in foil outside his door in case he was sleeping or out when I knocked and he didn't answer."

"And?"

"It was there the next morning. I didn't want to leave it

too long so I took it back. You know what food in the hallway can bring."

Jane knew. She had been in enough buildings crawling with them.

"Did you see that woman during that time when he didn't answer the door?" Defino asked.

"How could I remember? You're asking about a long time ago. I saw her, I didn't see her. I saw him, I didn't see him. He looked good, he looked not so good. And then I smelled something and it made me sick to my stomach, not so much the smell but because I was afraid of what it meant."

"Did you tell the police about this woman when they came around?"

"That's a good question. I told them he had friends, I told them about the pizza. If they had showed me a picture, I would have said, 'Sure. She comes around a lot.' But there wasn't any picture, and you know, they didn't start asking questions until a long time after poor Andy died."

When Mrs. C. started getting her back up.

"Thanks, Mrs. Bender," Defino said.

"You hear of a good apartment that I can afford, you let me know, OK?"

Defino smiled. "I'll do that, ma'am."

Out on the street they decided to show the sketch to Larry Vale. Defino liked the idea because they would disturb him during his emergencies-only period, thus disrupting his afternoon.

Vale called "Who is it?" from inside after they rang.

"Detectives Bauer and Defino," Jane said. She was sure she could hear the hiss of an obscenity as he approached the door.

"What now?" he asked. "Haven't I answered enough questions?"

Jane handed him the sketch and watched his face. It paled noticeably. Vale seemed transfixed by the picture, his eyes glued to it.

"Who is she?" Jane asked.

It wasn't that cold out but a tremor ran across Vale's shoulders. He backed into the apartment, letting them enter. "Where did you get this?" he asked.

"We're asking the questions," Defino said. "Detective Bauer asked you who this woman is."

"I don't know her name."

"But you know who she is."

"Just from memory. I saw her once or twice before the renovation."

"What was she doing here?"

"I don't know. I just recognize the face."

"And it scared the shit out of you."

"No, of course not." Vale had recovered and reverted to his usual offensive demeanor. "It was just a shock seeing a face from so long ago. It's a very good likeness."

"What was her relationship to Stratton?" Jane asked.

"To Andy? Did he know her?"

"Mr. Vale, this woman knew Andy Stratton. You know that and we know that. Now you tell us everything you know about their relationship."

He handed the picture back to Jane but she said "Keep it," and refused to take it. "Tell us what you know."

"As I said, I didn't know her. I saw her once or twice. If she knew Andy, that's news to me. I don't know her name. I don't know why she was here. I just recognize the face." He passed a hand through his hair. His color had returned as well as his composure.

"You saw her once or twice eight or nine years ago and you recognize her in that sketch? Come on, Vale, you can do better than that."

"I can't. I've told you everything I know." He put the sheet of paper on a chair. "Is that all? I have work to do."

"We'll be back," Defino promised.

"All we know for sure," Jane said, looking across the desk to Graves, "is that Vale knew who she was and seeing that picture shook him up."

Ellis McElroy had joined them in Graves's office and MacHovec was sitting quietly in a corner drinking coffee.

"It doesn't mean Vale killed Stratton," she continued, "or that Erica Rinzler did. Something was going on, maybe drugs. Vale's not going to give an inch till we have something that scares him more than the sketch."

"OK," Graves said. "We're not pressed for time. Keep at it." He turned to MacHovec. "Anything more on Rinzler?"

"Not right now."

"Have a good weekend."

11

JANE SLEPT A little later Saturday morning, dressed, and had breakfast. She called her father, thinking she might go up and visit, and found him busy with Madeleine, his neighbor and friend. What she really wanted was to go to Alphabet City and do a little canvassing on her own. She liked Defino and she trusted him as much as she trusted Marty Hoagland, her last partner, but the truth was she enjoyed being alone. She would miss having someone to talk to, but the joy of walking down a street, turning left or right at a whim, would more than make up for it.

Saturday errands took the better part of an hour. She was carrying her smaller, five-shot Smith & Wesson Chief, an antique from her earlier police career, not that she could tell the difference in the weight. The crap she had to carry daily had left a permanent dent in her left shoulder where she carried the bag.

Before leaving the apartment, she pulled out MacHovec's list of the three people at Social Services who had been friends of Erica Rinzler. Just on a lark, she looked up the first name, Arthur Provenzano. It wasn't in the Manhattan book so she tried Brooklyn. The name appeared with an address in the Park Slope section and she decided to give it a try. He answered on the second ring.

"Mr. Provenzano? This is Detective Jane Bauer of the Cold Case Squad in Manhattan. You work for Social Services, is that correct?"

"That's correct. Is something wrong?"

"No, sir. I have your name as having been acquainted with Erica Rinzler."

"Erica, yes. That was several years ago."

"I'd like to talk to you about her."

"I'm on my way out."

"Could we meet somewhere or could I come to your home?"

He made little sounds of irritation. "I'm going to be in the city this afternoon. I'm meeting someone at two at the Museum of Modern Art."

"Suppose I get there about twenty minutes before two. Would that work?"

"Yes, it could."

"Inside the lobby on the right near the inner door to the gift shop."

"Sounds like you know the museum."

His voice echoed surprise. How would a dumb cop know anything about an art museum? "I know it well. I'll have my shield on my jacket."

"See you then."

Good, she thought. He hadn't said no, he hadn't denied knowing the Rinzler woman. Maybe he was a lead. She would take the subway up to the Fifties when she was through with Alphabet City.

Feeling in need of exercise, she decided to walk from her apartment in the West Village. It was almost due east and she began by picking up Waverly Place, which ran along the north side of Washington Square Park. At Fifth Avenue, she zigged north a block and walked through the Washington Mews, a beautifully preserved block of old stables converted into chic and very expensive living quarters. She felt the uneven cobblestone surface beneath her feet and wondered what the horses would think if they knew who the current occupants of their quarters had become.

She worked her way over to Seventh Street and continued east, passing McSorley's Old Ale House, which famously had managed not to serve women for over a hundred years, until a group of determined women entered in 1970 and caused a revolution. She had been there on several occasions and never quite understood what the fuss was about. The waiters were surly, as though they still resented the intrusion of the second-class citizens they now had to serve.

Seventh took her along the southern edge of Tompkins Square Park. She continued to the east corner and then went into the enclosed children's section, where several women sat talking with strollers at their feet. As it was Saturday, a number of young fathers were also in the park, assisting their children on the slides and swings and other paraphernalia that had been developed after Jane's childhood.

Aware that her mission bordered on futility, she went from mother to mother, offering each the sketch onto which she had clipped her card. Head after head shook to indicate lack of recognition.

"Hang on to it," Jane said conversationally. "Maybe you have a neighbor who'll recognize her."

"When was she here?" a woman asked.

"Eight or nine years ago."

"I didn't even know my husband then."

"I was living in Chicago," another said.

"Ask around, OK? It's really important. We're looking into a questionable death."

She tried the men with no better results. One of them looked at Rinzler for a long time, then shook his head. "Good-looking girl," he said. But no dice.

She left the children's area and started through the main section of the park, immediately sensing a hostility that had been entirely missing among the people she had just questioned. They gave her charged looks and turned their heads away. She knew it was useless and decided not to make the effort. She had left a number of sketches and cards among people who might take her request seriously; that was enough for one morning.

She entered the lobby of the museum at one-thirty and pinned her shield and its leather case carefully to the lapel of her coat. No one near the gift shop entrance looked like her man, so she took a turn through the shop, wondering if she needed a calendar for her kitchen or study. A pack of notecards caught her eye and she bought them. The pictures were by Monet and projected a sense of serenity. She would use them to write to her daughter, Lisa. They had gotten along so well at the December meeting, she wanted to keep the good feelings flowing.

It was exactly one-forty when she slipped her change in her purse. The gold-and-blue enamel shield was visible on her unbuttoned jacket. She was still wearing the casual clothes she had put on in the morning for her walk to Alphabet City.

A thin, dark-haired man near the entrance to the gift shop was standing and looking around. She walked over and said, "Mr. Provenzano?"

"Oh, yes. Detective Bauer?"

"I see a couple of seats together over there. Shall we sit?"

"Sure."

They crossed the lobby and sat. "I'm told you were a friend of Erica Rinzler."

"I was. But I haven't seen her in years."

"Why did she quit? Or was she fired?"

"It was a murky situation. I don't know the answer to your question, but Erica said she quit and that was good enough for me."

"Any idea why she would do that?"

"Ah." It was clear this was something he would rather

not talk about. "There were rumors that she was falsifying records."

"What kind of records?"

"Where she went, what clients she saw, what she did. People she was supposed to have visited called and said she never showed up, but the record showed she'd been there. I don't know what was going on. She's a smart woman. She knew her business. She got along with people. Then . . ."

That was what you waited for, the pause, the hesitation. She said, "What happened then?"

"Maybe it got to be too much for her. Maybe she had a nervous breakdown. Maybe she fell apart. Maybe she burned out. I don't know what happened, but she wasn't the kind of person who would do what they accused her of doing."

"Did you have a relationship with her, Mr. Provenzano?"

"If you mean did we date, no. We went places together because we were friends. We talked at night sometimes, mostly about work, but also about city politics. You work for the city; you know what goes on."

Jane smiled. "I do indeed. Go on."

"That's it. We were friends."

"How did you find out she was quitting?"

"I came to work one morning and she was clearing out her desk. I said, 'Erica, what's going on?' She said, 'Arthur, everything ends eventually. My career just ended.' "

"That was it? No explanation?"

"Not at that point. I helped her pack a few things—she didn't keep much personal stuff in her office—and then she left. It was, I don't know how to put it, it was mind-boggling. One day she was an admired supervisor; the next she was leaving."

"Did you talk to her after she quit?"

"I did, yes. I called her at home that night. As I said, we used to talk at night sometimes. She picked up the phone and said, 'Arthur, I can't go into it. They're giving me my vacation pay and some accumulated days. I'm too young for a pension but there may be an arrangement where I can get it when I'm old enough.' "

"How old was she?"

"Thirties. I'm not sure of the exact number. I'm forty-four now and I always thought she was a little younger than I, so she'd be forty-one or -two now."

"Was that the last conversation you had with her?"

"I called her once more, maybe a week later, but her phone had been turned off. So yes, that was the last conversation. I never heard from her again." The thought clearly distressed him. "I miss her, you know?" He looked Jane in the eye. "We were friends. If something went wrong in her job, that didn't have to mean our friendship was over."

"I understand. Do you have any idea where she went?"

"No. I dropped over at her building on Thirty-sixth Street and they told me she had moved out."

"How long was that after she quit?"

"I don't remember. It's years since this happened."

"Do you have any idea where she might have gone? Was there a friend she could have moved in with? A family?"

"She talked about California. I guess everyone does, don't they?" He smiled sadly. "If she's there, I wouldn't have any idea where. She had a sister, you know."

"Where did the sister live?"

"In one of the suburbs. I don't remember which one, but Erica used to visit. She had a niece, I think, maybe more than one."

"Do you remember the sister's name?"

"Ah." He bent his head. "Her first name was Judy. Erica used to talk about her. Judy did this, Judy said that. But her last name." He looked toward the main door and his face brightened. "There's my friend." He stood.

"Mr. Provenzano, it's really important, the sister's last name."

He seemed agitated. "I really can't spend any more time at this." He looked over toward the door and began to walk away.

"Mr. Provenzano, please. Try to think of the name."

"Arturo," a man said, approaching.

"Hold on just one minute, Frank." Then, in a murmur, he said, "Judy, Judy." He shook his head. "You know, it could be Weiss or Weissberg. And his name was Steven. Judy and Steve. She said that a lot. 'I'm visiting Judy and Steve this weekend.' "

"Think about where they lived," Jane pressed, not wanting to let go while his brain was doing the right thing.

"Up the Hudson. She took the train. She would see the river. One of those upscale towns. What the hell was it called? Frank, you remember Erica Rinzler?"

"Yeah. She quit all of a sudden."

"That's the one. Where did her sister live?"

"Chappaqua."

"Yes." Arthur Provenzano smiled. "That's it. She lived in Chappaqua. Is that it?"

"That's great. Thanks a lot. Enjoy the museum."

That was a lucky break. Jane walked over to the Midtown North station house on Fifty-fourth Street and enlisted the aid of a detective with a computer. There was no Steven Weiss or Weissberg in Chappaqua, but there was a Weissman. She used the phone and called the number. No one answered. It was Saturday afternoon and they were probably doing family things together. Jane took the subway downtown, picked up a steak for dinner. There were baking potatoes in the refrigerator, a couple of fresh vegetables, and the makings of a salad. She would eat well tonight.

At five she tried the Weissman number again. This time a woman answered.

"Mrs. Weissman," Jane said after she had identified herself, "I believe you're the sister of Erica Rinzler."

"What is this about?" The voice sounded tense.

"Her name has come up in a police investigation. We'd like to talk to her."

"That's impossible," the woman said.

"I'm sorry?"

"You can't talk to Erica. It's too late. She's dead. My sister committed suicide several years ago."

12

IT HITS YOU like a thunderbolt. There's something there. There's a case. Maybe Anderson Stratton starved to death because he stopped eating and maybe someone saw to it that he died, but here was a suspicious death, a voice in her ear using the word *suicide.*

"Mrs. Weissman, I am looking into the death of a man your sister knew. I didn't know she had died. I'm sorry for your loss. Can you tell me what happened?"

"Not now I can't. It's five o'clock and I have to feed my kids. My husband and I are going out tonight. And I don't want to do this over the phone. I want to see you and see some identification. I want information from you."

"That's no problem. Tell me what will be convenient for you."

They arranged for the next day at eleven. Judy Weissman gave her precise instructions on trains and schedules. Then Jane called Lieutenant McElroy.

"So Mrs. Constantine may have been right. Looks like you got yourself a case."

"I'm taking the train up to Chappaqua tomorrow morning to talk to her. I just wanted to keep you informed."

"Good. We'll talk Monday morning."

She called Defino because she knew he would want to know. From the upbeat sound of his voice, she sensed he appreciated the call. MacHovec would not appreciate it. When MacHovec left Centre Street, he cut the cord that linked him to the job. On Monday morning he would reestablish it. He was a different kind of cop.

The next morning, Sunday, she took the train from Grand Central Terminal, watching the scenery go by most of the way. She had a book with her but she didn't read much. She had a lot to think about.

Before leaving the apartment, she had checked her voice mail at the office. Mrs. Constantine had returned her Friday call after Jane had left for the weekend, but it was too early to call before she left to catch the train.

At the Chappaqua station she looked for the maroon SUV that Mrs. Weissman had described and found it easily. Not many people were traveling this morning. Jane took out her shield and photo ID and made them visible as she approached the woman.

"Detective Bauer?"

"Yes. Good morning."

"I'm Judy Weissman. Let's drive somewhere. I don't want to have this conversation in my home. My kids are there and they don't know the story."

"This is a lovely town," Jane said as they left the station.

"And the schools are good. We wouldn't be here if not for the schools."

She parked on a picturesque street with little shops, people walking dogs, and a small restaurant two doors down the block. Inside they took a table for two near enough to the fireplace that Jane could feel the heat. They both ordered coffee.

While they waited, Jane explained that there had been a death in New York several years ago, a client of Erica Rinzler's. "There's been a controversy about the cause of the man's death," she explained. "As he was your sister's client in the Social Service system, we thought it might be productive to talk to her." She heard herself using the kinds of words and phrases that tended to irritate her when she was on the receiving end. But she had to be careful not to give away anything that might keep this woman from telling what she knew about Erica Rinzler.

"When I called you," Jane said, "I was hoping you could give me an address and phone number for your sister so we could talk to her. After what you told me, I'd like to hear the circumstances of her death."

"It wasn't long after she quit her job. She called me when that happened and said she'd have to give up the apartment because she didn't know when she'd get work and the rent would drain her savings. I told her to stay with us for a while. I felt she didn't really want to, but she put her furniture in storage and came up here."

"Did she look for another job?"

"She seemed somehow preoccupied, as though her mind were elsewhere. She never really talked about the circumstances of her leaving her job. I sensed she left under a cloud but I didn't want to ask. We were close, but still, I didn't want to intrude."

"What did she do while she was living with you?"

"I will say she went through the listings in the *Times* on Sunday and followed up on a lot of them. We had just gotten a fax machine and she sent her résumé so it would be there Monday morning when the office opened. She got some calls and she went into the city for interviews, but nothing worked out."

"Was she depressed?"

"I guess you could say she was unhappy. She had warned me she would have trouble finding a good job, but she never said why. I suppose if she was fired, she wouldn't be able to get a good reference, and after working for the city for so many years, that reference would be very important."

"I would think so. Did she tell you she was fired?"

"She said she quit. She said she walked in one morning

and there was a problem and it was the straw that broke her back. She had a pile of complaints about the office, the people she worked with, the clients—it went on and on. I just assumed she burned herself out."

"Where did she sleep in your house?"

"We have a guest room."

"You said she stored her furniture."

"It was in a place in Queens. She came to us with just a couple of suitcases, clothes mostly."

"Did she eat well? Did she participate in family conversations?"

"She was fine. You're asking to see how unhappy she was. If I had thought she was dangerously depressed, I can assure you, I would have insisted she see someone. She was good with my kids. She loved them and it was mutual. She was the aunt who came and gave them a good time. When she died, I made up a story. They were young, in grade school. I couldn't tell them the truth." She motioned to the waitress and asked for refills. "Would you like a roll or a piece of pastry?"

"No thanks."

She was an attractive woman and Jane could see the resemblance between this woman and the sketch of Erica Rinzler. Judy Weissman was wearing black wool slacks and a gorgeous sweater with shades of rose and purple over a collared pink shirt. "Before we go any further, I'd like you to tell me what you wanted to talk to Erica about."

"A man's body was found in his apartment in lower Manhattan about eight years ago. According to the medical examiner, he starved to death. He had mental problems so it was assumed his death was accidental. A member of his family thought his death might have been murder and we reopened the investigation. We learned that the deceased was a client of your sister. That's why we wanted to talk to her."

"I see. So she could help you research your case."

"Exactly. Did she ever mention any of her clients to you?"

"Hm." Judy Weissman sipped her coffee. "Not really. She would tell my kids about the poor people she worked with, how she was trying to help them get on their feet. But she never mentioned names. She was very discreet, very professional. I wish I knew what went wrong at her job."

"I'd like to know that myself," Jane said. "Are you able to tell me about her death?"

"I know very little about it. A few weeks after Erica came to us, she took the train into New York. She said she had an interview for a job and she might meet a friend for lunch. She said not to wait dinner for her. I never saw her again." Judy Weissman's eyes were wet.

"Where was she found?"

"In a seedy hotel on the west side of Manhattan, Fifty-fourth Street."

"How had she died?"

"A gunshot to the head." Her voice almost broke.

"Your sister owned a gun?"

"Apparently. I knew nothing about it."

"Did she leave a note?"

She shook her head.

"Did you find that strange?"

"I found the whole thing strange. I found it unbelievable. Why would she do such a thing? She'd had good interviews and she was looking in new areas for work. She could have gotten something that would have given her an income and tided her over till she found something better. No one even suggested that she should leave us. She was my sister. I wanted her alive. She was young. She had most of her life ahead of her. I just don't know why she did it."

"Mrs. Weissman, did she have files or records of any sort from her job?"

"I have a box of papers. After she died, I kept some of her things and sold most of the furniture. My children and I were her heirs. Our parents were gone. I've been through everything and there wasn't a clue anywhere to why she killed herself."

"May I see the papers?"

The woman nodded. "Come to the house with me. I'll give them to you."

"Thank you. I'll give you a receipt for whatever I take and I promise you'll get it all back."

"Maybe you'll find out why Erica took her life."

"That's possible." It was more than possible. This suicide, or apparent suicide to be precise, would almost surely become part of the investigation into Stratton's death. "There are two questions I need to ask you. One is, did anyone ever call your sister Bee-Bee?"

The surprise on Mrs. Weissman's face was genuine. "How could you possibly know that?"

"Someone described a woman, perhaps a caseworker from Social Services, as being called Bee-Bee. I gather that was a nickname for your sister."

"It was. When she was born, my mother had a private nurse to help out for a couple of weeks. I don't know where the woman was from but she refused to call my sister Erica. She called her 'Baby' but with her accent, it came out Bee-Bee. I loved that and I called her that all her life."

"And other people must have too."

"They did. Erica never liked her name that much —I don't know why; it's a perfectly fine name—and outside of work she often told people to call her Bee-Bee."

"One other thing: Someone found some beads in the apartment of your sister's client after he died. I'd like to show them to you." Jane took out the small plastic bag and set it on the table.

"Oh my," Judy Weissman said, her voice catching. She picked up the bag and looked at the tiny beads. "These could be . . . I'm almost sure these were Sandy's, my daughter's. She gave them to my sister. Erica wore them frequently. At least, she usually wore them when she visited. Sandy was thrilled. She had been afraid they were too small for Erica. My sister loved beads and wore strings of them every day, but most of them were much larger than these. Is this all there are?"

"There are a few more, perhaps ten or fifteen altogether. We assumed the string broke while the wearer was in the apartment of the deceased, and before she was able to save them, several fell to the floor and rolled into a corner behind a bookcase. The floor had a slight slant."

Judy Weissman fingered the beads through the plastic. "I never thought I'd see these again."

Jane retrieved the bag and dropped it in her handbag. "Why don't we go to your house so I can get that carton of papers?" She took out her wallet to pay for the coffee but Judy Weissman had flagged the waitress and handed her a bill.

The house was on a picture-perfect street with well-cared-for trees and lawns. Large cars and a few small ones sat on driveways, a couple of women pushed strollers, stopped and chatted in the middle of the street, moved out of the way for the Weissman SUV, and waved. The house was a traditional colonial with fancy embellishments, a porchlike structure over the front door to shield against inclement weather, a double front door with small stained-glass windows, and several chimneys indicating fireplaces inside.

They went through the garage, Mrs. Weissman warning Jane that there would be no discussion of Erica with the children. In fact, only the son was visible as he closed the refrigerator, said a quick "Hi," and dashed to the stairs. Steven Weissman carried the carton up from the basement to the kitchen where Jane glanced quickly through the contents, spying a tax return, an appointment calendar, and some letters. She wrote a receipt for the Weissmans and Steven took the box out to the car.

"You're looking into my sister-in-law's death?" he asked after he had shoved the box on the backseat.

"That wasn't our original mission, but we may have to. Anything you want to tell me?"

"I don't think she killed herself. I saw her every day she was here and that was a few weeks. If she was suicidal, then I'm not much of a judge of human nature."

His wife seemed troubled by his statement, but she said nothing.

"I'd like to ask you one last question," Jane said. "Erica's funeral. Who attended? I talked to a friend of hers yesterday and I don't think he knows she's dead."

Steven Weissman watched as his wife answered. "Very few people came. We notified almost no one. It was just Steve and me, a rabbi, and a couple of friends."

"Thank you both for your help. We'll keep you informed." Jane handed her card to Judy. Then she climbed into the SUV and Judy drove her to the station.

She spent what was left of the day and evening sorting the contents of the box. She was aware that what was here had been culled from a larger amount of documents. Anything that the Weissmans thought might be important enough to save or personal or even incriminating would have been removed years ago and locked away or destroyed.

The tax return, which had caught her eye first, was the last one Erica had made out, and she had done it without the help of a professional. That didn't surprise Jane. Erica, like Jane, was a salaried worker whose taxes were automatically withheld, along with Social Security and a few other things, from each paycheck. According to the return, she had modest interest from bank accounts and she owned stock in a few companies with well-known names and one that Jane had never heard of. The return was simple and anyone with basic arithmetic and a little time to devote to it could figure it out.

Among the letters were some from the Weissman children, sweet missives from camp and from holidays. It appeared that Erica's warm feeling for her niece and nephew were genuine. The letters were in a small folder and arranged by date.

Also arranged carefully were letters from a friend in California. Apparently, Erica and this woman, Ellie Raymond, had gone to school and gotten their master's degrees in social work together. The correspondence ended abruptly two years before Erica's death when Ellie Raymond announced she was buying herself a computer and would begin to send e-mail to Erica's office. The letters, Jane observed, all began "Dear Bee-Bee."

Jane made a note of the name and address. There was little else in the carton with similar potentially useful information. No check stubs or statements, no paid bills, and no address book or wallet. All of that must have found its way to another place. They would have to decide at some point whether to request that kind of material, but that was not a concern at this moment.

By the time she was tired enough for bed, Jane had organized everything in the carton. She had not called the second whip, nor had he called her. That could all wait for Monday morning.

She was about to turn her light off when she decided to call Ellie Raymond. The three-hour time difference meant it was only eight-thirty on the West Coast. Information had a listing for Raymond at the return address on the letters and Jane dialed. On the third ring, a male voice answered.

"I'd like to talk to Ellie Raymond," Jane said, not certain what the full first name was.

"She's out. Who's calling?"

"An old friend. Is there a time tomorrow that I can reach her?"

"She gets home around five."

Eight o'clock eastern. That was time enough.

13

JANE TOOK A taxi to work in order to get the carton of papers to Centre Street. The mood among the team became swiftly upbeat as she announced Erica Rinzler's suicide.

"Looks like we got a case," Defino said, eyes brightening.

"Who knows what case, but something sure smells," Jane said.

"Want me to call McElroy?" MacHovec asked.

"Sure."

But the second whip appeared at their door as she spoke. "Anything?" he said.

"Lots."

"Let's talk here. Captain Graves is out this morning."

She delivered her briefing in an almost staccato style. The call to Arthur Provenzano, the meeting at the museum, the name of the sister and her address, the bombshell of the suicide, the meeting in Chappaqua, the beads, the nickname, the papers, the friend in California.

"You putting in for overtime?"

Jane gave him a grin. "I'll get it back when I need a short afternoon. I had nothing on my calendar."

"Thank God for dull weekends. So what've you got in the box?"

She pulled out bunches of papers, some paper-clipped, some rubber-banded.

"Jeez," McElroy said, "you already cataloged it."

"Just made piles. I hate to tell you, but there isn't much. I think Sean should go over it; he's got an eagle eye. And we have to get the file on Rinzler's suicide. Should be an autopsy on that one. The sister said she was supposed to be having lunch with a friend that day. I don't know if we can track down who that was."

"If it was anyone. She could've told the sister a story."

"She met someone. I don't buy suicide."

"OK. I'm giving you a go on this. We'll talk to the captain this afternoon, but as far as I'm concerned, one cold case is as good as another." Before he was out of the room, MacHovec was on the phone.

The West Forties and low Fifties were filled with drab hotels that dated from before World War II. Comparatively small, they were built to serve tourists and businessmen on modest budgets. Lobbies were compact and inelegant. Some rooms lacked private baths. But all were close to the center of excitement: the theater, Fifth Avenue, and enough restaurants to satisfy any taste.

In the late twentieth century, most of the hotels had undergone renovations. While the rooms could never be considered luxurious, they became cleaner and more modern-looking. Overseas travel agents booked their clients there and the hotels began to live new lives. Judy Weissman had referred to the place where her sister died as "seedy." If it had not been gutted, at least they could see the room Rinzler had died in. Not that it mattered. The autopsy report would contain plenty of information.

"They'll dig up the autopsy," MacHovec said, hanging up. "Shouldn't take too long. Let me go through the papers." He reached for the piles on Jane's desk.

She turned to Defino. "West Fifties is Midtown North. Let's find out who caught the case."

MacHovec dropped the file he was holding and reached for the phone. He talked for a few minutes, giving a date and the name. "Yeah, that's the one." He started writing. "Good. Thanks. He around? . . . Fine." He hung up and handed Jane his notes. "Guy named Lew for Lewis Beech caught the case. He's due in at ten."

Jane looked at Defino. He got up and grabbed his coat.

They stopped at the desk on the way up to the squad room and asked a couple of questions. Det. Lewis Beech had been a member of the squad for eight and a half years, having been transferred from the City-Wide Anti-Crime Unit when he was awarded his gold shield shortly before the date of Erica Rinzler's death.

"Sounds like he was long on collars and short on squad experience," Defino said as they climbed the stairs.

"Well, he's eight years smarter now, so let's see what he remembers."

Beech was a blue-eyed fiery redhead in his thirties. He was on the phone when they arrived and he nodded at them to sit. "Don't give me that shit," he said into the phone. "I said I had to have it. *I have to have it.*" The conversation continued but he didn't seem any closer to getting what he wanted when he hung up than when they had arrived. "Sorry," he said. "I'm Lew Beech. You are . . . ?"

They introduced themselves. "We wanted to talk to you about an apparent suicide eight years ago," Jane said. She handed him a sheet of paper with the particulars.

He frowned. "Hold on. Let me get the file."

He returned five minutes later with a thin file. "I remember it now. It was a month or so after I got my shield. She shot herself in a hotel room. The maid found her in the morning. It was messy. The victim was a woman in her thirties, nice-looking, out of work, despondent—"

"Who said she was despondent?" Jane asked.

"She committed suicide. You're happy, you don't kill yourself."

"Go on."

"That's it. We talked to the family. The sister was too distraught to say much. The brother-in-law didn't believe it was suicide, but who ever does? Her prints were on the gun, she had rented the room that day for one night. That was it."

"She check in with a suitcase?" Defino asked.

"We didn't find one."

"She leave a note?"

"Ditto."

"We're working on a cold case this woman was connected to. We'll need the file."

Beech looked as though he didn't like that. "What case you working on?"

"Guy's name is Stratton. He died in the Nine. Across the street from Tompkins Square Park."

"What's the connection?"

"You gonna give us the file or what?" Defino said, clearly irritated. A detective at a nearby desk looked in their direction.

"What are you trying to do, make me look bad? I handle a dozen stiffs a year in this squad and they all turn out closed with results."

"How many homicides or suicides had you handled up to this case?"

Beech looked embarrassed. "That was my first."

"Give us the file."

"Yeah, OK. I'll have it sent over. Leave me your address."

"What the fuck was his problem?" Defino's temper had flared and for good reason. They had every right to the file.

"He may be eight years smarter but he's still an idiot."

"Want to walk over to the hotel she died in?"

"Sure."

The lobby floor was new and clean, the paint was light, the front door glass. They approached the desk where a couple with wheelies were checking in, showed their ID, and asked to speak to anyone who had been at the hotel eight years ago. A minute later a man came from an inner room and ushered them to the end of the counter for privacy.

"I'm William Steiner. How may I help you?"

"A woman committed suicide here about eight years ago," Jane said.

"Yes. Yes. You needn't go any further. That was a horrible incident. I was on the desk that morning when she was found. She shot herself. It was gruesome."

"You went upstairs to look?" Defino asked.

"I had to. I was the senior person on duty. I took a quick look and called the police. Two cars came, then a couple of detectives a little later. One of them had red hair. I've forgotten his name."

"Detective Beech."

"Yes, of course. It took most of the day before they removed that poor woman. There was crime scene tape everywhere. The van from the morgue parked outside. It was horrible."

"What did you know about her?" Jane asked.

"Nothing. She paid for the room with cash, said it was for one night. We gave all the documents to the police."

"Was the room reserved in advance?"

Steiner thought a moment. "I don't believe so."

"What floor was she on?"

"Six. The top floor."

"And no one heard a gunshot?"

"The hotel wasn't full that night. Most of six was empty. Nobody reported a loud sound."

"Did anyone find a suicide note?" Jane asked.

"I never went into the room after the police came. You better ask them. They took a lot of stuff, sheets, towels, I don't know what. They would know."

"Can you show us the room, Mr. Steiner?"

"Come with me." He stopped to pick up a ring of keys, then led the way to the elevator, which was near the front door.

"Has the building been renovated or changed since that happened?" Defino asked.

"We did a renovation about a year before the incident. Nothing has changed except to freshen up the paint and update the TVs."

On six they followed him down the hall to a door near the back of the building. He unlocked it and stepped aside for them. With the lights off, the room was dark. Its one window faced an airshaft. Behind the hotel a much taller building overshadowed the smaller one. The room had its own bathroom and here the effect of the renovation was visible. The tub, sink, and toilet were comparatively new and the floor tiles were late twentieth century.

A double bed, a nightstand, a small desk and chair, and a dresser crowded the small bedroom. A suitcase would have to be wedged between the bed and the wall to keep it out of the way. So much for guests with large wardrobes.

"Anything I can show you?" Steiner asked.

"Where was she lying?" Defino said.

"On the floor next to the bed, as if she'd fallen from a sitting position."

"What was she wearing?"

"Her clothes."

"All of them?"

Steiner took a breath. "I only saw her that once for a few seconds, but she appeared to be fully dressed."

"Shoes?"

"I think her shoes were on too."

Defino looked at Jane. She shook her head.

"Thanks," Defino said. "Thanks for your help."

"So no one found her asleep and shot her." They were on the street, Defino lighting up for the first time that morning. Maybe he was cutting back.

"That was the lunch date she told her sister about. Only it wasn't lunch. What the hell was going on?"

"I'm hungry."

"Right. It's that time of day."

The streets between Fifth and Sixth were full of restaurants. Defino agreed to forgo his usual pasta and they opted for a Chinese restaurant where Jane ordered a noodle bowl with seafood. Defino, who had chosen a beef and vegetable dish, eyed hers with skepticism. Jane could remember a time, when she was in her twenties, when she refused to eat anything she hadn't eaten at her mother's table. It had been a date who had challenged her, calling her a provincial. Angry at the characterization—she was a born-and-bred New Yorker, after all—she had allowed him to order for her and her world had changed.

"Real tough to prove that was a homicide," Defino said, forking food into his mouth while Jane used chopsticks. "All her clothes on looks like suicide."

"Even if it was suicide, something was going on that made her do it. I just don't like the fact that she left no letter. She was living with her sister; she loved those people. They deserved an explanation, and even if she couldn't give the true one, she could at least have said she was sorry."

"Maybe there was no paper to write on in the room."

"Good thought. We'll have to call Steiner and ask. But there must have been something in her handbag to write on, even a Kleenex." The contents would be detailed in the file. She hoped it would come soon.

They ate and talked, tossing ideas back and forth. What was Rinzler involved in? Was Stratton involved too or was he a convenient fall guy? And how did he help her?

"How the fuck are we going to find out who she met for 'lunch' eight years ago?" Defino asked, echoing her own thoughts.

"Her sister may know who some of her friends were."

"This wasn't a friend; this was a business associate."

"Gordon, there have to be papers, some kind of records. What the sister gave me was sanitized. She knows what was going on or, at least, she has an idea. That carton she gave me was the sweet and lovely side of Erica Rinzler, the letters from her niece and nephew, from her wonderful old friend in California. The tax return shows how honest she was. We need the papers from the black side, the names and addresses."

"Maybe she had them memorized."

"Even the Mafia has lists. She couldn't trust her memory with everything."

"The sister'll give you a hard time."

"I know, but there's more in that basement in Chappaqua, even if the husband isn't aware of it."

"You think she's keeping it to herself?"

"He told me he didn't think Erica was suicidal. The wife said it was a shock but didn't put it as strongly as her husband. It was a blow but she accepted it. You heard what Beech said. If she hadn't been despondent, she wouldn't've killed herself. That's how he knows she was despondent."

"He's a little light on gray matter. That good?" He nodded at her almost empty noodle bowl.

"Delicious. Shrimp and other stuff, lots of noodles, and the soup is out of this world. You should try it. Think of it as Chinese pasta."

He gave her a little grin. "I'll think about it."

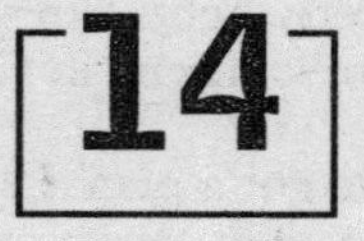

14

CAPTAIN GRAVES WAS back at his desk when they returned to Centre Street and they briefed him in his office. The Rinzler autopsy had arrived and MacHovec had gone through it and pulled out everything that had set his hair on end.

"So it looks like you've found a case," the captain said. "We just don't know if Stratton's part of it. And this Rinzler woman could be a suicide."

"Could be," Defino said. "But there are too many questions and no suicide note."

"They don't all leave notes."

"This one would have."

"I agree," Jane said.

"Let's not let Mrs. Constantine know what we know yet. String her along. As long as she thinks we're taking this seriously, she won't bother us. I don't want to find out it's a big nothing after we've told her we've got a case." Graves looked at Jane, who was now the senior detective in the group. "What's on?"

"I have to call Mrs. C. about where Stratton's money came from and how he got it. Gordon and I saw the hotel room this morning and we talked to the guy who was on the desk when the body was discovered. He's the hotel manager now. We'll call him back and ask if there was stationery in the room."

"She could have used an envelope in her bag," Graves said.

"True. But if there was stationery, we'll know she chose not to write. The file from Midtown North is on its way. The autopsy is here." She glanced at Defino. "Gordon and I think Rinzler's sister, Judy Weissman, is holding back papers that are more important than the ones she gave us. These are pretty light, letters from her niece and nephew. Oh, and there's a friend in California. I'll call her from home tonight."

"Sounds like you've got a plan. Let's get to it."

They went back to their desks and Jane made a few notes. Her head was buzzing. She had to call Mrs. C., but that could wait another minute. "Sean, indulge me."

He gave her his wicked grin.

"Judy Weissman said her sister's things had been stored in a place in Queens. That included furniture, which was later sold, and everything Erica kept from her apartment but didn't have with her at the Weissmans'. Maybe Weissman looked through the things in the storage facility by herself, no husband around, found some incriminating or not so nice stuff, and decided to leave it stored, probably in a small locker, since the big pieces were gone. It could be rented under Weissman or Rinzler."

"Got it." He pulled a phone book onto his desk—he kept a pile for the five boroughs in the corner of the room where his desk was—and opened the yellow pages. If anything was stored under one of those names, MacHovec would find it.

"That's good," Defino said, looking up from his typewriter and the Five he was working on.

Jane called the Constantine number and Mrs. Constantine picked up immediately.

"Mrs. Constantine, Detective Bauer."

"Oh, Detective. I thought you'd forgotten me."

"Not at all, ma'am. It was a busy weekend and I didn't get to the phone. I have a couple of questions about your brother's financial situation."

"Of course. It was quite simple. Andy lived off a trust fund my parents set up for him years ago. Of course, he hated having anything to do with money and he didn't want to go anywhere to pick it up, so I arranged to have money delivered to him once or twice a month."

"Do you mean you sent a check?"

"No, I couldn't do that. He would have to go to a bank to cash it, which would be just as bad as going somewhere to withdraw it. I sent it by messenger. It was delivered to his door."

"Did he open his door for the messenger?"

There was a brief sigh. "Usually not. Andy didn't like dealing with strangers. They rang the bell, announced who they were, and left the package. I assume Andy opened the door when he thought they were gone and took it inside. It was cash."

"Can you give me an idea of how much he received?"

"A thousand dollars a week, usually two thousand every two weeks, unless he said he didn't need that much or he needed more. I had power of attorney and I accommodated his needs."

"What did you do when you took that trip at the end of his life?"

"I gave him more than four thousand for the month. I took care of the rent so everything he got was for his own use. I have to tell you, when I went through the apartment after he died, I found bills tucked everywhere, in his drawers, under the mattress, in the pockets of his clothes. He lived on very little. It was a matter of pride with him that he wasn't rich. He liked being a common man."

"Thank you, Mrs. Constantine. You've answered all my questions."

The voice in her ear laughed. "I didn't let you ask them, did I? But if there's anything else, please call. Are you making progress?"

"We're learning new things, and for the moment we're continuing with the case."

"What about the little beads? Did you find out whose they were?"

It was a question she had hoped would not be raised. "We're still asking about them."

"Keep at it," Mrs. Constantine said. "My brother was murdered."

"One tough cookie," Jane said after she hung up. She turned to Defino and told him the money routine.

"Great. They left four thousand dollars in an envelope outside his door?"

"No complaints. It must have all arrived intact. Then, when he had too much, he stashed it around the apartment."

"Maybe he gave it away on the street."

"Could be."

Annie appeared at the door. "A file was just faxed to you. There's a note that the photos are coming through departmental mail."

"Good," Jane said, reaching for the file. "I've been waiting for this."

Erica Rinzler had checked into the hotel at four in the afternoon. That allowed time for her lunch beforehand with a friend. There was no record of any outgoing calls but the operator on duty remembered at least one call to her room from an outside phone. It had the smell of a rendezvous. No one at the desk remembered anyone asking for her room number or whether she was registered, so her visitor, if there had been one, had gotten that from the operator. Det. Lew Beech had not attempted to determine where the outside call had come from. In his defense, the number of calls coming in to the hotel that day had probably been large and without the cooperation of the caller, it would be impossible to isolate any calls to Rinzler's room. What troubled Jane was why he had not made at least a small effort. Didn't suicides generally hole up in a room that no one knew they were in?

Rinzler had been fully clothed. She was wearing a long, full skirt of a crinkly cocoa-colored cotton, a beige cotton sweater, stockings, and low-heeled shoes. A gold watch was on her left wrist and a number of rings adorned her fingers. Three strings of beads encircled her neck. Her clothes and the beads on all three strands were bloodstained. A coat, identified as Rinzler's by her sister, was folded over the dresser.

Only Rinzler's fingerprints were found on the gun, which was clean and well oiled. Besides prints from her right hand in the expected places where a shooter would hold a gun, there were also prints from both hands on the barrel, as though she had lifted the gun from her bag, which was also on the dresser. To Beech's credit, he had determined that Rinzler was right-handed.

That was the suicide scenario. If it had been murder, then Rinzler had sat on the side of the bed while the killer, to her right on the chair, forced her hand up to her temple and pulled the trigger, thus assuring that burned powder, nitrate residue, was on her hand as well as his. Both were viable scenarios.

The autopsy and toxicology reports indicated that Rinzler had been in good health and sober. The contents of her stomach included a partially digested spinach salad with bacon bits, the elusive lunch.

Jane picked up the phone and called the hotel. Steiner was there. "Mr. Steiner, Detective Bauer."

"Yes, hello. How can I help you?"

"Was there hotel stationery in Ms. Rinzler's room?"

"Definitely. That's always a priority in our hotel. We never run out and it's always on the housekeeping carts. We consider letters written from our hotel good publicity."

"Thank you." She hung up and turned to Defino. "There's always stationery in the rooms."

"And she didn't use it. One point for us."

"Bingo!" MacHovec put down the phone and turned to face them. "A small box rented by Erica Rinzler, paid for semiannually by 'a friend.' Here's the address of your treasure trove."

That meant a scramble for a warrant. Jane and Defino went directly to Graves. With luck, they could have a warrant by early tomorrow at the Queens courthouse. He put his glasses on and read MacHovec's notes.

"In the dead woman's name?" he asked.

"Apparently. We think the sister left the good stuff under lock and key. She may not have known what to do with it, but she knew it was potentially dangerous. I doubt her husband even knows it exists." She had to make a good case for Graves's support of a warrant or they'd never get it.

"It's worth a look. I'll ask Annie to run the paperwork over."

"Thanks, Cap."

Back at her desk, Jane dug into the file. The Rinzler file was much thinner and lighter in weight than a homicide file. The longest interview was with Judy Weissman, who, Jane realized, spoke to the police before looking through her sister's possessions. That would have come later when she learned where they were stored, and would have necessitated a longish drive from Chappaqua to inspect the lot. So what she said to the police after the suicide was her first reaction, probably honest, unclouded by later information that might have put her on her guard. She explained that her sister had resigned from her job, moved in with the Weissmans, and was looking for work. Erica had sent out résumés and had several interviews. On the day of her death, she had gone to Manhattan to have lunch with a friend, but Mrs. Weissman did not know who the friend was or where they had planned to meet. She had not been ill, had not complained of anything bothering her except her inability to find work, and the suicide was unexpected and very distressing. The interview had been carried out by Det. Lewis Beech.

The woman who had found the body had little to say and was too upset to put much into words. The hotel finally let her leave for the rest of the day after a detective essentially gave up trying to get anything out of her. Interviews with Mr. Steiner, then the deskman, and a handful of other employees yielded little additional information. No one had seen visitors going to or from Rinzler's room. No one had heard the shot. (The autopsy later determined she had died between six and seven that night.) All in all, it appeared to be a suicide and it was ruled as such.

And then eight years passed, Jane thought, and Mrs. Constantine gave us a push. She could hardly wait to get her hands on the contents of that locker. That might just tell the tale.

"You guys are lucky," Annie said at the door. "I got the paperwork for your warrant faxed to Queens and I just got a call you can pick it up at five." It was close to five now.

"I'll swear it out in the morning," Defino said. "I'll have it with me. Thanks, Annie. Good job." He had become both polite and deferential to the PAA after observing the power she wielded in the office.

"Sure thing, Detective."

"Well, you guys have fun on the road," MacHovec said, taking his coat off the hook. "You better have a good story when you come back tomorrow."

Jane hoped they would too. She hated going to Queens. It was a maze of streets and avenues and courts all with the same numbers. But she couldn't let Defino do this on his own, even though he lived in the borough and it was a trip for her. She wanted to be there.

"Can I get there by nine-thirty without killing myself?" she asked him.

Defino grinned. "Hell, with your ambition you can be anywhere by nine-thirty."

She waited till nine that evening to call the Raymond woman in California, giving her an hour after she got home to get herself together. The same male voice answered and called for his mother.

"Mrs. Raymond, this is Detective Jane Bauer of the New York Police Department."

"Police? What is this about?"

"It's about a friend of yours who committed suicide eight years ago."

"Erica. My God. What is it?"

"I'd like to talk to you about Ms. Rinzler."

"I— How do I know you are who you say you are?"

"I'm calling from my home tonight. I can give you the number and you can call me back. You can check my name with information. I'll be glad to give you my address as well. If you'd like to talk to me at my office, that will have to wait till tomorrow. I can give you numbers to call to verify my name and rank."

Silence, then, "Tell me your name again, please."

"Jane Bauer."

"And you're a police detective."

"Right."

"Are you investigating Erica's death? Because that was one damn peculiar suicide."

"We are looking into it, yes."

Silence. A faint sound. "You better be who you say you are."

"If you have any doubts, I—"

"No, it's OK. Go ahead. It's been years since she died and I am full of unanswered questions."

"Do you recall the last time you talked to Ms. Rinzler?"

"Yes. It was two days before she died. She was staying with her sister."

"Mrs. Weissman."

"Yes, Judy. Erica was never clear about what happened at the job. She was a social worker, a supervisor. They sent her out on difficult cases. She was top-notch in her job. I'm digressing. You asked about the last time I talked to her. We called each other from time to time and e-mailed each other a lot. I just got a yen to talk to her that day and she had given me her sister's phone number after she moved out of the apartment in Manhattan. I called her and we had a long talk. I knew she was out of work and had been for a few weeks by that time, but I can't tell you exactly how long. She was looking for work. She'd heard about some jobs in different fields and she was going to give them a try. I was as encouraging as I could be. We were good friends from college. She was my maid of honor when I married Walt. She came out and visited us a couple of times and she even talked about moving out here. I think I'm digressing again."

"Did she give you any indication in that phone call that she was depressed, despondent, out of sorts, down in the dumps?"

"You're asking if she was signaling that she was thinking of taking her life."

"Yes."

"She wasn't. She wasn't any of those things you just ticked off. I won't say she was jumping for joy, but she hadn't lost hope, she wasn't out of money, she didn't feel it was the end of the world."

"What did you think when you heard what had happened?"

"I thought— I was so shook up, I couldn't speak. I had to hand the phone to my husband. I thought I would pass out. This was my friend. We had spent our beautiful young years together, we had fallen in and out of love together, we had taken trips and gone to concerts and called each other in the middle of the night and cried on each other's shoulders and gotten jobs and griped. And now her sister was telling me she had committed suicide in some sleazy hotel in New York, and I couldn't figure out why." From the passion in her voice, she could have been reliving the experience.

"Did her sister indicate there might be a reason?"

"I don't think so. She just accepted it. She was kind of dumbstruck. It had happened; she had identified the body. God, I don't know how she did that."

"It's very difficult. I understand."

"And by the time she called me, it was over. The funeral was over. She was buried near her parents. She would never marry, she would never have children. I can't tell you what that did to me."

"Mrs. Raymond, did Erica ever talk about her clients? Did she mention that one had died?"

"Oh, the guy near Tompkins Park. She told me about it. She left her job after he died, but she never told me what the connection was, if there was one. Was there?"

"We don't know. We learned of Ms. Rinzler's death in our investigation of that case, and we're now trying to determine whether her death was actually a suicide."

"I've spent a lot more time thinking about this than you have. What I came up with was this: It's hard to believe she committed suicide. She wasn't at that low a point in her life and nothing was driving her toward it even though she was having problems. On the other hand, what's the alternative? That she was murdered? That's even harder to believe. Especially as she was in a strange place, that she hadn't told anyone she was going there, that the door wasn't broken down or anything. Who would murder my friend Bee-Bee?"

"That's what we'd like to find out."

"Do you think she was murdered?" the voice from California asked.

"We think it's a possibility. We hoped you might come up with someone who had a grudge, either from work or from her group of acquaintances."

"I can't imagine who." Ellie Raymond's voice was faint.

"Did she ever mention any other work she was involved in? Any project that she spent time on?" It was an awkward way of asking whether Rinzler had bought and sold drugs or was involved in some other illicit operation, but being direct might dissolve the bond Jane was forging with the woman.

"No, not that I can remember." There was a tentative quality to the response. "You think something like that had an influence on her death?"

"I have no idea yet," Jane said. "Mrs. Raymond, what is your first name, please?"

"Ellen."

"And do you have a daytime phone number where I could call you?"

"Sure." She gave it and assured Jane it was OK to call. "If I'm not there, leave a message on my voice mail and I'll get back to you. You really think Erica was murdered?"

"No, I don't. I think it's possible. I think there may be things that come up that you can help us with."

"I will. Anything. I'd like to put this to rest, whatever the answers are."

"We feel the same way."

It had been a productive conversation, more than Jane had hoped for. Her notes were copious. A few minutes after she hung up, Defino called.

"I'm OK to pick up the warrant. The courthouse is on Queens Boulevard. I should be OK for nine-thirty."

"No problem. And I'll tell you about my conversation with Ellie Raymond."

"It must have been a long one. I've been trying you for half an hour."

"See you tomorrow."

15

POLICE OFFICERS RODE the subway free. Flash a shield, commonly called tin, to the token seller and they allowed the officer to open the exit gate and walk onto the platform. Jane tinned her way to the Queens Plaza station in Long Island City, finally reaching the storage building a little after nine-thirty. Defino was walking off his breakfast, smoking a cigarette, which he dropped to the ground and stepped on as he saw her.

They went into the small, cluttered office where a forty-ish overweight man was smoking a cigar, the fumes of which filled the entire room. Defino handed him the warrant.

"We want the box in Erica Rinzler's name."

"You got a court order?"

"It's in your hand."

"Oh." He tapped ash into a crowded ashtray and left the cigar there as he read it. "What's the problem?"

"That's not your concern."

The man shrugged. "You got the key?"

"No. I've got cutters for the padlock."

The box was a large cube, about two feet by two feet on its face. Defino cut the padlock with difficulty and pulled the box out of its recess.

"You gonna look at it here?"

"You got a place we can sit down?"

"I'll show you."

He put them in an empty office. When the door was closed, they opened the box.

The contents appeared to be largely paper. A cursory riffle through it yielded no jewelry or cash, but an address book and an agenda, both bound in black, were there along with a spiral notebook from Columbia University. Some checkbook registers were squeezed in along the side. Among the papers were IRS returns and New York State and city tax returns from several years before Rinzler's death, along with handwritten worksheets.

"Looks like she didn't have an accountant," Defino said.

"The one Weissman gave me was also handwritten."

"Standard deduction. She couldn't have been cheating."

"People doing tricks don't want to call attention to themselves."

"Good thought."

Jane opened the spiral notebook. "Whatever she was into, this could be it."

Nothing more telling than initials appeared on the pages. She saw the words *pickup* and *delivery* on each page, along with dates.

Defino asked for it and flipped pages, shaking his head. "What the fuck was she dealing in?"

"Stratton's name anywhere?"

"A.S. I don't see it."

"Let's get the whole thing back to Centre Street."

"Right."

They gave the cigar man a receipt, emptied the box into a shopping bag Jane had brought with her, and took a taxi back to Centre Street. Losing the bag on the subway would be a disaster.

"So there was something," Lieutenant McElroy said as he flipped through the books and papers. "Any idea what?"

"We just looked at a couple of pages, pickups and deliveries," Jane said. "Could be anything. Could also be nothing, but then why would Weissman hide the stuff in a locked box under Rinzler's name?"

"Think Weissman was part of it?"

"Not likely. If she was in on it, she would have used this stuff. Rinzler must have decided to cut this off when she left Social Services. There was no forwarding number on her home telephone. No one could reach her. If she didn't turn on her computer, she didn't get any e-mail. It was cold turkey."

"You don't know that she didn't turn on her computer," McElroy said.

"True. But I'm not sure at this point that I can get anything out of Weissman, unless she doesn't know we took the box."

"I bet she won't know," Defino said. "The storage place may not even have a phone number for her. She pays her rent on the box, they're happy. This guy we saw this morning wouldn't break his neck to let her know we were there."

"Maybe I'll call her. Sean, lots of numbers here."

"I'll start after lunch."

The first thing they did was catalog the material. Then Jane started through the spiral notebook while Defino went through the address book. "You know what's missing?" she said.

Defino looked up. "From the locker?"

"From this stuff. Where's the file on Rinzler?" It was on her desk and she flipped through several pages till she found the description of the suicide gun. "Clean and well-oiled," she read. "The gun Rinzler allegedly used. There's nothing in here to clean a gun with, no oil, no bullets."

"The sister threw it away along with a thousand other things."

"I don't think so. She might not have known what the oil and soft cloth were for, but if there was a box of bullets, she would have known Erica had a gun or at least the use of a gun. She would have showed it to her husband

and he would have agreed it was suicide. She would have told Lew Beech."

"Give her a call."

She dialed the Chappaqua number, hoping Weissman had not heard from the cigar man.

"Hello?"

"Mrs. Weissman, this is Detective Bauer."

"Oh. Yes. Did something happen?"

"I have a question. Did you find any bullets among your sister's belongings?"

"Like for a gun?"

"Yes."

"No. There was nothing. My husband mentioned that. He said if she'd owned a gun, she would have bought bullets for it and we would have found them. And other things. He was in the army and he told me how you took your weapon apart and cleaned it and wrapped it up when you weren't using it. It's one of the reasons he thought Erica didn't commit suicide."

"Did your sister have a computer?"

"I didn't find one. She had one at work. I don't know what she would have needed one at home for. It's not like now when everyone has e-mail. At the time she died, we didn't even own a computer ourselves."

"Thanks for your help." She turned to Defino. "Her husband commented that there would have been bullets if she'd owned a gun."

"You're right, she didn't level with him. This box was her secret. But she's probably telling the truth about the gun. She would want to know if her sister committed suicide. I've got a million names and addresses in this book, including that Provenzano guy you talked to over the weekend. Most of these look like friends and neighbors. The Raymond woman's name and address are in here. I don't know why Weissman would hide them."

"Because she read the spiral notebook and the agenda and she suspected something was going on. She didn't know if the address book was just friends or if it was part of whatever Rinzler was involved in."

"I gotta tell you, MacHovec's gonna spend a week calling all these numbers."

"Well, let me get started," MacHovec said. "Just cross out the plumber and the electrician."

Defino dropped the book on his desk, then went back and opened the agenda. "Lunch, dinner, theater. Here's a name I saw in the address book: Mimi. In the address book she's got a last name. Erica and Mimi went to the theater together."

"Sounds like what people do in New York," Jane said.

"Yeah?"

"Yeah."

MacHovec was already on the phone, the address book in front of him.

If something was going on in Erica Rinzler's life, the spiral notebook was the key. It was written in the kind of casual code that one might use as a shorthand. The code was largely abbreviation. Rinzler did not anticipate that anyone besides her would ever read the notes. If *T* was Tuesday, then *Th* was Thursday. What wasn't clear was what was going on on *T* or *Th*. Those abbreviations were more elusive.

As she read, she was aware of MacHovec making call after call, most of them with no response. That wasn't surprising. Rinzler's friends would be at work or out pushing baby carriages in the afternoon.

The dates in the notebook consisted of months and days, but no years. Jane looked for abbreviations that could be either of Andy Stratton's names, but found none. What was most prevalent was the letter *L* near the dates. Who was *L*? Larry Vale? Had Rinzler delivered something to him or had she picked up something from him on the days she visited Stratton? That would account for her frequent visits. Visiting Stratton was the excuse to see Vale, but they would need concrete facts before they would get him to talk.

"Numbers changed, numbers don't answer, nobody home," MacHovec announced. "Eight years is a long time in this city unless you're in a rent-controlled apartment. Lotta crossed-out stuff too, like her mother. Who would cross out her mother even if she died?" It was an unexpected and atypical display of sentiment from the plainspoken detective. He turned a page and picked up the phone again.

"Gordon, remember how Larry Vale reacted when we showed him the sketch of Rinzler?"

"Yeah. He knew her and he was scared."

"I think she used her visits to Stratton to see Vale. She may have been picking up or delivering drugs when she went to the building." She pushed the notebook over so he could see it and pointed to the *L*'s.

"And when Stratton died, she had no excuse to go to the building anymore and she didn't want to be seen there without her client."

"Maybe he killed her. Maybe she knew too much." She opened the Rinzler file again and found the report on the gun. It had no known owner, serial number removed but possibly recoverable, manufactured about two years before the suicide, well taken care of, only Rinzler's fingerprints, none on the bullets. "Sean?"

He hung up again.

"Did Larry Vale ever own a gun?"

"We'll find out right now."

Jane got up and left the office. She needed a cup of coffee and a few minutes alone. The coffeemaker was just finishing its procedure, a few last drops falling into the carafe. She waited, then poured, and sat at a table, sipping and thinking. It had to be drugs. Rinzler had begun visiting Stratton and met Vale by accident. They talked. Maybe they had a thing together. He was smoking something or doing something and there was money in it. It was the Nine, for Christ's sake. Everybody was smoking something or doing something in the Nine except the old ladies who'd lived in their apartments since before the war.

Vale knew the neighborhood. He knew the park, probably had friends squatting in the abandoned buildings. He knew where to deal. Did Rinzler want the stuff for personal use or to sell to her friends? She could pick up enough on one visit to pad her income nicely and it was tax-free. Hence the weekly visits. She didn't give a damn about Stratton and his problems, but he gave her a convenient excuse to visit the building. Her reports would emphasize the necessity of seeing him frequently. And he wasn't complaining anymore about the visits of social workers. They should get Rinzler's files from Human Resources.

She went back to the office and called Mrs. Constantine. "Did your brother complain to you about the social workers after he moved into the building on Tenth Street?"

"He complained to me, he complained to them. He threw them out, I'm afraid. They tried one after the other."

"What did you do when he complained?"

"I called Social Services and told them they had to send someone else. Finally, he stopped complaining."

"Did you ask him about it?"

"Yes, and he said someone much better was coming to see him."

"Did you ever meet that person?"

"No. But he seemed content, so I let it be."

"Thank you."

"Call any time."

"Gordon." She turned toward him. "Vale was supplying Rinzler with stuff."

"OK." He rubbed his eyes.

"No gun registered to Lawrence Vale," MacHovec said.

"So he got it from one of his pals in the park. Thanks, Sean." She turned back to Defino. "He lived in a dangerous area on the ground floor. He needed a gun. There were break-ins and burglaries. He never used it or we'd know about it. Something happened in that four-week period when Mrs. C. was out of the country. Rinzler stopped coming to see Stratton and Stratton died. It's even possible Stratton's death was an accident, but when the dust cleared, they had a body in that building, Rinzler had a dead client, and Vale felt he couldn't do business with her anymore."

"And she didn't want it to end," Defino said. "She made threats."

"So he made up a reason why they had to meet, allegedly to set things right, but actually to get rid of her."

"Sounds OK. Doesn't give us a killer for Stratton but it gives us something. What we gotta do is figure out that notebook of hers."

"I know. It's giving me a headache."

"Give it here."

"See you folks tomorrow." MacHovec was putting on his coat.

"Jeez, is it that time already?" Defino looked at his watch.

"Almost," Jane said with a grin. MacHovec always rounded off time to the nearest ten minutes that would benefit him. She gave him a wave as he flew out the door.

"Let me Xerox that notebook. I'll take the pages home and think about it."

"Make two copies. I may as well keep the headache going."

After dinner Flora called. She picked a restaurant for tomorrow's dinner in the Village not far from the subway. She could get home and Jane wouldn't have a long way to go either. "How's six-thirty?"

"Fine. Give me time to get home and change."

"What? For me?"

Jane laughed. "For my sanity. See you tomorrow."

Hack called a little while later. "We on for tomorrow?"

"You bet."

"I don't know when I'll be done. It's a dinner meeting. That's all I do these days, eat and meet."

"Got your key?" She had given it to him during the time she was on medical leave recovering and had given up on trying not to see him.

"Got it. If you're not there, I'll let myself in. Flora's not going to keep you long. She needs her beauty sleep. She needs something." There was no love lost between them.

"We're meeting at six-thirty. I should be home by nine at the latest."

"Don't eat dessert."

She felt the flicker of lusty unrest at the prospect of seeing him. It had been a few weeks, sometime before New Year's, since she had last seen him. She wondered if they would move into old age still feeling a youthful passion for each other. She hoped so. In retirement, they would buy a shack on a beach on some Pacific island and walk on the sand till the tug of their bodies for each other was too much to bear and they would lie down, the ocean lapping at their feet, and satisfy their mutual lust.

Grow up, Janey, her internal adult admonished her. His wife will outlive him and you'll outlive them both. You'll be old and alone for years. Just get what you can now so you have something to remember. If your mind doesn't fail at the other end.

She read the pages Defino had copied for her, trying to make sense out of them. If Vale had acquired the drugs and sold them to Rinzler, his connections were long gone, maybe dead by now if they were users. If Rinzler was selling to friends, it wouldn't be easy to find them eight years later. Where would they start? With Mimi, who went to the theater with Erica? MacHovec hadn't gotten a response from any of the numbers he'd tried that afternoon. This case was as cold as the Stratton one. It hadn't even been a case until last weekend. It was all surmise and hypothesis, assumption and hope.

But something had gone on between Vale and Rinzler—of that she was sure. And somehow poor Anderson Stratton had gotten in the middle of it or facilitated it by being in that apartment. And maybe he had died for it.

16

"YOU GET ANYTHING out of that notebook?" Defino asked Wednesday morning.

"Nothing more than what we talked about."

"You want to go down and talk to Vale?"

"I don't know, Gordon. I hate to show him our hand. He'll get a lawyer and clam up. I have a feeling, whatever was going on, Vale knew about it. He knew everything. He never told us about Rinzler but he knew her. He never told Shreiber either. Irma Bender may have seen her, but she was just one of the people she saw through the crack, like the pizza man."

"Let's go see the pizza man," Defino said. "I feel restless."

You should know what I feel, Jane thought. Flora for dinner and Hack for dessert. "Fine. Let's do it."

They took the subway up to Fourteenth Street, then walked to the pizza place on the east side of the park. The address had been in Shreiber's file as well as the official Stratton file. As they turned the corner, Jane hoped they were still in business.

A hairy young man wearing two coats walked toward them eating a slice and Jane relaxed. With that kind of clientele, they'd be in business forever. Perhaps a dozen Formica-topped tables, most with four chairs, were arranged in the small restaurant. Behind the counter at the back were two pizza ovens. A man in his twenties stood behind the high counter, a newspaper open in front of him. He looked up at the prospective customers.

"Help ya?"

They showed their IDs.

"Morning, officers. Anything wrong?"

"Just some questions about a customer you had a few years ago, guy used to call for a delivery," Defino said.

"Who's that?"

"Stratton." Defino gave the address.

"A few years ago? That's the guy who died, right? That was more than a few years ago."

"You know him?"

"Yeah. I used to do the deliveries. That was before my father retired. What about him?"

"You ever see him? Talk to him?"

"Not at his apartment, but he used to come in, you know. He'd get a hero, sit at a table, sometimes with a friend."

"What friend?" Jane asked.

"The guy who was the super over where he lived. Sometimes a woman."

Defino put the sketch of Rinzler on top of the *Daily News*. He didn't say anything.

"Could have been her. It was a long time ago, not just a few years."

"She and Stratton seem like an item?"

"You're asking me to remember something that happened when I was nineteen? I don't know. He was a messed-up guy. I don't know what went on with him."

"When you delivered," Jane said, "what happened?"

"The first time was crazy. I went up the stairs, rang the bell, nothing happened. I knocked. He said 'Go away.' I said 'I can't go away, I've got your pizza. You have to pay me.' I waited a long time. Finally he opened the door a crack. He had a handful of bills. He almost threw them at me. Then he said, 'Look, next time you come I'll leave you an envelope. You leave the pizza, you take the envelope and go.' So that's what I did. Once in a while, there wouldn't be an envelope and he'd open the door and stick his hand out with the money. But most of the time I didn't see him. Sometimes I would go halfway down the stairs and wait to see if he opened the door. Then I'd go."

"So you didn't become friendly with him," Jane said.

"Friendly? I wouldn't call it friendly. It was strictly business. He tipped a lot, I can tell you. He never wanted change. He was a guy wanted to be alone. Hey, that was his business."

"That woman ever come in here by herself or with someone else?" Defino asked.

"Maybe. It's a long time ago. My father might remember. You want me to ask him?" He looked toward the kitchen.

"I thought you said he retired."

"He did. He just can't stay home and do nothing." He moved toward the kitchen. "Pop? You wanna come out here for a minute?" He looked at Defino. "You tell him this is a police case, you'll make his day."

An older man came to the counter, smiled, and said hello. Jane explained why they were there.

"Yes," he said nodding his head. "I remember him. My boy wouldn't remember. He was just learning the business, but I knew my customers. That man who died—they said he starved to death—he used to come in here sometimes and then he stopped. Then he only ordered by phone and my son would deliver, or maybe my nephew. I felt very bad when I heard the news."

Defino put the sketch back on the counter. "Do you recognize her, sir?"

"Could be the lady he came in with sometimes. This was seven, maybe eight years ago, right?"

"Right."

"So you'll forgive an old man if he doesn't recognize a picture of a woman he saw maybe two, three times a long time ago."

"Your son said Mr. Stratton may have come in with the super at the building he lived in. You remember that?"

"Larry, sure. We know Larry a long time, don't we?" He looked at his son, who said, "Sure, Pop."

"He still a customer of yours?"

"Now and then. He orders a pizza on the phone maybe once a week, maybe not so often. He comes in once in a while, sometimes with friends. They order dinner."

Defino turned to the son. "Did you deliver to Larry too?"

"Yeah."

"How did he pay you?"

"He opened the door. He always had the money counted. I never had to make change. He's kind of a gruff guy, you know? Doesn't make small talk."

Jane turned to the father. "Did anything happen to make Mr. Stratton stop calling?"

"Maybe he wasn't hungry no more. How should I know?" He shrugged. "You know, after that poor guy died, maybe a while after, a private detective came in here, talked to me and my son."

"Mr. Shreiber," Jane said.

"Shreiber, that was the name." He nodded. "I remember him. Asked the kind of questions you folks are asking. But I'll tell you what he didn't ask. He didn't ask about Larry, the super. He asked about Andy Stratton. And he didn't have a picture of no woman with him."

"The woman," Jane said. "She ever come in by herself? With anyone else?"

The old man scratched his head as he looked at the picture. "She wore beads, right?"

"Right," Defino said.

"She came in with Larry sometimes. I remember now."

"Thank you, sir. We appreciate your good memory."

"Me too. It's all I got left now."

Out on the street Defino folded the sketch and put it in his jacket pocket. "Son of a bitch. I knew that guy Vale was hiding something. Let's go put it to him. He knew Rinzler."

"OK. Maybe we can scare something out of him."

Vale was coming out of the door to the first floor as they reached the outside stairs. "You again," he said.

"Yeah, us again," Defino said. "We need to talk to you."

"You're getting to be a pain in the ass, you know that?"

"Watch your mouth."

Vale led the way to his door and used a key on two locks. "Sit wherever." He sounded as annoyed with Defino as Defino was with him.

Defino reached into his jacket pocket, took out the sketch, and unfolded it. Then he handed it to Vale. "Take a good look at her. You looked at her once and it didn't register in your brain, just on your face."

Vale was under control this time. "I'm looking."

"We know you knew her. Erica Rinzler. Don't fuck around with me, Vale. What was your relationship with her?"

"It's so long ago," Vale said. "She came to see Andy a couple of times and I must have run into her. Said hello. Shot the breeze. That was it."

"Maybe you went out together? Maybe you went in together, like to your bed."

"And if I did, what business is it of the police?"

"What business did you and she have together?"

"What kind of business are you talking about?" He still held the sketch in his hand but he looked as though he wanted to get rid of it. Defino made no move to retrieve it.

"Any business. Anything having to do with money."

Vale shook his head. "I don't think any money passed between us."

"What did pass between you?"

"Nothing, Detective." Vale leaned forward and handed Defino the sketch. "I met Ms. Rinzler a couple of times. Then she stopped coming. I think Andy was her only client in the building. When he died, no one from Social Services came."

"Did you go to her funeral, Mr. Vale?" Jane asked.

"Her what?" He paled. He seemed unable to control the blood flow to his face.

"Her funeral. Surely you know she died."

"How would I know that? I barely knew the woman."

"Why did Rinzler stop coming to see Andy Stratton weeks before he died? If she'd shown up, she might have been able to save his life."

"I don't understand why you're asking me these questions. I had nothing to do with her visits to Andy. I'm the super here, not a security guard. I don't make people go through a metal detector or sign in and out. You're harassing me, you know that?"

"You'll know when we start harassing," Defino said. "You know what?" He looked at Jane. "We should get those phone records from the year that Stratton died, find out if Mr. Vale called Ms. Rinzler at her home or office, or vice versa." He stood up, preparing to leave. "Let's do that."

"Good thought." She knew he was just needling Vale, but the idea was a good one. "Let's get back to the office."

"Thanks, Larry," Defino said as they filed out the door.

"Can I laugh now?" Jane asked. They were halfway down the block.

"Boy, I'd like to sock that guy in his gorgeous nose. Yeah, you can laugh. I'm hungry. It must be noon."

"Close to it. Let's eat and get back. I think MacHovec should check those phone records."

"Phone records'll take a while," MacHovec said. "We're talking eight, nine years ago. My friend at the phone company'll have to dig them out. But we'll get them. Meanwhile, I got an answer on one of the names in Rinzler's address book, Patricia Washington."

"Jesus," Defino said, "you didn't get an answer till the W's?"

"I got some others, but this one's the most promising. She worked at Social Services with Rinzler. Give her a try. She's on vacation this week so she's home." He handed the information to Jane. Defino turned to his typewriter;

there were Fives to type and he could take out his aggressive feelings toward Vale by banging on the keys.

Jane dialed the number and a soft-spoken woman answered.

"Oh yes, Detective MacHovec called. I knew Erica for a long time. What can I tell you?"

Jane looked at her watch. "Suppose we meet tomorrow morning, if that's all right with you. Anywhere you want is fine."

"How's ten? I live in Brooklyn, just over the bridge. Can you come here?"

"Sure." She got the address and walking directions from the subway. Even if the wind was strong, it wouldn't be a long walk.

Defino said they could meet here at Centre Street and go over together.

MacHovec cleared his throat. "Your boy Vale. I called the Nine. There's a little something here. He got hauled in way back, about ten years ago. Suspicion of using drugs. No charges ever filed. He's clear."

"They didn't find it is all. He laid off after that and when he went back in, he was more careful. Son of a bitch. We'll get him this time. Just wait."

The surprise of the afternoon was a call from the man himself. It came in on Jane's phone about four o'clock.

"Detective Bauer, this is Larry Vale from Andy Stratton's building." He sounded as though he'd had some acting lessons since they'd seen him at noon. His voice was friendly and engaging.

"Yes, Mr. Vale," Jane replied in a similar voice. She looked over at a surprised Defino and grinned.

"I wonder if you and I could get together and talk. I'd prefer it if Detective Defino weren't present. I'm afraid he sets my teeth on edge."

And I'm a pushover, she thought. "I think we could manage that. Tomorrow afternoon?"

He paused for a moment and Jane remembered that the afternoon was when he preferred not to be disturbed.

"Yes, afternoon will be fine. Come at your convenience. I'll be here from noon on."

"I'll see you about one. Anything special you want to discuss?"

"Yes. I've decided I want to tell you the truth."

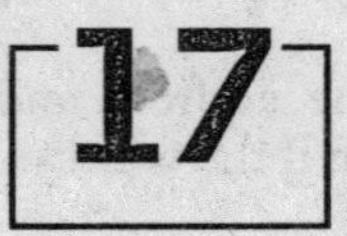

SHE REACHED THE restaurant just before six-thirty. Flora Hamburg was sitting at a table for four, her ubiquitous shopping bag on an empty chair. Jane found her way herself, gave Flora a hug, and sat at right angles to her.

"You look good, Jane. I was worried about the abrasions."

"Everything seems to have healed except this thing over here on my right cheek."

"I didn't even see it. Put a little color on it; no one'll notice. Drink?"

"Maybe some wine."

"I can't tell you how relieved I am that you decided not to pull the pin."

A few months earlier, Jane had been ready to leave the job and work for an insurance company. She had looked forward to the larger income, the office with the window, the regular hours, the kind of life most Americans lived. Her twentieth anniversary was coming up and with it the pension. Also, she would be spared running into Hack. At this moment, that seemed a long time ago.

"I think there's an artery in my gut that's tied to the job."

"Maybe it's in your heart."

"Maybe." She wasn't anxious to talk about hearts.

Flora ordered two glasses of wine and they studied the menu. Flora's tastes ran to simpler food. Mention sushi and she turned green. "Ah. A small filet steak. How does that grab you?"

"I'll do it."

"Tell me about the new case."

Jane went over it. Flora had a retentive memory and nothing got past her. Her looks were so deceiving, one might think she was a homeless old woman (packing a rod) or a grandmother whose mental capacity stopped at reading knitting instructions. In fact, those were merely her looks. Her mind was as sharp as Hack's, and her decades-long consuming commitment was moving women along on the job. If not for Flora, Jane would never have gotten her degree, or she would have started much later and perhaps given it up.

"So you've gone from thinking this was nothing but a busybody's intervention to acknowledging this Stratton may have been murdered."

"We still have nothing that says murder, but the suicide of the Rinzler woman has got us on edge."

"Interesting working on cold cases," Flora said, sipping her wine. "The crime scene's gone, half your witnesses are dead or gone, and if there was a wife, she's probably remarried twice since then."

"But the phone records will still exist. And tomorrow afternoon the super will give me his new version of the truth."

Flora smiled. "My little girl is a cynic."

"Would you have me any other way?"

"No, I suppose not." Flora reached into her shopping bag and pulled out a neatly folded tissue and blew her nose. What was in that bag had stirred the imagination of two generations of cops.

They had both begun with salads and now the meat was placed before them, an appealing dish with a mushroom sauce, baked potato, and a mélange of barely cooked vegetables. Jane was glad she had ordered red wine. Flora drank nothing but white.

"I surprised you last week, didn't I? Asking about your love life."

Her love life was no one's business, especially not Flora's, but Jane didn't know how to change the subject without being obvious. You didn't need to be as sharp as Flora to recognize a diversionary tactic when it hit you. "You surprised me, yes."

"I feel a little responsible, Jane. I pushed you into college. I read you the riot act whenever I thought you were wavering. Now I look back and I think maybe I kept you from meeting some guy and having a real life."

"You didn't. Everything I've done for the last twenty years came from me."

"From that artery in your gut or your heart tied to the job?"

"That's part of it."

"You're almost forty-one. You may regret never having had a child."

Jane took a deep breath. She had not told Flora, simply because the appropriate moment hadn't occurred. Maybe this was the time. "I have a child, Flora. A daughter."

Flora coughed and put her fork down noisily. She didn't say anything for almost a minute, as though she were running scripts through her mind. "You don't have to tell me, Jane. I didn't mean to pry. I was only trying to help."

"It's OK. I never told anyone. Only my parents knew. I got pregnant one summer before I came on the job and gave up the baby. She wrote to me a few months ago and I took a quick trip out to the Midwest last month to meet her and her parents."

"It takes something to shock me, you know that? Not that what you've said is shocking, just that I had no idea."

"She's a lovely girl. She treats her parents a lot better than I treated mine."

"You treated them fine. Your father is lucky to have you."

"That's now. I used to be a teenager."

"Well, you've got one on me. I never was. I was born, I went to school, I became a cop." It was a typical Flora recitation. Cut and dried, that was Flora's world.

"If you're forty today, you were a teenager twenty-one years ago. Anyway, this has all turned out to be right for me. I'm not sure I could handle a baby. I know I couldn't deal with a teenager. Christ, she might be like me. Lisa's a good student. She's going to have a degree in a couple of years. I'm proud of her and I'm glad she landed with the people who raised her. And who love her."

"Accepted. And I'm glad for you. This gives me some peace of mind. Eat your steak before it gets cold."

Jane smiled. No one knew whether Flora herself had a husband and family. She lived in Brooklyn, just over the bridge. Jane had never been invited there. They always met in the city, usually in a restaurant for dinner. Years ago, she had been summoned from time to time to Flora's office, generally to talk about career paths and college.

"You might like having a man in your life," Flora said. "A lot of women do."

Jane laughed. "You still after me? I have had men, Flora. I have had good ones and bad ones."

"Don't fuck where you work."

"You've told me that before. I've been out with cops and I've been out with civilians."

"And stay away from married men. At your age, they're all married or they have been or they're useless."

"You're really a treasure chest of directives tonight."

"I worry about you. I worry about you alone in that great apartment of yours with a fireplace. You're an only child. There are no nieces and nephews. Who'll look after you when you retire?"

The shack on the beach, Hack holding her hand as they walk through the sand. "That's a long way away." Her voice came out low, as though she were troubled. "Not everyone can live with another person, Flora."

"I know."

"Are you all right?"

"Me? Never better. I smoke too much, that's all. I get my annual X ray and I don't worry. Why?"

"You seem so concerned with my mortality tonight—"

"That you thought I was concerned with mine."

Jane didn't answer.

"I'm fine, sweetheart. Just wanted to get a few things out of the way. Finish your steak. It's good for you. They have great desserts here."

"Not for me, thanks. December was devastating. People came with candy and cookies. I want to be careful."

"OK. You can have a bite of mine."

The conversation moved to department gossip. This one was getting a divorce, that one was thinking of retiring. The gorgeous Captain Graves was driving hell-bent for his goal, chief of detectives. "But to become chief of D, he'll have to leapfrog over Hackett or kill him in a duel."

Jane hoped her face didn't show her thoughts the way Vale's did. Only this time it was red, not pale, that would give her away. "A duel would be interesting."

"Yeah. They could sell tickets and get rid of the deficit."

"OK, Flora. You're up to par."

"Glad to hear it." She motioned the waiter over and ordered dessert and coffee. Jane declined both. When Flora had finished her second cup, she looked at her watch. "You know what? It's early yet. Let me go over and see this great place of yours. Make me a fire. I'll take a taxi home or at least back to the subway."

Shit. Hack could be there. Hack could arrive while Flora was there. Hack could run into Flora in the lobby or the elevator or out on the street and it would be immediately apparent to Flora where he was going and why.

"The place is a mess, Flora. Really. I'd love for you to see it but come when it's in order."

"Nonsense. You're a neat person. And I never see clutter. It's one of my blind spots."

"It's filthy. I haven't run a vacuum since this case started. I spent all last weekend working on the case." She heard herself babbling, getting herself in trouble, but she couldn't allow a visit.

"OK. I know when I'm not wanted. I guess you've got the boyfriend I never met snuggling up in your bed."

"Hardly."

Flora got up, put her coat on, and took her shopping bag. As she stretched to get her arm in the coat, the holster at her hip flashed and a woman at a nearby table saw it and raised her eyebrows.

"This has been a good dinner, and I don't just mean the food."

"It was great. I'll cook for you next time. And make a fire."

"Gimme a hug and I'll be on my way."

"I'll walk you to the subway."

"And leave the boyfriend all alone?"

"That's his problem."

Hack turned up at the stroke of nine. Jane turned the coffeemaker on at the sound of the downstairs doorbell. She opened the apartment door and listened for the elevator or his footsteps on the stairs. These were the moments in her life that she had come to live for, the sounds of the doorbell ringing, the coffee dripping, the elevator rising, the door sliding open.

"Hello, sweetheart."

The voice of her lover, his arms wrapped around her, the door kicked shut. And then, because he was a cop, he left her for one brief moment to double lock the door.

My darling Hack. "Hi."

They went into the kitchen, where the smell of coffee was inviting, and Hack put the pint of ice cream in the freezer. He kissed her and kissed her again. There was more that was inviting besides the coffee. They went to the bedroom.

He touched her hair afterward, her ears, the sweat between her breasts. "Does the face still hurt?"

"No."

"Then I can rub against it."

"Only if you've shaved."

He laughed. He always shaved before he came over, almost always. He rubbed his cheek lightly across hers.

"Let's go get some ice cream and coffee and a dash of Flora."

He put on a pair of jeans he left in her closet and they sat at the table together. She told him about Flora, that she had almost come home with Jane.

"I know you love her, but she's a devious old gal."

"I'll have her over when this case is finished, let her see the apartment. How are you?"

They talked quietly. The ice cream was vanilla with rich chocolate syrup running through it. Hack was trim, with the muscular legs of a man who shunned elevators to low floors and taxis for short hops, a man careful with the calories, but ice cream was his downfall, or at least one of his deepest earthly desires. He asked her about the case. She went to her desk and got the copies Defino had made of the spiral notebook pages.

"You have to break the code. Looks like people's names."

"I'm talking to a friend of Rinzler's tomorrow morning. There was a period of time there, at least four weeks, when Rinzler may have stopped coming to see Stratton and he died of starvation. When the news came out about his death, either she was fired or she quit. Something happened in that period of time and we have to find out what."

"Maybe someone died of an overdose, maybe a lot of people—tainted drugs—and they shut down the operation."

"Could be."

"So you figured out that the *L* here is the super."

"Larry, yeah. Did I tell you he called this afternoon? He wants to talk to me minus Defino—Defino sets him on edge, poor guy. He wants to tell me the truth."

"And he thinks you're a soft touch. He may have a surprise coming."

"He's the key to this, Hack. I don't know what the hell they were doing, but he knows. *L* has got to be for Larry. It's on every entry. It's when she met with him, made an exchange, something like that. We'll figure it out. It'll just take time."

"You said a private eye investigated the case."

"A former cop."

"Why didn't he dig up what your team did?"

"One reason." She had thought about it; Shreiber was a good detective. Why had he trusted Vale and learned nothing about Rinzler? "When we first talked to the super—Shreiber told us to see him; he knew Stratton—we asked Vale who visited Stratton and he mentioned the little Chinese girl who brought Stratton's clean shirts to him. Vale made a mistake telling us that. We asked him how he knew the girl was going to Stratton's apartment. She could have been going anywhere. He said he saw her one day and he asked her."

"And that led you to her and she told you about Rinzler."

"Right. And then we learned everything else. Vale never told Shreiber about the child. If he had, Shreiber would have followed up on it, I'm sure. Vale slipped up."

"Lucky break. Even luckier that she remembered the Rinzler woman well enough to do a sketch."

"She's a smart girl. I like her. Rose. She's in college now."

"Looks like a good case." He pored over the Xeroxed pages as though the abbreviations might open up and make sense to him. "You think Vale killed Rinzler?"

"I think there's a good chance. They were involved in whatever the business was and probably sexually as well."

"Being involved sexually isn't always bad." He leaned across the table and kissed her.

"Not always."

"I can stay longer tonight if you don't think Flora'll come knocking on your door."

"I don't think she will. What if you get a call at the hotel?"

"I'm in the bar. Isn't that where off-duty cops usually are?" The sarcasm was thick.

"Usually."

The ice cream was finished. Hack had used his spoon to scrape out the last of it. They went slowly back to the bedroom and got undressed. Everything was slow this time, the kisses, the touches, the whispers, the rise, the arrival, and eventually the fall.

"I think it's the ice cream that does it," he said, holding her.

"Gotta be something."

"Go to sleep. I'm exhausted."

He had set his watch alarm for five but his internal alarm went off before it. She watched him dress—shirt, pants, shoulder holster, jacket, tie in the pocket. His hair was a mess. She got out of bed and smoothed it while he touched her naked body. The jeans were folded over a chair. Next laundry, she would wash them, keep them fresh for the next time, whenever that would be.

"What are you looking at?"

"Your jeans."

"I didn't hang them up. You mad?"

"Hack—"

"What, baby?"

She went over and put her hands on the jeans where they covered the back of the chair. "*L* isn't for Larry."

"Then what?"

"*L* is for laundry." She turned to face him in the dark. "Something was in the package of laundry. That's why Rinzler was there when Rose delivered it. It wasn't a coincidence. She was there to open the package. Whatever they were dealing, it passed through the Chinese laundry."

18

DEFINO LOVED IT. "You think there were drugs in with the shirts?"

"There was something. Maybe instructions about when to pick them up. Or where. Rinzler didn't give a damn about Andy Stratton. She was there for business."

"We're not going to get anything out of those folks in the laundry, you know that."

"Then we have to get it somewhere else."

"You gonna sweet-talk Vale this afternoon?"

"That's what he thinks."

"Wear your medals."

She laughed. They were on their way to Brooklyn. The train rattled and swayed through the tunnel under the East River. They exited in Brooklyn and set off.

Patricia Washington's house was a five-minute walk. She lived on the second floor of what had once been a two-family house that now had four apartments. Her apartment was in the back and overlooked a small garden.

"Good morning," she said pleasantly as she opened the door. Her eyes moved from one shield and ID to another and then to the faces. "Please come in. I have coffee on. Will you have some?"

"Love it," Defino said.

"Thank you. That's very nice of you, Ms. Washington."

They followed her into a small dinette furnished with a round table, four chairs, and a hutch whose shelves were full of individual dishes standing in tracks along the rear. Cups and saucers were displayed in front of them.

"Nice collection," Jane said, sitting down.

"Oh, thank you. Some of the plates were my mother's. They're quite old."

Washington poured coffee and offered cream and sugar. A platter of cookies lay in the center of the table. She had gone out early to prepare for this meeting.

"This is Detective Defino, Ms. Washington. We're working on the case together."

"You want to know about Erica." She had sat between them at the third cup, a woman in her forties wearing a beige pantsuit, the V-necked jacket with large white buttons down the front.

"When was the last time you saw her?"

"The day she left. There was such turmoil that day, tears, screaming, you can't imagine. She just clammed up, emptied her desk, and left. I went downstairs with her —I think maybe Arthur came too—and we got her a cab so she could get home with all the stuff."

"Is there a reason why you never saw her again?"

"I called her. She said she couldn't talk. She said she'd get in touch but it would take time. She needed a job, she needed a place to live that wouldn't cost so much. But she said she would call. I tried again a couple of weeks later and her phone had been disconnected and there was no forwarding number. I was very—" She took a sip of coffee. "I guess you could say disappointed. We had been friends, real friends, not just coworkers. I didn't understand what had happened."

"What was the nature of your friendship?"

"You mean like what did we do together?"

"Yes."

"We talked on the phone a lot. We went to movies. We went to dinner. We were friends. We had like an understanding. She was a Jew and I was black and there were things we shared. She was friends with Arthur too, you know, Arthur Provenzano."

"Yes. How long did you know her?"

"Oh, a long time. We'd both been at Social Services for years. Other people came and went but we stayed on. We joked that we'd still be there when they outlawed welfare. I probably will be. I have a lot of years now and I wouldn't want to lose my pension."

"So you never talked to her again after that last phone call. Did you hear anything?"

She looked a little confused. "Well, she died, you know."

"And what did you hear about that?"

"It was terrible. It was unbelievable. She went to a hotel on the west side and she— They said she shot herself. I don't know why she would do that."

"The last month or so of her life, did you notice a change in Erica?"

"I did, yes. She seemed tense. Sometimes she had phone conversations where she almost whispered. My desk wasn't too far from hers."

"Did you ask her about it?"

"It wasn't my business. I thought maybe she'd met someone, a man, and there were problems and she didn't want to talk about it."

"You didn't think it had anything to do with work?"

"No. If it had been work, she would have talked about it."

"Do you know why she left Social Services?"

"I wish I did." Her face had grown sad. "There were a lot of rumors but no one knew for sure."

"Tell us what the rumors were."

"Well, there were two main ones, that she quit and that she was fired. If she quit, it was probably because she got burnt out. She couldn't take the amount of work anymore, she thought she could do something better with her life and maybe make more money. But I don't think that was it. She would have told me. She would have told

Arthur. She turned her back on both of us." It was clear that had hurt.

"So you think she was fired."

"But I don't know why." It was almost a wail. "She walked in a minute after I did, she went to her desk, the supervisor called her in, and five minutes later it was all over. And if she was fired, she waived her right to a hearing."

"What's the name of the supervisor?" Defino asked, his notebook open.

"Miss O'Neill. Margaret. She was an old-timer. There aren't many of them left. They've all retired. And good riddance," she added. "They were by-the-book old maids. Listen to me talk, I'm an old maid myself." She smiled and her face lit up.

"Hardly," Jane said, thinking of her conversations last night, of how the world sees you in contrast to how you see yourself. "Did any of the rumors say that Erica had done something to get Miss O'Neill angry?"

"What I heard was that Erica screwed up on the job, that she failed to see clients but that her records showed she had seen them. You can't do that. I'm sure you understand. But Erica wouldn't do that. She had integrity. If she said she did something or went somewhere, she did. She had no reason to lie. Maybe there was a mix-up in a file, information recorded in the wrong place, but I can't believe Erica deliberately falsified anything."

"Did she ever mention a man named Larry? Or did you hear her use that name when she was on the phone?"

"Larry. It's so many years ago, I couldn't tell you for sure."

"Were there men in her life?"

"Sometimes."

"Did you know her sister?"

"I met her once. She's a nice woman, a good sister. Erica loved those children."

"Did you ever meet any of Erica's boyfriends?"

Washington shook her head. "I don't think so."

"Did you know her friend Ellen Raymond?"

"Ellie? The one in California? I never met her but Erica went out to visit her a couple of times. I think they knew each other from when they got their degrees in social work. They were old friends."

Jane pushed her chair back slightly and Defino took up the questioning. "Ms. Washington, I'm going to ask you something that may upset you, but we both want you to know that you're not under investigation for anything and what you tell us will stay with us. Did Ms. Rinzler do drugs? Smoke a little pot?"

She swallowed, reached for a cookie, took a tiny bite, and sipped her coffee. "Not in my presence. She knew what I thought of that. I have a brother with a problem. I wouldn't go near the stuff. And she didn't do hard drugs. I'm not saying she smoked anything; I'm just saying I never saw her do it."

"Is it possible she was dealing?"

"Erica?" Her voice was shocked. "Never."

"Is there anything else she might have been involved in that was, let's say, a little shady? Maybe she was importing diamonds or stolen artwork."

Washington laughed. "Detective, you're barking up the wrong tree. You've just got the wrong person. You know, our job is full-time. You're lucky to have the two days at the end of the week to clean your house and do your laundry and see a movie."

"But if she was skipping client visits, maybe she had more time than you're aware of."

"If that were true, of course there would be time." She looked troubled, a frown creasing her forehead.

"Do you know any other people Ms. Rinzler was friendly with?"

"Arthur was a friend. She was friendly with almost everyone at work, but she wasn't their friend, if you know what I mean."

"Did she ever talk to you about Anderson Stratton, the man who was found dead in his apartment?"

"Maybe a little. I think she liked him. Oh yes, she said he wrote wonderful poetry. I remember that. He was schizophrenic, wasn't he? You know what I remember? Several caseworkers were assigned to him, one after the other, and he threw them all out. They sent Erica because she was so good with people. And it was the right thing to do. She didn't get thrown out. I heard he starved to death. Is that true?"

"We don't know," Defino said. "That's why we're looking into his death. Did you ever meet any other friends of Ms. Rinzler's?"

"Just Mimi. We went to dinner and the theater together a few times."

"Do you know if Ms. Rinzler owned a gun?"

"I can't tell you that she didn't, but I never saw one, and she never said she owned one." Something seemed to click in her mind. "Do you think Erica was murdered?"

"It's something we're investigating," Jane said.

"My God. Does her sister know?"

"We've spoken to her sister. I just have one more question. How did you find out that Erica had died?"

She thought about it. "It was quite a while after it happened. Either I called her sister or she called me. I don't remember now. I never told a soul. I suppose I should have told Arthur, but he'd been transferred and I didn't see him much."

Defino took his card out and laid it on the table as Jane did the same. "You can call either of us," he said, "if something comes to you. Maybe you'll think of a reason why someone might have wanted to kill Ms. Rinzler."

Patricia Washington studied both cards. "I don't think so," she said. "No one could have wanted her dead."

They passed the living room on the way to the door and Jane noticed a pipe in a large ashtray, a brown tobacco pouch beside it on the end table. Maybe not quite an old maid.

"So we got zip," Defino said as they walked back to the subway.

"Except that something was going on in Rinzler's life the last month of Stratton's life."

"Which we knew. What do you think we should do about the Chinese laundry?"

"Let's not jump the gun. We should try to get the Social Service records for Rinzler, personnel and her clients."

"We'll need a warrant. They'll scream about privacy issues."

"Then we'll do it that way. And maybe find Miss O'Neill. She sounds like the nuns when I was a kid."

"I was thinking the same thing. Get my hand whacked again."

"It sure as hell didn't work on me."

19

AFTER LUNCH JANE took the subway up to Fourteenth Street. MacHovec was expecting to hear from his friend at the telephone company this afternoon and Jane promised to be back after her interview with Vale. That wouldn't take much time. By now, Vale had rehearsed his new story and unless he slipped up again, he would just repeat the new set of lies. Jane didn't think there was much chance he would tell her any truths.

He must have seen her approach through the living room window as he opened the door before she was down the steps. "Nice to see you, Detective," he said in the new, be-nice-to-the-cops voice. "Come in."

"Hello, Mr. Vale."

"Some coffee?"

"No, thanks."

"Well, let's sit in the living room and talk."

She took out her notebook, flipped to an empty page, and dated it. "I'm listening."

"You were quite right that I knew Erica Rinzler, Detective. I hadn't mentioned my relationship with her to the police or to that private detective. What was his name?"

"Shreiber."

"Of course, Mr. Shreiber. He and I got on very well, you know."

"That's because you neglected to tell him everything you knew. You didn't tell him about the little Chinese girl delivering Mr. Stratton's laundry."

"It didn't seem to matter. It must have slipped my mind."

"Let's get back to Erica Rinzler and your relationship with her."

"You might call it a brief affair, Detective Bauer. We were drawn to each other in a sexual way. Very drawn. Although she was ostensibly visiting Andy as a caseworker, she was really coming to see me. The relationship didn't last long, but it was quite intense."

"How long did it last, Mr. Vale?"

"I'm not sure I could put a number of days or weeks on it, Detective Bauer. I'm sure you know how these things are. The hotter and heavier they are, the sooner they burn out." He attempted a smile, drawing her into his little circle of disappointed lovers. He had paid her the compliment of comparing her to himself. "And when it was over, Erica stopped coming here."

"So you're telling me that her visits to Andy Stratton were excuses to see you."

"Precisely. Are you sure you wouldn't like some coffee? A glass of wine?" The charm was stifling.

"Let's stay on track here, Mr. Vale. My information about Ms. Rinzler is that she was a dedicated worker. You're telling me that wasn't correct."

"I'm sure she was dedicated. She said as much to me. But you know how affairs of the heart can affect one's work."

"No, I'm afraid I don't. Would you like to tell me?"

The attempt at a happy face faded. "When we broke up, Erica stopped coming to this building. That's all I know."

"What caused the breakup?"

"As I said, these hot fires don't last long."

"Mr. Vale, I appreciate your way with words, but that doesn't answer my question."

"She— I just got tired of the relationship. I knew it wasn't going anywhere. I told her it was over."

"What about your business relationship with her?" She kept her eyes on his face, looking for the telltale loss of color. "Did you break that off too?"

"There was no business relationship." His color remained neutral. "I told you, we had a sexual—"

"Come on, Mr. Vale. You and Erica were making a little money on the side, weren't you? It wasn't what you were doing in bed, it was what you were doing on your feet."

"Detective, I don't know what you're talking about."

"Was this little story about the affair the truth you wanted to get on the record?"

"It is the truth. I can't prove it. Erica's gone, but—"

"Were you at her funeral?"

"No. I didn't even know she was dead for some time."

"How did you find out?"

That stumped him. "I heard it. I don't remember from whom. Maybe Andy—"

"Andy was dead, remember?"

"Yes, of course. He died during that period, when she stopped coming."

"And you never looked in on him? He was your friend and you never thought to go up a couple of flights and see how he was doing? There must have been weeks when you didn't see him from this window."

"It was a busy time." It was starting to get to him. "I don't check up on the tenants unless they call for help."

"Larry," she said, her voice raised, "this wasn't a tenant. This was a friend. This was a guy who sat and talked music with you, remember? This was Andy Stratton who had dinner with you sometimes. Why the fuck didn't you go up and check on him?"

The outburst left him speechless. He stood and walked across the room, then back again. "I didn't expect this from you," he said.

"Just answer the question," she said in a normal voice. "Why didn't you go up and check on Andy? You knew he had problems. You didn't see him for weeks. I wonder if you didn't want him dead, Mr. Vale, you and Erica Rinzler both."

"I can't believe you said that." He ran his hands through his hair. This interview he had prepared to ace was turning into a nightmare. "I was busy. I had a lot of things on my mind. I regret that I didn't go up, I'll admit that. I had a lot of sleepless nights after Mrs. Bender called the police and they found Andy. But I wasn't responsible for his death. I didn't know how ill he was. I didn't realize that without constant observation he might do such a thing to himself."

"Who did Erica Rinzler get a gun from?"

"I— You mean the gun she killed herself with?"

"That gun, yes."

"I don't know. I suppose there are places. I don't believe in owning a firearm so I've never looked into it."

"She didn't believe in firearms either. Strange that she set her principles aside and acquired one."

"It is strange, now that you mention it."

"Did you ever see the little Chinese girl again after Andy Stratton died?"

"I don't recall. I don't go to the laundry. I wash my clothes in a machine."

"This has been very interesting, Mr. Vale. If you decide on another version of the truth, please let me know. You have my number."

Getting out of that overheated room and into the cold air felt better than anything else that day.

MacHovec had the phone records when she got back to the office. His friend had called and given him a synopsis of what he'd found; then he'd faxed the pages, which had just come in the last few minutes, and MacHovec was going through them, making marks in red.

"Can't prove they went to bed together, but they did a lot of talking," he said. "The records don't register what extension Vale called at Social Services but he sure as hell called the main number a lot over a period of maybe six months."

"I'm more interested in the business than the sex," Jane said. "Vale was pushing the sex part this afternoon, as though that and his unbearable charm would get him off the hook. He didn't admit to any business."

"Well, he called her at work and called her at night and on weekends at her home number. But that all stopped weeks before she died."

"How about before Stratton died?"

MacHovec checked some papers on his desk, came back to the faxed material, and said, "Before Stratton's body was discovered anyway. If we figure he was dead one or two weeks before he was found, yeah, hold on, no phone calls probably for the last week or so of his life."

"We need a time line," Defino said from his typewriter.

Jane agreed. "I can—"

"My specialty," MacHovec said. "How do you want it? Black and white or multicolor? I can do a rainbow."

Jane grinned at him. "Do your thing, partner. Anyone want to hear Vale's new story?" She briefed them, which took almost no time.

"So he decided we should think he and Erica were taking a tumble and that's what went on between them," MacHovec said.

"And that's *all* that went on between them. And since I'm a sucker for his sticky charm, I'll believe him. After this, he'll be asking for you, Gordon."

Defino laughed, a real laugh, his face brightening.

"What I want to know is: If Vale didn't kill Rinzler, who told him she was dead?"

No one responded. Jane took the phone records when MacHovec had given them the once-over. He had marked the calls between Rinzler and Vale on both their records.

Eight to ten years earlier there were fewer cell phones in use and these two had had only the phones in their homes and office. While Vale's calls to Social Services could not be identified as having terminated at Rinzler's desk, she was as sure as MacHovec was that they had. Otherwise, he was having quite a dialogue with Social Services.

On Rinzler's record Jane found several calls to Ellie Raymond's number in California. There were also frequent calls, mostly in the evening, to Patricia Washington and to Judy Weissman. The records were more detailed than telephone bills, which normally noted only long-distance calls. Here, every call placed from the number was listed. Jane went through many pages, writing down frequently called numbers. Something might come of that. She picked up the phone and called one, just to see who answered.

It was a woman with a young voice. "I'm sorry," Jane said cordially. "I thought this was my friend's number. I haven't called her in some time. How long have you had this number?"

"Two years, I think. Maybe three."

"Sorry for bothering you."

Defino was looking at her.

"I bet they just shut down whatever the operation was, turned off their phones, maybe even moved. I hope this doesn't all come down to sweating the Chinese laundry people. The review board'll have us up on charges."

"They'll use Rose on the front page of the *Daily News* with insets of you and me beating her."

"I'll vouch for you," MacHovec said, raising his head from his artwork. "And I'll try to find out who had those numbers eight years ago."

Jane looked over at his work. MacHovec was a man of several talents, most of which he kept to himself. The time line he was drawing could have come from the hand of an artist. He was using colored pens, rulers, and a roll of paper he had found somewhere and never used before. It gave him great length. When he was done, they could tack it on the wall.

He left before it was finished, just as Jane's phone rang.

"Hi," Hack's voice said.

It made her smile. "Hi. Where are you?"

"Still in that bar I spent the night in."

"Good place for you."

"I'm glad we're together again, Jane."

"So am I."

"I'll see you in a week or two."

"Good."

"I know you're in a crowd over there so don't say anything, but I'm all alone and I love you."

"That makes two."

"Bye."

She hung up and heard Defino's phone ring. He reached for it from his seat at the typewriter. "Yeah, Defino."

Jane moved over to MacHovec's desk to admire the time line. It began with Stratton's move into the apartment in Alphabet City about ten years ago. The next point on it was the arrival of Erica Rinzler as his caseworker. As Jane's eyes moved from left to right, she heard Defino's conversation.

"She can't. . . . Because I say so and you say so. Put her on the phone. . . . Dammit— . . . Then you tell her. She stays home. I come home and find her gone, she'll be in more trouble than she's ever been before. . . . I don't give a shit. That's the way it is. . . . She what? . . . Yeah, I'm on my way." He banged the phone down. "That kid'll be my death. She met some guy, wants to go out with him tonight. 'An older man,' " he said, mimicking his daughter. "I'll give her an older man." He had left the typewriter, pulled the page out, and dropped it on his desk.

"Gordon—"

"Am I wrong?"

"No, you're right. Just control your rage when you talk to her."

"Rage is right." He put his coat on. "Jesus, what else does she have in store for us?"

Plenty, Jane thought. "Good luck."

"Thanks. See you in the morning."

She watched him go, thinking of her father when she was a teenager. He had not shown rage, although Jane was sure he must have felt it. He had simply been incredulous. How had this happened? Their beautiful, wonderful, perfect daughter had acted like someone else's trampy no-good child.

She pushed MacHovec's chair away from the desk and put her coat on. It was quiet outside her office, the detectives on their way home to their good and bad children, Annie off to a fun evening with her friends. Not bothering to wait for the elevator, she went down the stairs. As she walked to the subway, she thought about Hack's call and the stack of phone records on her desk. A little while ago, a piece of equipment at the telephone company had recorded his phone making a call to hers and how long the call had lasted. Records existed of his office phone and cell phone calling her at home, this apartment or that, for ten years. If someone suspected their relationship and had the wherewithal, as MacHovec did, he could get those records without a warrant, just as Sean had today.

They were always careful. There had been nights when Hack had called from a pay phone to say he couldn't leave the group he was with and their date was canceled. The question was: Was it enough? She went down into the subway.

Carrying bags of groceries and a bundle of firewood, she moved through homeward-bound New Yorkers from the center of the sidewalk toward her front door. Preoccupied, she failed to notice a man coming from the other direction and they collided.

"I'm so sorry," he said, reaching to prevent one bag from slipping from her grasp. "I wasn't looking. You live here?" He was tall and handsome, dark hair a bit too long, well dressed, not more than thirty.

"Excuse me," she said sternly, pulling back.

"I'll help you in," he said cordially, pushing the door open.

"Out of my way," she ordered.

He gave her a warm smile. "Sorry. Have a good evening."

She stood and watched him walk down the street. He didn't look back. When he was gone, she went inside.

20

WHEN SHE TURNED off the alarm, it kept on ringing. Confused, she looked at the clock. It wasn't seven yet and it was the phone making the noise. She picked it up.

"Jane, Gordon. My daughter's not home."

"Jesus, what happened?"

"She snuck out after we went to bed. I checked her before I went to sleep. She must have waited awhile. We have carpeting. You can't hear a damn thing."

"You call the precinct?"

"Just now."

"Want me to call McElroy?"

"Yeah, thanks. I better stay here. My wife's about to collapse."

And probably Gordon too, Jane thought. "I'll come out."

"What for?"

"We'll figure something out. Let me know if you hear. Gordon, I feel terrible."

"Thanks."

She called McElroy, who was all sympathy. "Sure. Go out. Give him some support. I'll tell Annie."

"Thanks, Lieutenant."

She hung up and sat on the edge of the bed, her insides

doing terrible things. A teenaged girl and an older man. God, let her be alive, she thought. Gordon and his wife must be going through holy hell. She started moving, bathroom, clothes, bed, breakfast, although she wasn't hungry. The cop's rule was always eat first. You never know when you'll get your next meal when you're on a case. Let her be alive, please let her be alive.

Defino lived in Bellerose, a section of Queens on the edge of the Nassau County line. His resident precinct was the One-oh-five.

Jane took the F train to the end of the line in Queens and got off at Hillside Avenue. "End of the line" was the right description; you could be in Boston faster. From there she took the bus to 262nd Street. Then she walked. Boston, she thought. She could be in France by now.

Two police cars were parked at the Defino home, one in the driveway, one in front of the house. She took out her shield and pinned it to the lapel of her coat before she rang the doorbell. A uniform opened the door.

"Detective Bauer?"

"Yes. What's up?"

"She just came home."

"Thank God." Her throat choked up and she swallowed. "She OK?"

"We don't know yet."

That meant they suspected rape. From a nearby room, she heard a girl scream "It's your fault. It's all your fault," and Defino's familiar voice telling her to calm down. Jane moved toward the fracas. They were in the living room, the family and two uniformed cops who looked very unhappy. The girl looked awful. Her hair needed washing, her face was streaked with tears. Her clothes were a caricature of the cool teenager.

"Gordon," Jane said, and silence fell like a blanket as everyone turned toward her.

"Jane. She's back. Toni, this is Jane Bauer."

Defino's wife's face was as streaked with tears as her daughter's. She came over and said hello. "Thank you for coming. I nearly died of worry."

"What happened?"

"We don't know yet. She went out with some man. He kept her overnight and just dropped her off a couple of blocks from here. At least that's what she said. Gordon says she has to be tested for rape." She spoke softly so no one would hear.

"Did she say she'd been raped?"

"She said she was and then she said she wasn't."

The conversation had begun again, but at a lower volume. The daughter was still accusing her father of being at fault. Defino looked ready to take on the world. If he could find the man his daughter had been with, he'd be dead.

One of the uniforms came over to Jane and drew her into the kitchen. "We've got to take her to the hospital for an examination."

"I know."

"She's pretty adamant."

"I'll take her if I can convince her to go. Why don't you guys back off a little. This is hard enough without all the blues around."

"Sure thing."

"But I'll need you to drive us." She went back to the living room.

"I just want to take a shower and go to bed," the daughter wailed.

"You're not taking a shower," Defino thundered.

The girl burst into tears.

Jane took Defino by the arm and walked him to the kitchen. "Listen to me. I know what's worrying her. Let me talk to her. I can take her for the exam. You stay home."

"I want to know."

"I'll tell you what you need to know."

He looked angry enough to hit her. "What does that mean?"

"If she was raped, you'll know."

He went to the sink and took a glass of water. He drank it thirstily, then put the glass down on the counter. "What the fuck does she mean that this was my fault?" he said, leaning over the sink.

"We'll find out. Let's just make sure she doesn't take a shower."

"Come on. I'll introduce you."

They went back to the living room. Toni was sitting, holding her child's head against her breast. Toni was a handsome woman, a little plump but not fat. The girl was like Defino, a spindle. Her hair was brown, like her father's, and streaked with blond.

"Angela, I want you to meet Detective Bauer, my partner."

The girl looked up and nodded.

"Hi, Angela. Would you come and talk to me for a minute?"

Angela seemed anxious to get out of her parents' presence. She got up off the sofa and followed Jane to the kitchen where they both sat at the table.

"You need to have a rape test done," Jane said quietly.

"I wasn't raped. We didn't do that. We just—"

"Maybe there's DNA. We need evidence. We have to find this man."

"Please leave me alone. Please tell them to leave me alone. This isn't my fault." She seemed ready to cry again.

"If you were raped, your parents will be told. They won't be told anything else." She kept her eyes on Angela.

"Do they have to do it now?"

"They have to do it before you clean yourself off."

Tears rolled down her soiled cheeks. "Let's just go, OK? I want to get it over with. And they don't come."

"They won't."

They went in the radio car. Jane had instructed the cops in the front seat not to banter and they sat without saying a word. Defino, under protest, stayed home with his wife. As they drove, Jane asked Angela quietly what had happened.

She had met the man, Bill Fletcher, after school a couple of days ago. Yesterday, he walked her almost to her house and asked her out for the evening. He was cute and said he could get them in to a TV show in Manhattan. But her parents wouldn't let her go. He called her—she had told him she couldn't call him because her father was a cop and he could trace calls from the house—and she said she would meet him at the corner at midnight. That was too late for the TV show, but he would think of something else that was fun.

"Where did he take you?" Jane asked.

"To his house, or somebody's house. It was dark and I don't know where we were. We just hung out. He made scrambled eggs and gave me some Scotch. And then—"

Jane waited.

"I was tired and he was tired and we just kinda laid on the bed."

"That's all you did?"

"No."

The car turned into the emergency area and they all got out. One of the cops had phoned ahead and a young nurse was waiting for them. She put her arm around Angela and talked to her softly. It took time. There were papers to fill out, a counselor to talk to. Jane stayed in the examining room, sitting by Angela's side, feeling the pressure of her hand when she felt pain. When it was over, the nurse motioned her outside.

"She wasn't raped. There's some bruising, also on her arms, I noticed, and a little fluid. I don't know if we'll get anything from it."

"Thanks."

"And by the way, your girl's a virgin."

"Double thanks."

The cops drove them back, silent once again.

"Angela," Jane said, "why did you say it was your father's fault?"

"Because this morning, when Bill dropped me off at McDonald's, he said—" She took a breath that was almost a sob. "He said my father should mind his own business. He said Daddy was . . . how did he put it? He was sticking his nose into places it didn't belong."

"Was he talking about your father's police work?"

"I think so. He said something else. I can't remember." She shook her head. "Oh yeah. It was about me. He said, 'If your old man doesn't lay off, you won't get off so easy next time.' "

"There won't be a next time, Angela."

"What is my father working on?"

"An old case. It's from years ago. It has nothing to do with what's going on now."

"He almost raped me," Angela said, sniffing. "I fought him off."

Jane put her arm around her.

"I just remembered. He said something else. He drove me to McDonald's this morning and he pushed me out of the car and he said, 'Remember what I told you.' And then he said, 'A B C D.' "

A chill passed through Jane's shoulders. A, B, C, D. Alphabet City.

Toni took charge of her daughter when they got back. After she slept, she would have to go down to the 105th Precinct and make a statement. Defino would go with her. He walked outside the house with Jane and lit a cigarette. His hand wasn't steady.

"All right, tell me."

"She wasn't raped. But he threatened her. He said next time—"

"Fuck him, there's no next time."

"Calm down. He sent you a message. That's what this was all about. He wants you off the case you're working on."

"He said that?"

"Words to that effect. And when he dropped her off this morning, he reminded her to tell you what he'd said. And he finished with A, B, C, D."

"Who the fuck is this guy?"

"I don't know. But just maybe they got some DNA from him."

Defino looked at her starkly. "But she wasn't raped."

"She wasn't raped." Jane put an arm around his shoulders. "Relax, Gordon. Your daughter's a virgin." Without warning, tears started down her cheeks. "Shit, what the fuck is wrong with me?" She reached in her pocket for a tissue and blotted her face, feeling more embarrassed than she had for years. Crying in front of another cop, in front of her partner, for Christ's sake. "Sorry."

"It's OK. We're all OK. Thanks for telling me."

She gave him a squeeze. "I'm going back to Centre Street."

"I'll drive you to the station."

"Go sit with your wife. She needs you a lot more than I do."

"You look like hell," Captain Graves said. Jane, MacHovec, and McElroy were in the whip's office for debriefing.

"I thought she was dead, Cap. I know Gordon did too. Here's the way it played." She went through the whole thing, landing hard on the end: A, B, C, D.

"Alphabet City," the whip said.

"Eight fuckin' years and these guys are making threats?" McElroy seemed astounded.

"They must be back in business, or they never went out, just closed down the operation and opened it up again somewhere else. Or there was a death and they're still liable. Sean, you have kids?"

"Yeah, but not at home."

"Your wife?"

"I'll take care of it." He flipped some pages. "I'm getting the names and addresses of the phone numbers Vale and Rinzler called. I called a lot of them this morning and they've all been reassigned. Maybe Monday if we're lucky."

"Monday is two weeks," Graves said. "Decision time on the Stratton case. We've got something going here. I'm going to reopen the Rinzler suicide case and have it reclassified as a possible homicide. We have enough to support that position."

"I can work with that," Jane said.

"I'll call Mrs. Constantine on Monday. Meanwhile"—he looked at his watch—"have a nice weekend."

Defino called at night. He sounded as though he hadn't slept in days. He had taken Angela to the precinct and filed a complaint. She had been interviewed by two female detectives, one from the precinct squad, the other a specialist from the Borough Sex Crimes Unit. On Monday, she would sit with an artist and try to get a good likeness of Bill Fletcher. Defino was itching to get his hands on Vale.

"Vale was supposed to take care of you by sweet-talking you, and this mutt Fletcher was supposed to take care of me."

"Vale and Fletcher have to be connected."

"Vale put him on my tail. Captain Graves called. He wants me off the case."

"Shit," she said softly.

"I told him to forget about it. I'm on and I'm staying on."

"What about your family?"

"I've worked it out."

That meant he had enlisted the aid of friends and colleagues to see to it that the Defino children got to and from school safely. In addition, a uniform or a detective would be inside and outside the house for some time to come.

"Gordon, we have to go for Rinzler's case files and personnel files."

"Personnel files won't give us anything. Miss Margaret O'Neill just wrote down what looked good at the moment."

"Then we have to try to find her."

"It'll take more than sweet-talk to get anything out of her, if she's what Washington described."

"Let's make the effort."

"I'll see you Monday. You're a stand-up gal, you know that?"

21

BEFORE RETURNING TO work at the beginning of the month, Jane and her former partner, Marty Hoagland, had arranged to make one of their two annual required visits to Rodman's Neck, the NYPD shooting range, the following Saturday. Three hours would be spent in classes on new laws, regulations, and tactics, another three on live fire exercises with her Glock and her off-duty S&W.

Rodman's Neck was up in the Bronx, an almost impossible location to reach without a car. Marty would pick her up. Sitting back on her sofa across from the fire, she keyed his number to confirm their appointment.

His wife answered and they chatted a while before she called Marty to the phone.

"Hey, Jane, how's things? We got a date next Saturday."

"Right. When should I be ready?"

"Six-thirty. We can talk on the way. Shouldn't be too much traffic on Saturday morning."

On the following morning, Jane started calling Erica Rinzler's friends. She had luck with the first number, Mimi Bruegger.

"Ms. Bruegger, this is Det. Jane Bauer of the New York Police Department."

"Oh God. Is it my mother?"

"It's all right, ma'am. Nothing's wrong. I'm part of a team that's investigating the death of Erica Rinzler."

"Erica." She sounded incredulous. "Erica died years ago."

"I'm aware of that. We have reason to believe that her death may not have been a suicide." There was a silence. "Ms. Bruegger?"

"Yes, I heard you." She had a childlike voice and could have been mistaken for a teenager. "I guess I'm confused. I couldn't believe she'd killed herself when I heard it, but as time went on, I got used to the idea. Are you telling me she was murdered?"

"It's possible. Could we get together and talk, ma'am?"

"Sure. Let me look at my calendar." She put the phone down and Jane heard her talking some distance away. "I'm pretty busy this coming week but I could get away this afternoon."

"Tell me where and when."

"Uh. My husband's a member of the Harvard Club and I can use their facilities. It's on West Forty-fourth between Fifth and Sixth. It's comfortable and we can talk privately."

"That sounds good."

"I'll meet you inside the front door at two."

"I'll be there."

It was one of the places in Manhattan she had never been in, although she knew where the building was. It was a large, old brick building with a somewhat forbidding edifice, near the New York Yacht Club and down the block from the old Algonquin Hotel. She had been to a couple of meetings at the hotel but had not set foot in the clubs. She wondered how long women had been allowed to enter. Probably Flora knew. It was the kind of thing she kept up with.

She picked up the F train at West Fourth Street, rode it to Forty-second Street, and walked north two blocks and then east to the Harvard Club. It was as imposing as she recalled but no one stopped her as she entered. As she looked around, a small round woman in a long mink coat walked over to her.

"Detective Bauer?"

"Yes, ma'am." Jane showed her the shield and photo ID. "Ms. Bruegger?"

Mimi Bruegger smiled and held out her hand. "Come on. We can keep our coats."

They walked past a coat check and ended up in a large, old-fashioned room with comfortable furniture, a man's kind of room. They took possession of a sofa and a chair for their coats. Mimi Bruegger was wearing a black skirt and a frilly blouse. Her blond curls bobbed when she talked.

"Want some coffee?"

"I'm fine."

"OK. I told my husband what we were going to talk about. Dave knew Erica and he was really stunned when we heard she'd committed suicide. No one ever asked us anything. Why did it take so long for the police to get involved?"

"We've been looking into another death and Ms. Rinzler's name came up through her job at Social Services."

"You mean like through a client?"

"That's right."

"She was such a doll, my Bee-Bee. You know she was called Bee-Bee."

"I've heard. It was a childhood nickname."

"You've learned a lot. Who've you been talking to?"

"Some people who knew her at work. Ms. Bruegger, how long did you know Erica Rinzler?"

"Oh gosh, years. We went to high school together, then Brooklyn College. I left after two years and went to the University of Michigan. It was my first time out of New York, can you believe it?"

Jane could. She had lived a similarly insulated life. "What about Erica? What did she do after college?"

"She went to social work school and got her M.S.W. I think she took a little time off after college and went to Europe, not too long. She had wanderlust. She just wanted to get away."

"And then she went for her M.S.W. Do you remember where?"

"Columbia."

The spiral notebook was from Columbia. "Did she get a job right away with Social Services after she got her degree?"

The little woman nodded. "Pretty soon after, I think."

"Did she ever marry?"

"No. She wanted to. There was a guy when she was in her early twenties, a real nice guy, but it didn't work out. They dated, but it just never amounted to anything." She spoke with sadness.

"Did she complain about not having enough money to live on?"

Mimi's laugh was almost a giggle. "Who doesn't? Although I don't complain much anymore." Her diamond engagement ring flashed as she spoke.

"What I mean is, was she thinking of getting a job that paid better or maybe something part-time to give her a little extra money?"

"She may have said something like that but nothing specific. She loved her job even though sometimes it was hell."

"In what way?"

"The battle-ax she worked for was impossible. Some of her clients were difficult to deal with. You know, mothers who desert their families, kids who get into terrible trouble. You're with the police; I'm sure you could tell me a thing or two."

"But she never said she was doing additional work."

"No."

"Did she talk to you about her clients?"

"In a general way. She never mentioned names. She was very circumspect."

"Did she call you after she left the job?"

"She called me that night or the next day. She said she had quit, it had just gotten to her, she couldn't stand it anymore, Miss What's-her-name would see to it her job was a dead end, that sort of thing. She sounded awful, angry, upset. I told her to calm down. I said let's get together and talk this out. Come and stay overnight. You know, the things you say to a friend."

"And?"

"And the next thing I knew, she was living with her sister upstate. I don't mean it was a permanent thing; she said it was temporary. But she'd left her apartment, she'd cut off her phone, and she didn't even have a forwarding number. Can you believe that? I said, 'Bee-Bee, what are you doing? You can't cut yourself off from the whole world just because you lost your job.' And you know what she said? She said, 'I didn't lose it. I shoved it up their ass.' "

"Mrs. Bruegger, did you see Ms. Rinzler after she quit?"

"Yes, I think I did. I think she came in one day for an interview—she was looking for a job—and we had lunch."

"How long before her death was that?"

"A couple of weeks. I talked to her after that. And then her sister called." Her cheery face had become almost tearful. "I couldn't believe it."

"Did Erica ever tell you she owned a gun?"

"Erica didn't own a gun." Mimi waved a dismissing hand in the air. "That's a crock, you know that? I don't know how she came to kill herself, and I suppose no one will ever know, but she didn't go out and buy a gun. You can't get a gun in New York State if you're not a cop, can you?"

"It's difficult. Did Erica smoke a little grass now and then?"

"Probably. Everybody did, at least when they were young and single. But she'd never do anything stronger than that."

"She ever supply any for anyone you know?"

"Bee-Bee? Forget it. It was purely recreational."

Jane took out her card and handed it to Mimi. "If you think of anyone who was friendly with her near the end of her life, man or woman, I'd like to know."

"She had a friend in California, Ellie Raymond."

"Yes."

"There may have been a man for a while, but nothing with promise. What Erica wanted was to have a baby. She thought about it. She talked about it. But like so many things in her life, it was just talk. It never amounted to anything."

"You didn't happen to talk to her the day she died, did you?"

"I talked to her a few days before, but I can't remember how many. I called her at Judy's."

"Was she depressed?"

"You know what? She wasn't. She was confident she'd find something."

"We've heard that she went into New York on the last day of her life to have lunch with a friend. Do you know anything about that?"

"It wasn't with me. I don't know who it could have been. But she had other friends."

"Thanks, Mrs. Bruegger."

"Sure you don't want any coffee?"

"I'm sure, thanks."

"Well, I think I'll just stop in and have some myself. If you find anything out, I hope you'll let me know."

Jane said she would. She walked through the building to the front door, looking at the men who had gone to Harvard.

It was late afternoon, after she had done her Saturday chores, that the phone rang.

"Detective Bauer, this is Judy Weissman. From Chappaqua?"

"Yes, Mrs. Weissman." She tensed, wondering if Weissman had heard about the storage company.

"I told you something when you were here last week. I apologize, but I seem to have made a mistake."

"About what?"

"Those beads you showed me, the ones I said were my daughter's."

"Yes."

"I said something to Sandy yesterday about the little beads she gave to Aunt Erica. She said my sister gave them back; they were too delicate and she was afraid they would break. Sandy has them. The beads you showed me couldn't have been hers."

"I see. Thank you, Mrs. Weissman. I appreciate your call."

"Is it meaningful? I mean, you seemed pleased when I identified them as belonging to Erica."

"If it's meaningful, we'll find out. At the moment, it just leaves us not knowing where they came from. If you think of anything else—"

"Sure. Bye-bye."

Jane hung up and got the little plastic envelope out of her bag. They were too small for a grown woman to wear, especially not with the larger, colorful beads everyone remembered seeing on Rinzler. Rose was sure they hadn't been hers. Shit, maybe they had nothing to do with anything.

MacHovec had completed the time line on Friday while Jane was out in Queens. He had Xeroxed it in eight-and-a-half-inch widths and left a copy on each desk. She took hers out and spread it on the sofa, kneeling in front of it to see the whole thing at once. At the left end was the date when Stratton moved into the apartment in Alphabet City. Little notes indicated when he saw the psychiatrist at the beginning of his stay. A pencil notation showed when Rinzler probably began to visit him. That reminded Jane that they had to get the Social Services files that would tell them exactly when she made her first visit. A lot of data had to be filled in, she thought. Lew Beech had done none of this. He had been working with an apparent suicide. Erica's clients were unimportant to him.

Actually, between the visits to the psychiatrist and the finding of Stratton's body, little was certain. Stratton's body had been found on November 17. The medical examiner had estimated the time of death to be two weeks earlier, approximately November 3, but that was a rough estimate. Mrs. Constantine had left for France on October 15 but had not spoken to her brother for several days although she had called his number. That was a nearly five-week gap and it wasn't clear when her last telephone contact with him had been or when she had actually seen him last, which could have been some time earlier. It was possible he hadn't been eating well for some time, but if Mrs. C. hadn't been there to notice that he was losing weight, they couldn't put a date on when the deprivation had begun. And if she hadn't spoken to him, she might not know that the Social Service worker he got along with so well had stopped coming.

That was the question, wasn't it? When did Erica Rinzler stop coming? If they knew that, they could begin to find out what had happened before that date to keep her away from Stratton. Was it the breakup with Vale? Jane wasn't convinced there had even been an "affair," as Vale chose to call it, with Rinzler. It was a cinch the Chinese laundry didn't have a record of the last time Stratton's shirts were brought in or delivered. So much was murky and no way to verify when important events occurred. Even when they got the records from Social Services, nothing Rinzler wrote down could be relied on to be any more accurate than Vale's truths.

So, she thought, if we assume Stratton died around November 3, then he stopped eating around the time his sister left the country, October 15, give or take. And maybe that was why he didn't answer the phone when she called. He was too weak. Or he didn't care. Perhaps he wanted Rinzler for himself and when he learned of her affair with Vale, he became depressed and stopped eating.

That would work. What it didn't explain was why Rinzler didn't show up to check on him or send someone else in her place. Mrs. C. hadn't mentioned any change after Rinzler took over Stratton's case.

Jane went back to the time line. To the right of Stratton's body being found on November 17 was a notation that Rinzler parted company with Social Services on the eighteenth. That meant someone at the Nine had notified

Social Services and they had wasted no time giving her the ax. Maybe Vale had told the cop that Stratton was under the Social Services umbrella. It wouldn't take long for Miss Margaret O'Neill to get word.

Less than a week after the body was discovered, Rinzler had moved out of the Murray Hill apartment and up to Chappaqua. So we're about up to November 23, give or take a couple of days, Jane thought. The date of Rinzler's death was December 19, just over three weeks after she moved to her sister's, slightly more than a month since Stratton's body was discovered.

Jane's eyes moved left, to the earlier part of the time line, before Mrs. C. went to Paris. That had to be the period when Rinzler stopped visiting Stratton. He needed a good two weeks to die. In the middle of October of that year something happened to make Rinzler give up her visits to Alphabet City. Things happened daily in New York that were so terrible, so incredible, that any of them might frighten a social worker. Hack had suggested tainted drugs, sudden multiple deaths of users, a good possibility. Whatever the event was, it affected Rinzler or Vale or both of them. Or maybe Stratton. And that was the task of the team, to figure out what the hell it was.

22

THAT EVENING, JANE called the number MacHovec had located for Miss Margaret O'Neill. The woman answered quickly.

"Miss O'Neill, this is Detective Jane Bauer of NYPD."

"Has something happened?"

"No, ma'am. I'm part of a team that is investigating the death of one of your former employees."

"I have nothing to say."

"Miss O'Neill, I haven't even told you who I'm calling about."

"You don't have to. I'm retired, my tenure at Human Resources is over, and I don't want any involvement in the lives of people who worked for me."

"It's about Erica Rinzler."

"I assumed as much." There was a tired sound to the comment.

"I wonder if we could get together and talk tomorrow. It's quite important."

"I go to church in the morning," she said archly, a reminder of where her caller should be.

"Of course. I didn't mean the morning."

"I don't want you coming to my apartment. I don't need police there."

"I'll meet you anywhere you choose."

"There's a coffee shop on University Place." She gave an approximate location. It was not far from Washington Square and the NYU campus. Jane could walk there if the weather was nice.

"That's fine. What time?"

"One o'clock."

"I'll be there."

Later, Hack called.

"I'm going up to Rodman's Neck with Marty next Saturday."

"It's that time of year, isn't it? Maybe I'll see you there. How's the case coming?"

"Remember I told you about the little beads? Rinzler's sister called and said she was wrong; they weren't her daughter's. So we're back at square one."

"I heard about Defino's daughter. Were you there?"

"Yeah. She wasn't raped but she's scared to death. We all are. It's connected to the case, Hack. Did you know that?"

"Tell me."

She went over it, concluding with the letters of the alphabet.

He gave a short whistle. "I hadn't heard. Carry that cell phone with you, Jane. Put your weapon in a holster. Don't leave it in your bag. If they're after Defino's family, they could be after you and the other guy. MacHovec?"

"Yes. He said he has no kids at home."

"I don't like this," Hack said. "You don't go after a cop's daughter unless you're very stupid or very desperate. Is Defino in control?"

"Would you be if it were your daughter?"

"I withdraw the question. You have any lead on what that Rinzler woman was doing?"

"Nothing yet. We'll go after her work and personnel records on Monday. And I'm talking to the retired woman who was her supervisor tomorrow afternoon."

Hack laughed. "If you squeeze anything out of her, let me know. She won't tell you a thing."

"I have to try."

"I know." Jane heard a click and realized he was talking from a pay phone. "Talk to you again."

She went to the closet and pulled out a belt-carried pancake holster. She hadn't worn it for months, but Hack was right; keeping the gun in her bag was a mistake.

The holster was fairly new, still stiff, and still smelling fragrantly of leather. She sat down at the kitchen table and used some saddle soap on it. Tomorrow, when she met the infamous Miss O'Neill, she would wear it. You couldn't be too careful when interviewing an informant.

The coffee shop wasn't exactly where Miss O'Neill had placed it, but Jane found it. She had alternately walked and run from home and felt surprisingly refreshed when she arrived. When she went inside the little restaurant, she picked the woman out immediately. The hair was short and white, the face set, the bearing regal.

"Miss O'Neill?"

"Show me your identification."

"Yes, ma'am."

The woman pored over the shield and glanced at Jane's face to compare it with the photo before she handed it back and said, "Sit down."

A waitress came and took their coffee orders. Jane added a piece of Danish; the trek over had whipped up some appetite. Miss O'Neill looked at the pastry with disdain. Sugar was surely not part of her Sunday diet.

"For how many years were you Miss Rinzler's superior?" Jane asked.

"I don't remember the number of years, but for as long as she held a supervisory position. When she was promoted, she began to report to me."

"Did she ever present any problems to you or Social Services?"

"Aside from an occasional tardiness, I had no complaints."

"Was she fired or did she resign?"

"She left by mutual agreement."

"What was the reason on your side?"

"Her client died."

"And that client was—?"

"Mr. Stratton. I knew there would be hell to pay. His sister was always after us. She's a very influential woman, knows everyone from the governor down, it seemed. It was Miss Rinzler's duty to observe and report. She did neither."

"How often did she visit him?"

"More often than most clients. I couldn't tell you exactly and you won't find it when you subpoena the records because she falsified them."

"How do you know that?"

"If she had seen him two weeks before his body was found, she would have found the body."

"Perhaps she went and he didn't answer. How would she know something was wrong?"

"There was a super in the building. He would have the key. And she could have notified Mr. Stratton's sister."

"The sister was out of the country," Jane said, watching the stony face.

"There are other avenues. Miss Rinzler was not an inexperienced person." Her voice rang with anger.

"Did you ask her to explain herself?"

"When I asked, she resigned."

And that was the meaning of mutual agreement. "Was that it?" Jane asked. "Or was there more?"

"I conducted a thorough investigation after she left. Miss Rinzler had documented visits she never made. Two clients called, asking for her, and said they had not seen her that month. Their records claimed she had visited them both. She lied, she betrayed her clients, she deceived me and the city of New York." It wasn't clear which was worse. "She did not deserve to work for the Department of Human Resources." Miss O'Neill would have had a fine career as a hanging judge.

"I sympathize with your point of view," Jane said, hoping to ingratiate herself with the woman and realizing it was a task too difficult to accomplish. "Can you tell me if Miss Rinzler was involved in outside activities that may have bordered on the illegal?"

"I don't know what she did outside the department. I was concerned only with what she did and didn't do on department time. But I have reason to believe she was. I think she may have been using her visits to Mr. Stratton for reasons other than those she was empowered to do."

"What would make you think that?"

"She went there too often."

"I thought you said she didn't go there often enough."

Miss O'Neill's face flushed. "That was at the end. Before that, months before that, she may well have been visiting Mr. Stratton at the expense of other clients."

"To what end?" Jane asked, wishing the woman would open up and speak ordinary English. If Rinzler was fucking Vale, O'Neill could think of a polite way to say it, even if Jane couldn't.

"I think I've said enough, Detective Bauer. I'm sure

you'll be reading the records, if you haven't already. Perhaps you'll find something I overlooked."

Jane signaled for the check and took her wallet out. "Thank you for meeting me. It's been very helpful."

"You didn't ask me about her suicide." The tone was more than accusatory; it was damning.

"Is there anything you can tell me about it?" Jane asked, playing the good child.

"I believe she came to terms with her problems. I do not endorse suicide but I believe in Miss Rinzler's case it represented an admission of a guilt she could not bear to live with. She should have taken advantage of the mental health resources that were available to her as well as to her clients."

"Then you believe she took her life."

"Didn't she?"

"Apparently she did." Jane waited for the next piece of wisdom. When none was forthcoming, she picked up the check and walked to the cashier.

What was bothering her was a missing point on the time line. At home, she spread out the sheets once again and observed the events from left to right. Finally, she called Mrs. Constantine.

"Are you working on a Sunday afternoon?" Mrs. C. asked.

"I am, ma'am. And I have a question. We have the date you left the country before your brother's death and you told Detective Defino and me that you tried to call your brother before you left and didn't get through to him."

"That's correct."

"When was the last time you were in contact with Anderson?"

"Mm. I can't give you an exact date, Detective Bauer."

"I understand that. I just want to know whether it was days, weeks, or months before you left the country." She laid it out so there would be no ambiguity.

"Probably a week or more."

"Was that your general practice, to call every week or two?"

"I had no general practice. I called when I wanted to, when I felt it was time to call. There was a time after Andy moved into the apartment when I called almost every day and he asked me to stop. He said I was hovering; he could take care of himself. Whether he could or not remains to be seen. I knew I wanted to talk to him before I left for Paris, but I was very busy and didn't find the time to get down to his apartment."

"And you weren't concerned about leaving him without having spoken to him for a week or more?"

"The super looked in on Andy and the social worker came every week. I felt he was well taken care of."

"Thank you, Mrs. Constantine."

"About the case?"

"Captain Graves is making all the decisions. He'll be in touch with you."

"Thank you for calling."

OK. Mrs. C. hadn't spoken to her brother for "a week or more" when she left the country. Make it more rather than less. That gave him four weeks to starve to death. If Rinzler stopped coming around the time Mrs. C. stopped calling, and if Vale stopped checking on Stratton, if he ever had, no one saw Stratton until Mrs. Bender smelled his decomposing body, a total of six weeks from the last personal contact.

Jane penciled in the presumed dates: last phone call from Mrs. C., Rinzler's last visit. When Jane and Defino had spoken to her at her apartment, Mrs. Constantine had been careful not to disclose her last contact with her brother. Perhaps it embarrassed her that she had not tried harder to speak to him or visit him. She didn't know that Rinzler would never come again, that Vale was irresponsible, that Andy was so weak or depressed that he felt he could not or would not respond to the phone. It was looking more and more as though he inadvertently starved himself to death, unless they could show that Rinzler or Vale intervened to see that Stratton did not eat. And at this point, it would be difficult or impossible to determine whether someone prevented him from taking his medication or whether he just gave it up of his own volition.

Jane gathered the pieces of the time line and put them in the folder she had taken home with her on Friday. She didn't fault Mrs. Constantine; it had to be difficult looking after her brother while trying to live her own life. He had spurned assistance and psychiatric care, occasionally acted irrationally, complained about professional help. She had had her hands full. It was just bad luck that a confluence of events occurred at a low point in Stratton's life: she left the country, Rinzler bowed out, and Vale didn't bother.

And then there was the Chinese laundry. What had little Rose been delivering in those packages wrapped in brown paper and string? And for whose benefit?

23

EVERY DETECTIVE ON the squad had heard about Defino's daughter by Monday morning, and many came to express their sorrow and outrage. When the furor died down, Graves called the team into his office. On the agenda were getting a subpoena for the records from Social Services, which would be done immediately, reclassifying Rinzler's suicide as a homicide, and informing Mrs. Constantine that the investigation was continuing.

"And I want you all on your guard," the captain said. "If someone got that close to Gordon's family, they can get that close to you and yours. Get up to Rodman's Neck and do some shooting. If you're not qualified this year, do it now. Anything else?"

"I was looking at the time line Sean drew over the weekend, Cap. I called Mrs. Constantine and asked when was the last time she talked to her brother. She's vague about it, I think intentionally. It sounds like she left the country one to two weeks after the last time she talked to him."

Graves had a copy of the time line on his desk, the pieces neatly taped together. He unfolded it, put on his glasses, and looked at the crucial section. "So she could have been out of touch close to a month before he died."

"Right."

"And Rinzler may not have been there anytime during that period."

"Yes."

"So he could have starved to death without any assistance is what you're telling us."

"Precisely."

"I won't mention that when I talk to her. But it looks likely. In any case, we're centering our investigation on Rinzler now."

"And the Chinese laundry," Defino said. "I'm not sure where we are after Friday, but Jane thought the *L* in the notebook may have referred to the laundry, not to Larry Vale."

"Uh, yes, I think I have that. So the Chinese laundry may have been a center of operations for whatever Rinzler was involved in."

"And that prick Vale."

"And there could have been drugs in the laundry packages."

"Or whatever," MacHovec said.

"Right, whatever. Tompkins Square Park, you think drugs. OK. Annie's getting a subpoena prepared for the Human Resources files. Sean, have you had a chance to check out this Bill Fletcher?"

"I'll do it this morning."

"It's probably not his name so I don't expect you'll find anything. Any questions?"

Three heads shook. They got up and went.

The transformation of the cold case into a hot one put pressure on everyone. Someone out there was threatening the detectives in the most personal way.

"I talked to Rinzler's boss yesterday," Jane said when they were back in their office.

"With the Irish name?" Defino said.

"That one, yeah. I almost went to confession after I saw her. Man, does that woman know right from wrong."

Defino laughed. "Like the nuns."

"Just like the nuns. She couldn't tell me anything but I had to try. Oh, I almost forgot. I saw Rinzler's friend Mimi on Saturday. Met her at the Harvard Club."

"Oh-ho," MacHovec said. "You're movin' in high circles."

"Why not? It was free. Anyway, she thought Rinzler never used anything stronger than grass and didn't deal."

"What else would she say?" Defino asked. His phone rang and he picked it up. It was his wife and they spoke briskly for a minute. "She's a wreck," he said, hanging up.

"So are all of us. We'll work fast when the records come. Where was I?"

"Dealing grass at the Harvard Club," MacHovec said.

"Mimi says she wasn't the friend who had lunch with Rinzler that last day. Rinzler had boyfriends from time to time but nothing panned out. Erica wanted to have a baby, but she never did anything about it."

"Shit, she could have had one with Vale. She had enough time," Defino said sarcastically.

"I don't know if there was anything there, Gordon. Wait a few days, Vale'll come up with another story."

"So Mimi's a zero. The California friend is a zero. Washington was a zero. Everyone else in the damn address book moved or changed their number. If this case comes down to breaking the Chinese folks, we're not on the winning side."

"And we won't get any help from Rose. Those are her parents and grandmother. And she doesn't know what she was carrying in those packages."

"It's gotta be in the spiral notebook." Defino sounded discouraged.

"Sean," Jane said, "ask the Nine if anything happened around October fifteenth, give or take a week. That's when Rinzler stopped seeing Stratton."

"Uh-huh." He sounded distant. "I'm just checking on this Fletcher character. Lotta Fletchers in the system, including a William B. He's over fifty. How old was that guy?"

"Late twenties, thirty. Good-looking, good dresser. What else would my daughter fall for?"

"Guy's probably got ten aliases. Sorry. What was that date, Jane?"

"October fifteen, plus or minus a week." She turned to Defino. "I need the typewriter. Write up my Fives for Mimi and Miss Goody Two-shoes."

"It's all yours."

Getting the Social Services documents required a dash over to 100 Centre Street to swear the subpoena before a judge, then a quick trip to Water Street to serve the papers and conduct a search, after which they had to return to the judge's chambers to demonstrate their need for the seized records. Finally, they made it back to 137 and Jane and Defino fell on the documents like hungry dogs, Jane taking the work files. The two complaints Miss O'Neill had mentioned were up front among the latest items in the Rinzler file. Defino found the same complaints in his file. Personnel took a dim view of social workers who falsified visits.

One of the clients was a woman named Olga Federov. From the name and address in the Brighton Beach section of Brooklyn, Jane decided she must be a Russian immigrant. She dialed the number.

The woman who answered still had an accent.

"Ms. Federov, this is Det. Jane Bauer of the New York Police Department."

"Oh my God, police. What's the matter? I didn't do nothing."

"Ms. Federov, we're investigating a problem at Human Resources and the name of your caseworker, Ms. Rinzler, came up. This was a few years ago."

"Rinzler? From social work?"

"That's right."

"She's gone. I don't see her long time. I don't know what happened to her. We had deal and then she didn't come."

"A deal?"

"I mean like she was supposed to come and help me but she never did."

"She was your caseworker?"

"Yeah."

"Did the checks keep coming?"

"Yeah, I got checks. No more though. I got work."

"That's very nice. And you don't know why she stopped coming?"

"No idea. I call, I tell them, somebody else comes."

"Thanks, Ms. Federov." She made a note next to the name and called the other one, Sunny Kim. The woman who answered had a soft, almost wispy voice.

Jane went through the introduction.

"You are police?"

"Yes, Ms. Kim. I have some questions about a social worker who visited you several years ago, Ms. Rinzler."

"Rinzler, yes, I know her."

"You complained when she didn't visit you."

"My mother call, not me. She supposed to come. She never come."

"Did you get your checks?"

"Checks?"

"From the Department of Social Services, your welfare checks."

"Oh yes, I get checks. But I need Mrs. Rinzler and she not come."

"Thank you, Ms. Kim."

"Anything?" It was Defino.

"Two women. They wanted Rinzler and she didn't show up. They got their checks; they just didn't get her."

"What were their names?"

Jane read them off.

Defino turned pages in the notebook, running his index finger down the pages. "The Russian woman is here."

"What does it say?"

"O.F."

"And Sunny Kim?"

"Not here."

She took the book from him. "It doesn't compute. According to the complaint, Rinzler was supposed to visit Olga the second week of October. The date here was months before, looks like March or May, I can't read her handwriting. Why the gap? Did she get off welfare in the spring and go back on in the fall?"

"It happens."

She went backwards through the book, looking for *S* or *K* for Sunny Kim. It wasn't there. "Maybe it was too recent. Maybe she made the appointment just before she left the department."

She went back to the file, pulling out another name, Maria Brusca. She dialed and heard a woman answer.

"Is this Maria Brusca?"

"Who's this?"

"This is Detective Jane Bauer of the New York Police Department. Maria's not in any trouble. I just need some information from her."

"She's not in trouble?"

"No, ma'am."

"Then I think you got the wrong Maria."

"Are you her mother?"

"Yeah."

"Can you tell me where I can find her?"

The woman muttered something. "I haven't seen her

for three, four months. I haven't heard from her for a coupla weeks. You wanna know where I think she is?"

"If you can tell me."

"What do you want her for?"

"I have some questions about a social worker who saw her several years ago, a woman named Erica Rinzler."

"Rinzler! She was the one made all the trouble."

"What kind of trouble?"

"I can't talk about it. If Maria wants to tell you, it's her business. But I don't know if you'll find her."

Jane asked again where she was.

"Give me your number. I'll try to find her."

Dead end, Jane thought. She gave the number and hung up. If they found no one else, she could pay the woman a call. The phone number was the same; it was likely the address was.

She turned to Defino. "You know what's funny? I've called three women. Not one of them is black. What are the chances of that, calling three welfare recipients and getting no blacks?"

Defino looked interested. "Not very good. Maybe white folks were Rinzler's specialty."

"Kim must be Korean. The first one was Russian. This last one has an Italian name. Let me try another one."

"There's an M.B. in the book."

"Could be the same one. Let me try a man this time." She keyed the number for Tobias Goldsmith who, from the record, had been in his seventies eight years ago.

A woman answered.

"I'm trying to reach Mr. Tobias Goldsmith."

"That's my father. Can I ask who this is?"

She explained.

"My father died last week. I'm at his apartment, cleaning up. Can I help you?"

"I'm sorry for your loss. We're investigating a social worker who visited your father eight years ago, a woman named Erica Rinzler. Do you recall that name?"

"Yes, I do. She came to see my father many times. She

was very helpful. He appreciated it. Someone replaced her, I remember, but Dad always wished she hadn't quit her job."

"Did she ever disappoint your father? Did she fail to come when he expected her?"

"Not that he told me. It's just one day someone else came and said Erica had left Human Resources."

"Thank you very much."

"No problem?" Defino said.

"Maybe she was better to men than women. This guy thought Rinzler was great." She pulled another woman's name. The address was in Manhattan, not too far from where Jane lived. A man answered and Jane asked for Jackie Warren.

No response. He dropped the phone and called, "Jackie?"

"Hello?"

"Ms. Warren?"

Abruptly, "Who's this?"

"This is Detective Bauer of the New York Police Department."

"Why?"

"I have some questions I'd like to ask you concerning a social worker who used to visit you."

"What kind of questions?" Her voice was hostile.

"We're looking into her career and some questions have come up. Do you recall a Ms. Rinzler?"

"When was this?"

"Several years ago."

"I can't remember. Is this important? I'm very busy."

"Suppose I drop by this evening."

"At night?"

"Is that a problem?"

A sigh. "No, it's not a problem. Don't come before eight. What's your name again?"

Jane gave it, confirmed the address, and promised to come at eight.

"Black or white?" Defino asked.

"I'll know better when I see her, but I'd bet she's white. She's single, has a child. Sounds like she has a guy who answers the phone too."

"Everybody needs a secretary," Defino said.

"Right. She in that spiral book?"

He started through it from the back. "There's a J.W."

"That's it. Rinzler must have specialized in young non-black females. And Stratton. I don't think it's drugs, Gordon."

"I never thought so," MacHovec chimed in. "Maybe she was selling them guns for protection."

"It's as good as any other idea. Let me see if the Xerox is free. I'll make some copies to take home."

When she came back, MacHovec was gone.

24

JANE KEPT HER daytime clothes on for the appointment. Usually, she changed into jeans or sweats, but she decided to look as though she was working. After dinner, she walked over to the address for Jackie Warren. It was in the West Village, as her apartment was, but farther west in a run-down area just ripe for gentrification, which would mean the end of tenants like Jackie Warren.

The front door was ajar, a hole where once a lock had protected the tenants. Jane rang the bell for Warren. No one answered but she had no guarantee that the bell had sounded upstairs. She walked up to the fourth floor and rang the doorbell. That one sounded loud and clear. Inside, there wasn't a sound. Jane rang again and knocked.

"Ms. Warren? Jackie?" No answer. She looked at her watch. Five after eight. No one had come out of the building as she walked down the street and she had seen no one inside. She leaned against the wall, then thought better of it. Roaches crawled up and down walls; she could do without that.

She knocked on the other door on the floor. It was opened by a small Hispanic woman. Jane asked her about Warren and the woman shrugged and answered in Spanish. Essentially, she said she didn't know, but she gave a lot of peripheral facts to embellish her answer.

Jane gave it till eight-thirty, then left. As she walked through the dark streets, from the less safe to the safer, she thought about what had just happened. Jackie Warren knew she was coming. She had spoken English with native competence. She had ascertained the time of Jane's arrival so she would be sure not to be home. Finally, Jane thought, she had stirred something up. The case of Erica Rinzler's homicide had taken a small step forward.

"How long did you wait?" McElroy asked the next morning.

"Half an hour. She knew I was coming at eight. She didn't want to talk to me."

"What's next?"

"We're going through Rinzler's work file, checking out her clients. The Warren woman was one. I talked to two other women and the daughter of a man who died last week. The man liked her; the women had beefs."

"Well, keep it up. Captain Graves talked to Mrs. Constantine yesterday and said we were continuing the investigation, so she's happy for the moment." And he was off.

Jane and Defino went through Rinzler's work records and pulled out the names that appeared in the spiral notebook. They were all female. Jane checked the address book, but found none of them there. They were clients, not friends.

Before they got to calling anyone else, Jane's phone rang.

"Are you the detective who called me yesterday?" a woman asked.

"I'm Detective Bauer. Who is this, please?"

"Maria Brusca's mother."

"Mrs. Brusca. Thank you for calling back."

"I found her. Were you telling the truth when you said she wouldn't get in trouble?"

"Mrs. Brusca, we're only interested in her social worker of several years ago. I think Maria has information we can use."

"All right, I'll give it to you." She read off an address in the West Forties. "Listen to me. I'm telling you the truth. My daughter is a, you know, she's a call girl. Don't tell her I told you. I cry about it every day of my life."

"I'm sorry, Mrs. Brusca. That must be very difficult."

"It's not difficult; it's impossible, but what can I do? She comes from a good family. We gave her everything we could. When the trouble started, it looked like that social worker woman was going to help, but she made it worse. I don't know what else to say. She'll tell you what she wants to tell you. Don't call till after noon. She's sleeping now. She needs her sleep."

"Does she live alone?"

"No, she's got a roommate, another woman. If you talk to Maria, would you tell her to come home?"

"I will. Thank you, Mrs. Brusca." Jane hung up and closed her eyes. "Her mother says she's a call girl."

"Who?" Defino asked.

"Maria Brusca. She's in Rinzler's book. I talked to her mother yesterday. Want to go over this afternoon?"

"Sure. We'll have lunch first."

MacHovec checked out Maria. She was a known prostitute but otherwise had never been convicted of anything else. The first time she had been hauled in was seven years ago, about a year after Rinzler's death. The last time Rinzler had seen her was just before the crucial blackout period marking Andy Stratton's death. "Maybe Rinzler was running a prostitution ring."

Defino looked up. "Yeah, why not? Girls for white men with money."

"She was walking the streets the first time they brought her in. Maybe she upgraded."

"We'll find out," Jane said. She called Jackie Warren.

The phone was answered sleepily on the fourth ring.

"Ms. Warren, this is Detective Bauer."

"Who?"

"We had an appointment last night at eight."

"I couldn't make it."

"I may have to take you down to the station house if you don't cooperate."

"Look, I don't know anything about the Rinzler woman, OK? So get off my case." She hung up.

"Let's get over there, Gordon. She knows something." Jane was putting on her coat as Defino pushed away from his desk. "Yesterday she'd never heard of Rinzler. Today she used her name. I want to get there before she runs out again. Sean, tell Annie where we're going."

They ran down the stairs, hailed a cab, and went across town. Manhattan was narrow at that point but it took time. Streets in the Village were one-way and garbage trucks held up traffic on narrow streets with cars parked on both sides, legally and illegally.

"That's it," Jane said, shoving bills through the small opening in the transparent plastic divider that protected the cabbie from them or them from the cabbie; you couldn't always be sure.

They went out their respective doors, into the building, and up to the fourth floor. Defino was breathing normally at the top of the stairs. He was in good shape. Jane took a moment to regain hers, then pounded on Warren's door.

"Police, open up," she called.

Inside, something dropped with a metallic sound, a man started shouting, and a toilet flushed. Then the door opened.

The woman was white, dark-haired, and angry. "What do you want?" She pulled her bathrobe around her.

"We need to talk to you, Ms. Warren. Do we come in or do you come out with us?"

The woman opened the door all the way and slammed it hard behind them. "Sit down and ask your questions."

"Mind if I look around?" Jane asked.

"What for? You got a warrant?"

"I'm not taking anything. I just want to look."

The woman said nothing. Jane walked into the kitchen, where a man in an undershirt was sitting at a table drinking coffee. He gave her a one-second glance and then turned toward the window with its view of a fire escape. A bathroom was off the hall and the bedroom was the last room in the apartment. A queen-sized bed was unmade, clothes lying on the floor, a large television set opposite the bed.

Jane went back to the living room where Defino and Warren were looking at each other warily like boxers in the ring. "Where's your son?" Jane asked.

"What son?"

"The son the Department of Social Services sends you checks for."

"He's in school." Jackie Warren's face now looked more scared than angry.

"Show me his bed."

"Uh, he doesn't have one here. He's with my mother."

Jane took out her notebook and a pen and made a show of flipping pages. "Her address?"

"Look, you can't see her now."

"Why not?"

"Because she's moving. She's not feeling well."

"She's not feeling well and your son lives with her?"

Warren put her face in her hands. She was digging a nice little hole for herself.

"Where's the boy?" Defino said. "We need to know now."

"Jeez." Warren sat down on the sofa. She looked disoriented. "You have no right coming here like this."

"We had an appointment last night," Jane said. "I think you're the one who broke it."

"Look, the boy— I put him up for adoption."

"When was this?"

"When he was about two months old. I just never told Social Services he was gone."

"You've been getting checks for him for eight years?" Defino asked.

"Something like that."

"Terrific."

"Look, I need it. I don't earn much. Jack has problems."

"Tell me about Ms. Rinzler," Jane said, sitting on a chair.

"I don't know what to say. She was OK. She started coming when I was expecting and after I gave birth, she stopped. I don't know why. Then someone else started coming. I borrow my neighbor's kid if I know they're coming and I keep a folding bed in the closet. It's not a lot of money, but it helps."

"Did Ms. Rinzler know you gave your baby up for adoption?"

"Honest, I can't remember. It's a long time ago." She looked pitiful but maybe she had practice. She needed the social worker to believe she had serious problems. "How could she know? She would have stopped my checks, right?"

Defino was getting restless. "Maybe you were sharing the checks with her."

"With Ms. Rinzler? I told you, I needed the money. I still do. I got a lot of problems."

"So do I," Defino said, standing up.

"Thanks, Ms. Warren," Jane said.

"You gonna tell them?"

"We'll make a decision when we get back to the office."

They walked east, looking for a taxi, finally finding one on Hudson Street. They checked in at Centre Street, picked up the address for Maria Brusca, then left for lunch.

"I'm disappointed," Jane said as they ate.

"You thought she knew something and all she was doing was covering her ass."

"Looks like it. Nice scam. She pulled it off for a long time. I guess if she was pregnant, Rinzler wasn't her pimp."

"Maybe that's how she got pregnant."

"I'll keep it in mind."

They took the subway to Forty-second Street and walked west to the address Mrs. Brusca had given Jane.

"This is where a call girl lives?" Defino said. "For five hundred bucks a night I could do better than this."

Jane shared his skepticism. They went inside the front door, then up the stairs. Brusca's apartment was in the front on two. A bleached-blond woman wearing jeans and a man's shirt tied at the waist and with hair pulled back in a ponytail opened the door and looked from one to the other, then at their shields.

"Shit. What now?"

"Ms. Brusca?" Jane said.

"She's not here."

"Who are you?"

"I'm Darlene."

"Can you show us some ID?"

They followed her inside. The living room was a wreck. If a call girl was living here, she must be sending all her profits to a third-world nation.

Darlene went to the kitchen and came back with a handbag. She pulled out a driver's license with a photo. "Will this do?"

Jane nodded. "Where's Maria?"

"I don't know where she is now. Maybe uptown with a friend. Her mother called; and after they talk, she's good for nothing."

"Where can we find her?" Defino asked.

"I don't know the address. I can tell you where she'll be tonight. And her street name's Sparkle. Don't ask for Maria."

"Give us the location."

Third Avenue between Thirteenth and Fourteenth was a hooker stroll on the East Side.

"What does Maria look like?" Jane asked.

Darlene went into the bedroom and came out with a photo. "I can't give it to you. She'd kill me."

"How long have you known her?"

"Three, maybe four years."

"Was she ever a call girl?"

"She said she was, but not while I know her. Look, I got things to do. You done here?"

They said they were.

Downstairs, Jane said, "I'll go over there tonight."

"I'll come with you."

"Gordon, you've got a family you've got to be with. I can handle myself OK. She's a pross. I'll find her. Shit, that Rinzler really walked on the edge."

Back at Centre Street, Jane adjusted the time line, adding the new names in pencil and the dates from the official records. She tried some more numbers with no success. Several were reassigned, some didn't answer. MacHovec kept checking the names out, most of them turning up no records. If the women were prostitutes, they had somehow managed to keep their names out of police files. Not a likely scenario considering the number of women.

Something was wrong and they all knew it. Almost in desperation, Jane dialed the number in California for Ellie Raymond.

"Detective Bauer," she said. "What can I tell you today?"

"Maybe if I knew what to ask, I wouldn't have to," Jane said, matching the pleasant tone of Rinzler's friend. "I talked to Mimi Bruegger over the weekend."

"Mimi. I remember her. Erica knew her forever. They were close."

"Ms. Raymond, we think Erica was involved in some business that she kept to herself." She let it hang, hoping Ellie would bite.

"She did say she had more money coming in. I remember I said, 'What are you doing, betting on the ponies?'

She laughed and said it was something like that. I didn't press her. If she'd wanted to tell me, she would have. I figured she'd gotten a tip on a good stock. It happens to people, just not to me."

Jane smiled. She liked this woman. "When did she tell you this? Was it just before she died?"

"No. Could have been a year before. It's hard to pinpoint. She never said anything more about it but she visited us and brought us all presents and took us out to dinner, so whatever happened, it was good."

"Sounds like it. And she was in a good mood?"

"On that trip? Oh yes."

"And if it wasn't the ponies or the stock market, you don't know what it was."

"Not the faintest."

"I know this is far-fetched, but did she ever say anything about a Chinese laundry?"

"You mean like taking her clothes there?"

"Anything at all."

"We didn't talk about things like that."

"OK. Thanks, Ms. Raymond. I'll keep you updated."

Her elbow on her desk, Jane put her forehead in her palm.

"Getting to you?" Defino said.

"Yeah. Raymond just admitted Rinzler said she had some extra money coming in. She didn't tell me that the first time."

"When did it start?"

"Maybe a year before her death. I need a break." She went to the coffee room, poured a cup, and sat at a table. She was the only person there, which was what she wanted, no conversation, no clever remarks, just silence with a distant buzz.

The players were Erica Rinzler, Bill Fletcher, maybe Larry Vale. They were buying or selling some product and they were using the Chinese laundry, possibly as a meeting place, perhaps as a storehouse for the product. Little Rose may have been the unwitting delivery person for that product, or perhaps her packages contained messages for Rinzler from Fletcher.

Arthur Provenzano's name flitted through her mind. Was it believable that he had not heard of Rinzler's death? And could Patricia Washington know more than she had told them? Maybe there were questions they had failed to ask her.

Jane shook her head. Rinzler had to be the central operative. Vale, if he was involved, was some kind of facilitator. Maybe his job was just to make sure that Stratton stayed alive and malleable. He may even have been the one who saw to it that Stratton took his drugs. Fletcher must have worked with Rinzler, either buying or selling the product. In addition, he was a hatchet man, a useful guy to have around when things went bad.

So what had happened? Some *event*. She thought of it that way, in italics. Maybe someone caught on and robbed the Chinese laundry. Since neither money nor shirts were taken, the owners would not have reported the robbery. But they would have let Rinzler know. Rinzler had to keep away from Stratton and the area, Vale stopped looking after Stratton, Fletcher tried to smooth things over. End of operation, end of Stratton. The laundry stayed open but its ties to Rinzler and the others dissolved. Rose grew up and went to college knowing nothing.

"Just about what I know," Jane said aloud, finishing her coffee. God, I hope I find Maria Brusca tonight.

25

JANE ADDED HER off-duty S&W to the ankle holster, dressed warmly, and took a taxi to Third Avenue and Twelfth Street. It was dark and the women were walking to keep warm or standing in storefronts to stay out of the wind. Legs were visible beneath short skirts, and an occasional flash of sequins jazzed up the mournful atmosphere.

She had memorized the photo as well as she could and she tried to identify the face from across the street. In the picture, Maria Brusca was a good-looking, dark-haired girl in her twenties with a nice smile. Few of the faces had smiles tonight, except when a car pulled over to the curb and a woman was summoned.

Jane crossed the street and stopped to talk to the women. She asked for Sparkle. Several of the women knew her. One walked down the street, looking for her, but came back alone.

"She could be working."

"Did you see her tonight?"

"I don't think so."

Jane went down the block asking her questions. No one had seen Brusca that night.

"She's usually here by now," one gum-chewing girl with bright red hair volunteered. "Maybe she's sick."

"I heard she was visiting a friend this afternoon. You know who her friend is?"

Shrugged shoulders. "You want her to call you?"

"No thanks. I'll keep looking." Maria knew from her mother who was looking for her.

Jane kept walking, turning onto Fourteenth Street, trying to match faces with the one in her memory. The girls were black, white, and Hispanic, shivering in the cold regardless of race and ethnicity. Winter was an equal opportunity season.

She stayed an hour, then got a cab over to Brusca's apartment. In front of the door, she listened for sounds. Somewhere inside a radio or TV was playing. She rang the bell. The sound inside the apartment went dead. She waited, then rang again.

"Maria?"

"Who's there?" A hostile, or perhaps frightened voice.

"I want to talk to you."

"Go away."

"I'm not leaving. Open the door so I don't have to shout."

The door opened and the dark-haired young woman stood before her, wearing a terry-cloth bathrobe. "Show me ID."

Jane had her shield in her hand. She held it up along with the photo.

Maria backed up, let her in, closed the door, and bolted it. "What do you want from me?"

"Just some information."

"You the one who called my mother?"

"Yes."

"Before we talk, you have to promise me something."

Jane knew what it was and she promised.

"My mother thinks I'm a high-class call girl. You ever tell her different, you're in big trouble."

Threats didn't sit well with detectives. "Maria, I have the shield; you have the problem and the record. I have no reason to talk to your mother about anything if you tell me what I want to know."

"She said it's about that social worker."

"We're investigating her. Your mother said she ruined your life. What did she do to you?"

"Oh Jeez," the girl said under her breath. "She made me promises and she broke them. When I needed her, she wasn't there. She never came back."

"Do you know why?"

"Nobody told me. They sent someone else."

"What was that person's name?"

She closed her eyes, then shook her head. "It was years ago. The only one I really remember was Miss Rinzler. I trusted her, you know? I never made that mistake again."

"Is your mother on welfare?" Jane asked.

"My mother? No. My mother makes out OK. She would die before she would go on welfare."

"What was your connection to Social Services?" It seemed odd that a mother was self-sufficient and a child wasn't.

"I had problems, OK? I needed to work things out. I needed help. That's all I can tell you."

"Maria, you're not going to get in trouble. I'm here about Erica Rinzler, not you. What happened between you?"

She took a deep breath and her body quivered. "Nothing. She just took off. I can't tell you no more."

"Did Ms. Rinzler ever bring anyone along when she came to see you?"

"Like another social worker? No. She came alone. We talked about my problems and then she left."

"Did she ever talk about a man named Bill?"

"She never talked about other people."

Jane took her card out of her pocket and gave it to Maria. "If you decide to tell me more, you can reach me here. If you leave your first name, I'll get back to you."

Maria looked at the card, then nodded her head and put it on the end table next to the sofa. "Could you go, please? I still got time to make a few bucks."

Jane left.

Standing in the doorway downstairs, she buttoned her jacket up high and put her gloves on. A taxi might come along, but she'd have a better chance of finding one on an avenue and once she was on an avenue, she could pick up the subway on Forty-second Street and tin her way home. It would take less time and be just as warm.

She walked down the few stairs to the street and turned east. It was damn cold; maybe a taxi would be better. Hands in pockets, she walked with the wind from the Hudson River at her back. It was quiet, almost no traffic, and few pedestrians.

When the shot rang out, it was so stunning, so unexpected, that she stopped dead for two seconds before reacting. Then she turned and started running back to the building she had just left, pulling her cell phone out of her pocket as she ran. With her teeth, she ripped off her right glove, then started dialing 911. She identified herself as she went up the outside stairs. "Gunshot on West Forty-third between Ninth and Tenth, maybe number four-one-one. I am going to apartment four-A." She folded the phone closed and dashed up the stairs. No one had passed her on the street or on the stairs, no one had been running west as she approached the building. That meant the shooter had gone up to the roof or down the fire escape or into another apartment in the building, but she didn't have time to look for him. She reached two in seconds and continued up. The door to Maria Brusca's apartment was ajar and Jane went in, weapon in hand.

"Maria?" she called loudly. "Maria? It's Detective Bauer. Are you here?"

She heard a sound, a whimper, and she followed it to the bedroom. The girl was on the floor near one of the two twin beds. Jane flicked the light on and knelt beside the bloody form.

"Maria? Can you hear me?"

The girl moaned and her hand curled around Jane's.

"We'll get you to a hospital. Who did this to you?"

There was no sound.

"Maria?"

The fingers relaxed. From the distance, sirens cut

through the night, coming closer. For the girl on the floor, it was too late.

Jane held the girl's wrist, seeking a pulse, then set the hand down. She got up and backed out of the bedroom, touching nothing, and walked into the living room. Her eye fell on the end table next to the sofa where, not ten minutes ago, Maria had placed Jane's card. It was gone.

26

BEFORE THE COPS pounded up the stairs, Jane dialed Larry Vale's number on her cell phone. He answered brusquely on the third ring.

"Mr. Vale, this is Detective Bauer."

"What the fuck do you want?"

"Just wanted to see if you were home."

"Why?" His anger flew across the city. "Somebody rob a grocery store in my neighborhood?"

"Something a lot worse. Sorry I disturbed you." She hung up. The first cops were rushing through the open door. "She's dead, gunshot. In the bedroom. Don't bother calling a bus."

Two more cops entered the apartment, then another two right behind them. While they checked out the apartment, Jane called McElroy and briefed him.

"You think it's this Fletcher guy?"

"Has to be. He watched Gordon, now he's watching me. He must have followed me upstairs, gone up to the next landing, and waited till I left, then come down and knocked on her door. She probably thought I had come back. I'm sure it didn't help that she told him she hadn't answered my questions."

"I think we have some DNA on him, but it doesn't help if he has no record. We still have to find him."

"I called Vale a few minutes ago. He's in his apartment in Alphabet City. It couldn't have been him unless he flew."

"So we gotta find Fletcher."

" 'Fraid so. I'll stick around, make sure they don't destroy the crime scene."

"Good idea. You in Midtown North?"

"Yes."

"Don't set your alarm tonight."

What he meant was that it would be a long night. Before the body could be removed to the morgue, much work had to be done, including sketches, lifting of prints, photos, and a close inspection of the furniture and its contents, the closets, and anywhere else that information on the deceased and the killer might be found. The crime scene guys would be busy for hours.

Jane had suggested to the last cops in the apartment that they check out the roof and fire escape, but she held little hope for finding the shooter. He had been waiting for her to leave and then he came in, asked Maria a question or two, and shot her. Jane thought Maria had probably been trying to run away from him, which was why she lay on the bedroom floor.

"Door to the roof's locked," one cop said, coming back. "He must have used the fire escape. We'll check it out."

"It's in the bedroom."

It took twenty minutes for a pair of detectives to arrive. Jane briefed them and they dismissed the uniforms. A crime scene van was on its way but wouldn't arrive for some time. They were based in Jamaica, Queens. Jane walked around the apartment herself, having borrowed a pair of plastic gloves from a detective. She turned the coffeemaker off. They didn't need a fire on top of a homicide.

Nothing seemed out of order. Dirty dishes lay in the sink and a dish of sliced turkey and salad was on the kitchen table, along with a mug half filled with coffee. She stayed out of the bedroom, where the detectives were working, but looked in the bathroom. No drugs were in the medicine chest except some cold remedies and aspirin. The makeup, she thought, would be in the bedroom. She took her cell phone out again and called Defino.

"Holy shit," he said. "Now he's following you."

"Looks like it. McElroy said they had some DNA from Fletcher."

"Yeah, they called. And Angela sat with an artist. We've got a drawing."

"And it's not Vale."

"Nah. Vale's too old."

She told him she'd called Vale.

"Good thinking. So we gotta find this scumbag Fletcher."

"Hold on."

"Looks like he used the fire escape," the cop who had checked the roof said, entering the apartment. "The bottom section's pulled down. We walked around out back, but nobody's there. He probably went up to Forty-fourth Street and melted into the crowd."

"Thanks, Officer." She went back to the phone and told Defino what she had just learned.

"So he's a gymnast."

"Not necessarily. It's an easy walk down and not much of a jump to the ground. We'll check out the other apartments. Boro Homicide Task Force will send over a couple of teams to do the canvass before it gets too late. I'm not expecting much."

"What else is new."

She stayed around till they called the morgue at two A.M. Everyone had been busy. "I'll have to call her mother," she said to the detectives who had caught the case.

"You sure you want to?"

"I'm sure I don't, but she gave me Maria's address. I owe her."

Life was full of debts, she thought as she went down the stairs. She knew the detectives would have done it and she wanted them to, but it was a matter of honor. And a matter of responsibility.

As the first member of the service at the scene, it was Jane's duty to be at the morgue to identify the body she had found, but she felt a personal responsibility to Maria's mother to be there at the same time. At six A.M., Jane met Mrs. Brusca at the morgue at First Avenue and East Thirtieth Street. She was a thin woman with a face that reflected all the worry her daughter had caused her. Jane had arranged for a car from her precinct to drive her over. A single woman bearing the worst burden in the world, Mrs. Brusca could not have managed to get there on her own at any hour.

With one bony hand she clung to Jane, the other, holding a tissue, blotted her eyes and face. "Tell me what happened," she said, almost in a whisper.

"I talked to her in her apartment. I left her there, walked down the street, and heard a shot. I went back and found her."

"Was she . . . was she alive?"

"She was alive. I held her hand. She only lived a minute after I got there."

"Thank God you held her hand."

She identified her daughter and nearly collapsed. They sat her down, gave her water, and let her rest. Jane remained with her, saying nothing.

"What did she tell you?" the mother asked finally.

"Nothing."

"She didn't tell you what happened?"

"No."

"Who killed her?"

"Someone who thought I was getting information from her."

"For this they killed my child?"

"It looks like it."

"You gonna get him?"

"Yes. We will. And we will charge him and we will try him and I will testify against him."

"It won't bring her back."

Jane held the pale hand. "I know."

"You come around, I'll tell you everything I can. God forgive me. I want him dead."

"Thank you." They stood. "I'll call before I come."

27

SHE WAS EXHAUSTED, but she knew she wouldn't sleep. Her body and brain were so keyed up, she needed to keep moving. She went home, took a shower and changed her clothes, then went to Centre Street. It was ten o'clock when she walked into her office. Captain Graves was there, leaning against the wall and talking to Defino and MacHovec. Annie and McElroy were there too. They all turned as she slipped inside.

"You should be sleeping," McElroy said.

"I can't sleep. I was at the morgue with Mrs. Brusca. I just cleaned up and came here. What do you want to know?"

"What did Maria tell you?" Graves asked.

"Zero. Rinzler was helping her with her problems, whatever they were, then she disappeared and someone else took her place. I don't think she even knew Rinzler was dead."

"Can you talk to the mother?"

"She said she'll talk to me, yeah. I can't bother her

today, Cap. She's making arrangements. Maybe tomorrow. Maybe after the funeral."

"I've asked for priority on the autopsy."

"When we get the tox screen," Defino said, "we'll find out what her drugs of choice were. That'll be a while."

Jane hung up her coat and slid into her chair. A sketch of a man lay front and center. She drew in her breath.

"What?" the whip said.

"Is that Fletcher?" She felt her shoulders quiver.

"Yeah," Defino said. "Angela says it's a good likeness."

"I know him. He ran into me, purposely, I'm sure. Last Thursday night, the night he saw your daughter." She told them about the encounter, the man in the street who barged into her, who asked if this was where she lived.

McElroy muttered something blasphemous and Graves concurred in cleaner language. Annie just opened her eyes wide.

"Sending us a message," Defino said. "He knows where we live. Vale gave him a heads-up, that swine."

Jane held the sketch in her hands and looked into the eyes of the good-looking man who had murdered Maria Brusca last night. "You think we ought to ask Rose if this guy ever hung around the laundry?"

"Don't do that yet," the captain said. "Wait till we know more. We blow the laundry, we're stuck. Sean, that laundry ever attract any police attention?"

"No, sir," MacHovec said firmly. "The sector cops know where it is, they've dropped in, but there's never been any trouble."

"No fires?"

"No record of any."

"Maybe we should shove that sketch under Vale's nose and see what his response is," Defino said.

"He won't respond." Jane heard how tired her voice sounded. "He's learned his lesson. We show up, he's on his guard. We're not getting any more from him."

"Right now my greatest concern is the safety of the three of you." Graves was serious. "It's possible Fletcher is the only one tailing you so he can't be in two places at once."

"If he's followed me," MacHovec said, "he knows I go home at night and go to work in the morning. That's it. He can shoot me, but it won't stop the investigation. And that's what he wants, to shut us down."

Jane's phone rang. Graves nodded and she picked it up. The woman at the other end was sobbing. "What's going on? I just got home and my apartment's a crime scene. Where's Maria?"

Jane glanced at Defino. "Darlene, there was a shooting in your apartment last night."

"*Where's Maria?*" she shrieked.

"Maria died. I'm very sorry."

"You came here to talk to her and she's *dead*?"

"Yes. That's what happened. Can I come and get you and we can go somewhere and talk?"

"You can fucking stay away from me." She slammed the phone.

"Maria's roommate," Jane said, hanging up. She rubbed her forehead. "We should call the Midtown North detectives and see if they found anything in their canvass."

"Right," Graves said. "And I'll be back when the autopsy's faxed to us."

Annie stayed behind as the men left. "You OK?" she asked in a small, wavering voice, leaning over Jane's desk.

"I'm fine. Thanks, Annie."

Annie left, MacHovec watching her. "You and Annie tight?" he asked.

"Not at all. She was just being polite," a concept MacHovec would have a hard time understanding. She took her bag out of the drawer and found the cards last night's detectives had given her and handed them to Defino. "I don't remember which was which, Ramirez and Fanelli. I was just glad it wasn't Lew Beech."

Defino took the cards and made the call, asking for Fanelli. Jane sat back and listened. No one in the building saw anyone go in or out of Brusca's apartment, and that included Jane. When he got off the phone, he said,

"Someone heard you when you got there to talk to Brusca, but she didn't open her door."

"What about the gunshot?"

"Several of them heard it. No one opened up. One person called nine-one-one."

"Thank God for small favors."

"Yeah." He looked at his notes. "No one saw anyone going down the fire escape but most people sleep with the shades down and it was outside the bedroom windows. Not too productive."

"They start canvassing early?"

"Yeah. The Boro Task Force guys hit everybody in the building early this morning. Fanelli had all their notes."

And nobody saw anything, or nobody wanted to get involved. Par for New York. "Gordon, you up for an early lunch? I don't think I've eaten since last night."

He pushed himself away from his desk and went to get his coat.

They returned to Centre Street after lunch. Graves had just received a preliminary report on Maria Brusca's autopsy.

"One bullet, markings like an S&W, close range, chest entry left side, nothing surprising. No recent sex, no needle marks."

"She was avoiding me," Jane said. "Her mother told her I was looking for her and her roommate told me where to look when she was working so she kept away from the stroll last night. Her friends hadn't seen her."

"She had a smoker's lungs, no sign of disease. Reasonably healthy." He scanned the sheet in his hand. "The ME thinks she gave birth to a full-term baby."

"When?"

"Not recently."

"She's a pross," MacHovec said. "It goes with the territory."

"Anything else?"

"Put yourself in a cab and go home."

She smiled, almost laughing. "See you all tomorrow."

* * *

The cabbie was Pakistani and kept his mouth shut. She came close to nodding off as he drove across town, but he braked suddenly and woke her up. In New York, it was more dangerous to ride in a cab than to have a killer on your tail. No one was following her now; she checked several times.

Riding up in the elevator she thought about what the ME had determined. The toxicology screens wouldn't be ready for so long that if they pursued this, they would find the killer before they learned Maria's drug preferences.

She started shedding her clothes as soon as she locked the door, dropping her coat on a chair in the living room and pulling her sweater over her head as she stumbled toward the bedroom. God, she was tired. She thought about having a taste of Stoli, but decided she didn't need any help falling asleep. She was right. All she had to do was close her eyes.

The phone woke her. Disoriented, she thought it was morning, but it was too dark and the clock said eight something. She grabbed it before she lost the call.

"It's Hack. You all right?"

"I pulled an all-nighter. Just trying to catch up."

"Sorry. Shall I call back later?"

"No. Talk to me."

"I was thinking about those little beads you showed me last week, the ones they found in the Stratton apartment."

"So have I."

"When my daughter was born, she had a bracelet with her name on it. In between the beads that spelled out Hackett were beads like the ones you showed me."

"They came from a baby."

"They could have."

"Rinzler was selling babies."

"Could be."

"Jackie Warren sold hers."

He didn't respond.
"You know what happened last night?"
"The shooting on Forty-third?"
"That one, yeah. I was followed, Hack. The girl was shot just after I left that building. She must have opened the door thinking I'd come back to ask her something else."
"You better watch yourself, Jane." He sounded stern, almost angry.
"I am. I took a cab home from Centre Street and no one followed. Graves said I could voucher it. He was afraid I'd collapse on the way."
"You want me to come over?"
"I always want you to come over. Where are you?"
"On the train to Long Island."
"Don't come back. I'll see you another night."
"Watch yourself."
"Thanks."
She hung up and rested on the pillow, the room still dark. Several of the clients in Rinzler's file had been pregnant or had had babies. Here was another. Whether Maria's baby had been born eight years ago or two would have to be determined. If it was the former, her mother would know. But maybe Maria's problem was that Rinzler had promised to sell the baby and then she left the department before the sale was completed.
Jane got out of bed and dressed. She ate some cheese and drank a Coke, hoping the combination—protein, sugar, and caffeine—would give her enough energy to do what she had to. Bellevue Hospital was over on the East Side. She needed a maternity department, a nurse to look at the beads and confirm what Hack had observed.
The streets were busy, people walking, stopping in shops that kept late hours, leaving restaurants. A cab zipped down the street and Jane flagged it down. "Bellevue," she said briskly.
"You sick?" the cabbie asked.
"No. I have to see someone there. Don't go through any red lights."

She found the maternity floor and went to the nurses' station. One nurse was sitting with her head in her palm, catching some shut-eye. Another was writing on a chart. She looked up.

Jane had her ID out.

"Something wrong?" the nurse asked, looking edgy.

"Just want to ask you a question. Do you have a baby name bracelet around?"

"Sure." The nurse rummaged in a drawer. "Here's one." She pulled out a box and opened it. "This what you're looking for?"

Inside the box were dozens of bracelets that looked like tiny watchstraps. They had Velcro closings and a little white strip on which a name could be written.

Jane had the plastic bag in her hand with Mrs. C.'s beads. "I thought you used beads," she said, her disappointment audible.

"When you were born. No more."

"Thanks."

"That's it?"

"I'm afraid so. Have a good night." She dropped the beads in her bag and walked to the elevator. She had been so sure the beads meant something. It was the wrong night to think. Maybe someone would come up with a clever idea tomorrow.

28

"SO YOU THINK she was selling babies," Captain Graves said. They were gathered in his office, the bag of beads in his hand.

"I thought so," Jane said. "Now I'm not so sure. She held up the bracelet she had taken from the nurse. "I still can't figure where those beads came from."

"Maybe they're nothing," Defino said. "She could still have been selling babies."

"Until something happened and she had to stop."

"How does the laundry fit in?" Captain Graves asked.

"Maybe that was the transfer point. The new parents came to the laundry and picked up their baby. We'll never get anything from the owners."

"Or Rose," Defino said. "She was an innocent. You think she was carrying babies in the laundry bag?"

Jane shook her head. "Too heavy, too dangerous. But Rinzler may have been sending messages back with her. We never asked her, Gordon, if she took anything back. We only asked about her delivery."

"What kind of messages? Rinzler wrote English."

"They understood days of the week and lots of other things. And maybe the messages were passed on to Fletcher."

"Fletcher was young eight years ago."

"Old enough to shoot Rinzler, if we're right."

"Find a client of Rinzler's who'll come clean," Graves said. "We need evidence, not theories."

They all pitched in, MacHovec going carefully through the address book once again, from the *A*'s. Peripherally, Jane was aware that he was having little success. Defino had grabbed some of Rinzler's files and was attempting to reach old clients, also with no success. The remainder of the files lay in front of Jane, some of them going back ten years. She picked a name and number.

"Hello?"

"Mrs. Tedesco?" The sound of the woman's voice had startled Jane, whose attention was divided three ways.

"Yes. Who's this?"

"I'm trying to reach Andrea."

"Andrea doesn't live here anymore. Who's this?"

Jane identified herself.

"You're a cop?"

"Yes, ma'am. I need information on a social worker your daughter saw about nine years ago, a Ms. Rinzler."

"I remember her. She's the one—" The voice turned off like a bulb going out.

"The one who what?"

"What is this about?"

"We're looking into some irregularities in the Department of Human Resources. We need a little information about Ms. Rinzler. We're not investigating your daughter."

"I don't know if she'll talk to you."

"If you give me her number, I'd like to call her."

Silence. "I have to call her first."

"Where is she living now?" Jane asked conversationally.

"Out of state. Give me your number and I'll call you back."

"Got one," Jane said, hanging up. "The girl's out of state, or at least her mother says she is. Gordon, give me that spiral notebook. Something just occurred to me."

He handed it over and she went to the last page and inspected the dates yet again, the dates that had not made sense the first several times she read them. Using her fingers to count with, she reversed chronological direction on two of the women who had been Rinzler's clients.

"I've got it," she said. "Remember I thought it was crazy that these women hadn't seen Rinzler for several months before she quit? That it was too long a time?"

"Yeah. As if they'd dropped out of the system."

"They didn't. I was looking at these dates as if they were in the past. They weren't. They were in the future. These were the women's due dates. Look at this." She shoved the book and her calculations over to his desk.

"Nice," he said. "So it wasn't that she had seen these girls last spring or summer. It was next spring or summer when they were expecting. She was seeing them right along."

"And making arrangements to sell their babies for them. That's why she worked only with white and Asian women. Their babies are more salable. She took them on as clients knowing they were pregnant with babies she could sell easily for a good price. And when whatever happened to stop her from seeing the clients, several of them were left holding the bag. They had expected to give birth and get rid of the child right away. Suddenly, someone else showed up from Social Services, they had a baby coming, maybe in a week or two, and it was theirs and they didn't know what to do."

"Makes sense. But we still don't know what the event was."

"The connection broke down. Whoever was matching babies to adoptive parents got cold feet. Someone found out about it and threatened to blackmail them and they stopped cold turkey. There are lots of possibilities."

Defino's phone rang and he picked up. Since last Friday, he and his wife spoke many times a day. As Jane went back to the files, her phone rang.

"Detective Bauer? It's Mrs. Brusca." The woman sounded on the verge of tears.

"Yes, Mrs. Brusca," Jane said gently. "What can I do for you?"

"You want to talk?"

"Anytime you're ready."

"Can you come here?"

"Sure. Give me the address."

The apartment was in Little Italy, a section of Manhattan north of Chinatown and south of the Village, between Soho on the west and the Lower East Side. It was closer to Centre Street than Alphabet City and was known for its Italian restaurants and occasional gangland killings. People who lived there said you could walk the streets at night and feel safe and that was true, most of the time. But as the city changed, so did Little Italy. It was shrinking as the larger Chinese community, which bordered it on three sides, spread.

The residential buildings were old, dating back to the early part of the twentieth century. The ground floors were largely stores, Italian groceries with cheeses and spices and all the things Defino thought life was not worth living without. Jane found the doorway with the number Mrs. Brusca had given her and went inside and rang the bell. An answering buzz opened the inner door.

Jane had suggested that she go alone. The woman was in a fragile condition and might not want to speak with a man around. Defino didn't seem to mind, as though taking on another person's burden was too much for him at this time in his own life.

The woman who opened the door looked even more ashen than she had the previous morning at the morgue. She was wearing a limp cotton housedress and slippers and she apologized for the way she looked.

"I didn't have it in me," she said. "I couldn't get dressed. I couldn't make my bed. My cousin is coming over this afternoon. She'll help me so I can get to the funeral home."

"I'm so sorry," Jane said. "Can I make you something to eat or a cup of coffee?"

"I don't think I could keep it down."

They sat in the living room. Pictures of the dead husband and the dead daughter were on every surface. Jane paused and looked at a few.

"She was very pretty. She looked like you, Mrs. Brusca."

The woman's eyes filled and she grabbed a used tissue from her pocket and pressed it against her face. "She did. Everybody said so." Mrs. Brusca took a deep breath. "I'm going to tell you everything I know, OK?"

"Fine. I want to hear it."

"She was seventeen that summer. She was so beautiful, better-looking than me even if she had my features. First it looked like she had a lot of boyfriends. Then it was just one, a handsome boy. He seemed nice until what happened. They went out together all summer and then into the fall. He was a little older, you know? Dark hair, dark eyes. All the girls loved him, but he loved my Maria. Sometime in the winter she got pregnant. There was holy hell around here. My husband, I thought he would kill her. He wanted to kill the boy too. We talked about an abortion but I didn't want her to do that. That was my grandchild she was carrying. How could I let her do that?"

"It must have been very difficult."

"Difficult," she repeated with bewilderment. "It was a nightmare. It was like a zoo around here. Nobody was talking to anybody except when they were screaming. Somebody I know told me to call Social Services, they would help. They talked to her, they sent someone over. Then one day there was this new woman, this Miss Rinzler. She took over Maria's case. She sent her to a doctor. She said if Maria didn't want an abortion and didn't want to keep the baby, she could arrange to place it. That's how she said it, to place the baby. We thought that sounded good. The baby was due in the fall. Miss Rinzler said she found a good Catholic family, Italian Catholics; my husband didn't want Irish, and we agreed."

"Did you meet them?" Jane asked.

"No. I don't even know where they lived, but I think it was out of state. She took care of everything. She said Maria would get five thousand dollars for the baby. Maria dropped out of high school in the fall; she was this big." Her mother placed her hands six inches in front of her own stomach. "She couldn't go to school no more. She went into labor in October and she had a little girl. What a beauty that baby was." Mrs. Brusca pulled out the tissue and used it on her eyes. "I just saw her once, right after she was born. My husband wouldn't even go to the hospital." She sniffed. "When we left the hospital, we gave the baby to Miss Rinzler outside on the street, all wrapped up in a bundle. She made all the arrangements. Maria got five hundred dollars before she gave birth and she would get the rest when she came home. But it never happened."

Jane waited. The dates were right according to MacHovec's time line. The birth had occurred during the period that Rinzler stopped seeing Stratton and her other clients. "So Miss Rinzler took the baby with her," Jane said. "Did anything happen after that?"

"She called a couple of times and asked us to be patient. Then she came and told us a crazy story and then she came back a day or so later and told us another one. But she never paid us."

"Do you remember what the stories were?"

"First she said the new parents backed out. So I said, where's the baby? She said the baby was fine and she would find other people who wanted her. There was a long waiting list for newborns."

"And then?"

"And then she came back and said she couldn't find a set of parents and I said, what have you done with the baby?"

"What did she say?"

"She gave us a lot of claptrap. I didn't believe her, Detective Bauer. My husband wouldn't be a part of any of this, so it was just me and Maria that talked to her. I don't think people back out of adoptions. That was a healthy, beautiful baby. Why would they back out?"

"What did she say she had done with the baby, Mrs. Brusca?"

"She said it was in a safe place, that it was being cared for, but she couldn't pay us till someone adopted it. I could understand that, but nothing ever happened. We never heard from her again. She stole our baby from us. We were left with five hundred dollars and no baby. I think maybe she kept it for herself."

In her mind Jane could hear Mimi Bruegger saying how much Erica wanted a baby. "Did you ever hear from her or anyone else about the baby?"

"No. I called her office and she wasn't there. I couldn't tell Social Services what had happened because Miss Rinzler said that what she was doing wasn't exactly legal, and if she did it the way the law said you should, there would be lawyers and contracts and complications and maybe Maria wouldn't get the five thousand."

And maybe Maria would get more, Jane thought. Five thousand wasn't a fortune for a healthy white baby. Rinzler was probably pocketing a good bit herself. "How did it end up?"

"They sent someone else over maybe a week or two after I complained that Miss Rinzler had stopped coming, and we never saw Miss Rinzler again and never heard from her. I almost had a nervous breakdown over that, and you know what happened to Maria. You think that woman stole our baby?"

"It's possible, but I don't know for sure at this point. Did you ever tell anyone at Social Services what happened?"

She shook her head. "We were afraid of trouble. Maria was like in a stupor. She cried all the time. I was a wreck. I didn't know who to talk to over there. You could go to their office and wait hours to see someone. I didn't like the new woman they sent over. We told her Maria had a baby and she gave it up for adoption and that was the end of it. She stopped coming and I was glad to see the last of her."

"I'm sorry about this, Mrs. Brusca."

"She'd be eight years old now." The eyes filled with tears. "Then my husband had a heart attack six months later and he died. I had to go to work full-time and Maria never really got over it. She took a job, but it paid nothing and she hated it. Then a friend of hers told her how to make good money." The damp tissue came out again. "I don't think good money is worth what she did, even if she was high class. It's so dirty. How could she do a thing like that?" She put her head in her hands and cried quietly. Then she said, "Why did my daughter die, Detective Bauer?"

"Because we've opened an investigation of Miss Rinzler's work and we've found out some things that are very troubling. We think someone involved with her doesn't want the truth to come out."

"An investigation?" She sounded incredulous. "My daughter died because of an investigation? Something troubling happened and my daughter is dead?" Her dark eyes pierced Jane's.

"I'm sorry." Jane felt worse than she sounded. "I can't go into it, but it's a very serious situation, as you can see."

"So now they'll be after me, you think?"

"No one saw me come here. I made sure of that." Jane stood and Mrs. Brusca put her hands on the arms of her chair and raised herself to a standing position although she looked a little wobbly.

"God bless you," she said. "You find him, OK?"

"I'll do my best."

29

"SO MAYBE THAT'S it," Defino said. "She stole the babies. She gave the mothers five hundred dollars and took the rest for herself, and disappeared with the babies."

"I don't think that's what happened with Jackie Warren. She said she gave the baby up for adoption and she didn't complain about Rinzler."

"She was on the take, right?" MacHovec said. "Still getting paid welfare for the kid?"

"Right."

"So that was her quid pro quo. She got her five hundred and decided to make Social Services pay the rest."

"Wouldn't someone have complained?" Jane said. "You think all those women gave up their babies and not one of them was paid? You'd think there'd be one or two that would report Rinzler to the police."

"They were scared," Defino said. "Rinzler told them they'd get in trouble if they talked. Maybe they thought they'd end up in jail."

"Something's missing. It still doesn't explain why she stopped visiting Stratton. I need to talk to Rinzler's sister again." As she reached for the phone, it rang. She answered, identifying herself.

"This is Mrs. Tedesco. Are you the one who called me this morning?"

She backtracked quickly. "Yes, ma'am."

"I called my daughter. She'll talk to you, but she wants an assurance she won't get into trouble."

"I can give her that assurance. She can call my captain if she wants."

"OK. That should do it. She's in Philadelphia, well, near Philadelphia. Here's her number." She dictated and Jane wrote it down.

"What's her name, Mrs. Tedesco?"

"It's Bradley now, Mrs. Vincent Bradley. This is between you and her. You don't talk to her husband. You don't talk to the neighbors."

"I understand. Can I call her now?"

"She's waiting by her phone."

Jane went back to the records. This was another client of Rinzler's who had been dropped. She dialed the Pennsylvania number and a young female voice answered immediately.

"Mrs. Bradley?"

"Yes. Tell me who you are."

Jane went through it all, giving her Graves's number.

"You want to talk to me about that Social Services woman?"

"Yes, I do, ma'am."

"I can't do it on the phone. Can you come here?"

"Yes. How's tomorrow?"

"I can do it in the morning. How early can you get here?"

"By ten. How's that?"

"Ten is good. Will you drive?"

"Yes. Tell me how to get there."

They went through it in detail. It would mean renting a car, getting things vouchered. Defino said he wouldn't come. He needed to be available if Toni called. It would be a week tomorrow since the incident with Fletcher.

Jane checked in with Graves, who had just talked to Andrea Bradley. He told her to rent a car and they'd work out the paperwork on Monday.

"Do I carry a weapon?" she asked. She was crossing a state line and that got tricky.

"I'll make a phone call. Take it unless I call and tell you not to. Take your cell phone with you and watch yourself."

Annie reserved a car and started the paperwork.

"You do a lot of traveling," Annie said, writing down the details.

"I'm single. They can't leave their wives."

Annie grinned. It was their mutually shared identity.

Jane went back to her office with a cup of coffee. The day was moving toward its end and she wouldn't be back here till Monday. She Xeroxed a few things she wanted to have at home and perhaps take with her tomorrow. Then she dialed Judy Weissman's number in Chappaqua. Waiting for an answer, she sipped her coffee, which was nearly cold.

"Hello?"

"Mrs. Weissman, this is Detective Jane Bauer."

"Oh yes. Do you have information for me?"

"Not yet. I have some questions about your sister. Everyone who remembers her says she wore beautiful strings of beads."

"That's true. Beads were her passion. Some of them were valuable, but mostly, she just liked color and texture. It reflected her personality."

"Where did she get them?"

"Everywhere she went. She had some turquoise I would have killed for. We gave her some crystal beads once that turned colors in the light. But mostly she made them up herself."

"How did she do that?"

"She was a beader. It's gotten very popular in the last few years but she was doing it ten, twelve years ago. There's a place in the East Fifties she would go to. I don't remember the name of the store but it had one of those cute names like Bead Heaven or Beading Like Mad. It's just slipped my mind. I went there once with her to pick out stones for a necklace she was making me for my birthday."

"I see. That necklace of your daughter's, did Erica make that one?"

"No, my daughter made it. Erica was teaching her how to do it. She does beautiful work now. She's very artistic."

Jane wrote down "Bead shop East Fifties" and passed it to MacHovec, who reached for the yellow pages as she continued her conversation. "Mrs. Weissman, you were aware that your sister was involved in something outside her regular job, weren't you?"

The silence told her she had hit it. "I—" Another silence. "You found the box, didn't you?"

"Yes."

"Who gave you permission to get into it?"

"A warrant signed by a judge."

"You got a warrant for that box?"

"Yes, we did." She was aware that Defino was listening. "We've gone over everything in the box. Most of it looks pretty innocuous, the tax returns, the address book. How did you know to separate that from the other things she stored?"

"She left me a note." The voice had changed. Judy Weissman was crying. "I never told anyone, not even my husband. Bee-Bee wrapped that notebook in plastic and then rubberbanded a note to it. It said something like, 'Judy, if anything happens to me, burn this.' I found it after she died. That's why I thought maybe she really did commit suicide. I don't know what the notebook meant. It was written in a kind of code and I didn't really examine it. I just took that and a few other things and stored them in a small locker in the same place."

"Under her name."

"Yes. I called them the other day because the bill is due soon and I wanted to check on the amount. They told me the police had taken the contents of the box. Was she— Do you know what she was doing?"

"Not at the moment. Mrs. Weissman, did your sister ever adopt a baby?"

"Erica? No. What would make you think she did?"

"I'm just exploring possibilities. She never had a baby in her possession that you know of?"

"Absolutely not. She worked five days a week. She couldn't have managed a child. But she loved children. She loved my children. I know she wanted her own someday."

"Thank you for your time. I'm sorry I didn't tell you about the box, but we needed to see what was in it." As she hung up, MacHovec pushed a slip of paper with an address onto her desk. String Me Along on East Fifty-third Street. "Thanks, Sean." She put the slip in her bag, checked her watch, and gathered her papers in a folder, including a copy of the time line. "I'm outta here," she said, grabbing her coat. "See you Monday. Annie?" She dashed toward Annie's corner office. "Where do I pick up my car?"

The bead store was a new experience. Every wall was covered with strings of beads arranged by color and medium. All the glass beads were gathered in one area, the stones in another. Rainbow followed rainbow. Women of various ages pored over the strands, picking one, then another, then returning one to its hook to hang with ten other identical strands. Some beads were of irregular shape, some round or faceted, all the same on one string. In a glass-topped counter, large individual beads lay in open boxes, potential pendants. Jane could appreciate the draw of this hobby. The colors alone were magnetic.

"Can I help you?"

She had the plastic bag in her hand. "Do you recognize these?"

The woman held the bag up to the light. "We don't carry these anymore, but we did a few years ago. I can show you what we have now. They're similar but they're made by a different company."

"How long have you worked here?"

"Fifteen years."

"Do you recall a woman named Erica Rinzler as a customer?" Jane showed her the sketch.

"I do. She bought a lot from us. I haven't seen her in years."

"What would you do with these beads?"

"In the bag? You could put them between larger beads to show off the big ones. They're a little like the old baby bracelets, but they don't use them anymore. We have letter beads here if you wanted to make one of those. You expecting?"

"Not a baby," Jane said, leaving the woman looking puzzled. "Thanks for your help."

At home she called her father, organized her papers for tomorrow, ate dinner, and sat down to read a current biography. She could thank Flora for teaching her to read. Before she met Flora, she read little besides the *Daily News* and the dozens of sheets of institutional crap that flooded her in-box daily. In one of their early meetings, Flora had laid out part of a life plan for Jane to follow.

"You're a smart girl, Jane," she had said. "Now it's time you became a smart woman."

She had been right. Jane was in her mid-twenties when they had that conversation. The turmoil of her youth was behind her and Hack had not yet become part of her life. It was the job and guys, although by then she had become discriminating. She wanted them single and even if the sex was good, she dropped them if they were boring or did nothing but drink.

College had opened not just her eyes but her whole consciousness. Music actually predated the sixties and art had been around since the cavemen. The *Daily News* wasn't the only paper in town and books were more than romances about silly girls who wanted to get laid and married in one order or another. A course in literature had almost been her undoing, but she had made the effort and found that among the books she could not finish were many she put away to read again one day, knowing she would find something new the second time.

She had become the smart woman Flora wanted her to

be, achieving the gold shield and the B.A. And Hack. She hadn't gone after him. It hadn't occurred to her that that was an option. He had come for her. She had often wondered why. He was everything she could want in a man except that he was married. But what had drawn him to her? She wasn't cute and flirtatious. She hadn't even guessed he was interested until he spelled it out for her one day at the Academy when they ran into each other ten years ago, a year after they met in a class at John Jay College and she had thought he was a Madison Avenue businessman.

He had educated himself the way she had and he had gone on to law school, preparing himself for a high-powered job with the department that was now within reach. He was tough and political but he listened to her and took her seriously, disagreed with her sometimes and nodded appreciatively when she said something that captured him. He treated her like an equal. That had been Flora's message, just not for that kind of relationship.

Hack was the best sex Jane had ever had, even now when he was fifty. Thinking about him, her groin ached. Would the ache go away if they lived together? If she told him she wanted him forever, he would leave his wife the next day. She did want him forever, just not always in the same apartment with her, in the same routine. She needed time alone, time between visits, time to make the visits sweeter.

He had told her up front that he was married, something the others hadn't bothered to say. The love was long gone, he said, but he loved his daughters and didn't want to lose them.

The enduring mystery was what he had seen in her to make him initiate the affair and then to keep him interested after a decade. It was the freckles, he told her, the freckles now long gone, visible only in the memory of a loving father and the imagination of a lover.

30

FRIDAY MORNING SHE was up before sunrise. Taking her notes and driving instructions with her, she hailed a taxi and picked up the rental car. Annie had ordered a good-sized vehicle. It was good to have Annie on her side, although she had done nothing except be courteous to achieve it. MacHovec had screwed himself early on and Annie was not the forgiving type. Defino was somewhere in between, probably more positive now that his daughter had suffered. Annie knew how to pick and choose.

Jane found her way to the Lincoln Tunnel. Beside her on the passenger seat was a map the rental company had given her, marked to show her route. The drive would take a good two hours but the radio and her thoughts would keep her company. She remembered the way to the New Jersey Turnpike and she headed south, a stack of bills handy to pay the tolls.

The question of whether Rinzler had "stolen" Maria's baby, as Maria's mother believed, still rankled. Rinzler wanted a child. What better way to acquire one than wait for the perfect baby, pay five hundred dollars for it, and take it for her own. Except that there was no baby in Rinzler's life. Now that Judy Weissman had acknowledged that she knew her sister was involved in something dark, Jane believed Weissman would come clean. She had seemed startled at the thought that Erica had adopted a baby. Surely if a baby ended up in Chappaqua, Jane would know by now. The Weissmans' younger child was much more than eight years old, so that possibility was not viable.

The trip took more than two hours and Jane got lost once, near the end, but arrived close enough to ten that she didn't have to apologize. The woman who opened the door of the attractive house on a tree-shaded street was near Maria Brusca's age, but lived a life so different from Maria's that no comparison could be made aside from race. Andrea Bradley was slim and well dressed in a black pantsuit, diamond stud earrings, and two rings on her left hand, one of them a large diamond solitaire.

"Your ID?" she said before letting Jane in.

Jane displayed it and the woman inspected it carefully, comparing photo to face, then opened the door. A small boy came running to see who the company was. Shy, he grabbed his mother's leg and looked up at Jane, who smiled back.

"Go and tell Mrs. Ruskin you're ready to go out," Andrea Bradley said and the little boy dashed away. "They're leaving. Coffee?"

"I wouldn't mind some. It's been a long drive."

"I'm sure it was. Come in the kitchen."

She served coffee only. Jane would have to seek out lunch before she started back.

"Tell me what you want to know and I'll do my best to fill you in. It's been a while but my memory of that time is pretty good. I don't talk about it, even to my mother, but it's the kind of thing you don't forget."

Jane began by explaining that it was Rinzler they were interested in. "We want to know your relationship with her and what happened between you."

"You probably know I got pregnant. I was in high school. I was scared silly, and I wanted an abortion. A friend took me to a clinic and when I got there, I chickened out. After that, I told my parents. They were shocked, to put it mildly. I went to Catholic school and their daughter didn't get into that kind of trouble. Eventually, my mother and I went to Social Services and a caseworker was assigned to me."

"Do you remember who that was?"

"Mm. A woman with a Spanish name. Cordero or Cortaro. Something like that."

"When did Rinzler come on the scene?"

"Maybe a month later, I can't be sure. She showed up instead of the regular caseworker. She asked me if I wanted to keep the baby and I said I didn't. It was already too late for a safe abortion. Miss Rinzler said she could help me."

"What did she suggest?"

"She said she could arrange an adoption very quietly. I would get five thousand dollars, five hundred before I gave birth and the rest right after. I could even approve the parents from what she told me about them, but I would never know who they were."

"And you agreed?"

"We all agreed, my parents too. It seemed like a good way to go. Miss Rinzler said we couldn't talk about it because it was marginally legal but she said she'd done it several times and it had worked very well. The people adopting babies were all screened and had good homes. She found a couple with dark hair and eyes, people in their thirties, I think. He had a good job and she hadn't been able to get pregnant although they'd tried for years. It sounded right. Maybe there was more, but I can't remember at this point."

"And then what?"

"She gave me the five hundred in crisp bills. I'd never seen a hundred before. My mother put it away. Two weeks later I went into labor." Her face had changed as she spoke, her lips tightening, her brow furrowing. She was leading up to the bad part.

"You OK?" Jane said.

Andrea Bradley nodded. The house was quiet. A few minutes earlier a door had slammed and a car had backed out of the driveway. They were alone now, the investigator and the woman who might have the answers to the important questions.

Andrea got up from the table and poured more coffee. She had made a potful. When she came back, she sipped some and looked across the table at Jane. "It was a boy, really beautiful. I thought when I saw him that I should keep him. My parents and I talked about it—they were really supportive—and I knew they were right. Having a baby to care for at seventeen would have been the end for me. The day I left the hospital, I carried him out. He was seven-nine, really a healthy baby with dark fuzzy hair and big eyes. Miss Rinzler was waiting outside for us. She took the baby, looked at him, and promised to come by in a day or two with the money.

"My father was annoyed. He said he thought we'd get it right away when we gave up the baby, but she said the parents would pay when they accepted him. So we went home."

"And then what?"

"She called and said there was a small hitch, that the parents hadn't been able to get the plane they wanted and they would be a day late. We should be patient."

"Do you remember the dates of these events?"

"He was born October twentieth."

"Go on."

"Well, there isn't much else to say except she made up a story and never paid us."

"What was the story?"

"She said the baby died." Her voice shook as she said it.

"Did she tell you how?"

"She said it was SIDS, sudden infant death syndrome. She said the nurse who was caring for the baby found him dead in his crib. She was very sorry but she couldn't pay me because the parents never took possession of the baby. I just went off the deep end."

"What did you do?"

"I hit her. My father had to pull me off her. I wanted to kill her. How could that happen to my week-old baby, my beautiful little boy?" Tears filled her eyes. "I just punched her and punched her till Daddy separated us."

"Did she hit you back?"

"No. She just tried to protect her face from me."

"Did she tell you what happened to the body?"

"No. I asked her. I said I wanted to bury him properly, but she said it had been taken care of. She didn't bury him," Andrea said with raw anger. "She tossed his body in the garbage. If there was a body, she would have given it to us."

The phone rang and she jumped, startled out of her anger. She left the table and answered. It was obviously her husband. They talked a few minutes before she came back.

"What did you do after that?" Jane asked.

"We talked about it endlessly. My father wanted to go to the police but my mother and I wouldn't let him. There could have been all sorts of trouble. I wasn't sure what my responsibility was. I had given away my baby and I had no documentation or anything. I was afraid I'd go to jail. I was really scared."

"Did you ever hear from Miss Rinzler again?"

"Never. That was it. I got my high school equivalency that summer and started college. I met my husband a couple of years later but I never told him. My parents and I agreed we would never talk about it. As far as we know, there's no record of it. It's like it never happened. Then my mother called me and said you were looking for me."

"Your name came up because we were looking through Miss Rinzler's files. We're interested only in her activities."

"Were there more like me?"

"There may have been," Jane said. "That's what we're investigating."

"So what happened to her?"

"She left the department."

"I'm glad to hear it. I hope she isn't messing up somewhere else."

"I don't think she is."

"More coffee?" It was clear she wanted to be rid of Jane.

"No thanks. I appreciate your cooperation."

The interview hadn't taken all that long. It was still too early for lunch, so Jane found her way back to the road and started home. Even with a lunch stop, she returned the car before three and then took a cab to Centre Street.

"You're back already?" MacHovec said as she walked into the office. "You must've been doing eighty."

"Sixty-five. Here's the story." She hung up her coat. "Rinzler told her the baby died and she reneged on the forty-five hundred dollars the way she did with Maria Brusca."

"She was doing the deal herself," Defino said. "Picking up a lot of change tax free."

"She told this woman the baby died. She told Maria Brusca the parents backed out and then she disappeared. Jackie Warren said she gave up her baby for adoption but didn't tell Social Services and she's been collecting checks for eight years. Either she lied to us or she may have been one of the last people Rinzler paid the whole five thousand."

"You think the Tedesco baby died?" Defino asked.

"I don't know what to think. Rinzler made up such a bad story for Maria Brusca, she must have realized she had to do better next time. Maria's baby was born October nineteenth. Andrea Tedesco's was born the twentieth."

"That's some business, a baby a day. Five grand every day of the week."

"Could have been a coincidence. Most of the dates in the spiral notebook didn't cluster like that. Maybe she just got lucky in October."

"Or unlucky."

"Right." She looked at her watch. "I'm leaving. I'm going up to Rodman's Neck tomorrow morning."

"I'm going next Saturday," Defino said.

MacHovec was silent. His life outside this office remained strictly his own business.

31

It was the second day in a row that she got up before the sun. They had to be at the range by seven forty-five and Marty had promised to pick her up at six-thirty.

She walked out on the street, laden with her gear, just as he came to a stop at the curb. He got out and gave her a hug. It had been a while and much had happened since their last meeting.

"You're lookin' good, babe. Got everything?"

"I counted it twice. Let's get going."

"Both your handguns, belt, service weapon holster, ammo pouches, memo—"

"*Marty!* Shut up and get in the car. Who made you my mother?"

"Just a friendly reminder. Those range officers can be pretty sticky about the stuff. Got all your guns on your ten card?"

"Got it, got it." The ten card listed all the handguns bought or sold during a cop's time on the job.

That said, Marty headed across town to the FDR and took it north to the Triboro Bridge where he picked up the Bruckner Expressway. That led to the Cross Bronx, then the Hutch, the common name for the Hutchinson River Parkway, and finally to Pelham Parkway, well east in the Bronx. Finally, they reached City Island Avenue and drove over the bridge onto City Island itself, a small, peaceful anomalous refuge in a borough that had few. An almost defiant group of stalwart citizens lived there as though in a suburb of the big city, dining on fresh fish in one of the many good restaurants, even swimming in the sound.

At the range entrance, a uniformed police officer, who asked to see both their shields and photo ID cards, checked them in at the gate. Besides doing everything Marty had annoyingly reminded her about at the start of their trip, Jane also had her Mace canister for inspection, her bulletproof vest, her helmet, and her nightstick, a ton of equipment. From the parking lot they walked back along the path to the mess hall, carrying their gear. Along with the other cops, they were grouped according to class first or the shooting cycle first. Both she and Marty got the class first, which Jane had wanted to get out of the way.

The Rodman's Neck Firearms Range was a large open facility dotted with small utility buildings, bleachers, and various types of mechanized and static ranges. Owned by the city, the land jutted out into Long Island Sound and was surrounded by open water and marshes. It was used year-round by all New York City police for firearms training, essentially the shooting cycle. The ranges were varied and could handle all types of small arms; handguns of all caliber; shoulder weapons like shotguns, machine pistols, and machine guns; assault and sniper rifles. The grounds included an armory and range officers trained to inspect and repair all types of weapons.

The range officers of all ranks wore a unique uniform and insignia: tan slacks and shirts and green utility jackets. Their patches were green and gold and their collar brass the insignia of the military police, two crossed pistols. Some wore the old-style crossed dueling pistols and some the new revolver. Their hats were green or tan baseball-type hats with their rank pins affixed: three stripes for a sergeant, a gold bar for a lieutenant. Most of them wore boots rather than shoes.

The morning part consisted of the classroom training,

weapons inspection, weapons and tactics instruction, the explanation of new regulations and laws, and films and slides demonstrating safety procedures. Every gun was inspected and if a defect was discovered, it was repaired on site. The same was true of the ammo the cops brought. It was cleaned and examined for faults. In the afternoon, they would shoot their old ammo first and pick up all fresh ammo to take home and hope to God it grew old in a drawer.

Jane got through the classroom stuff without falling asleep during the slide show. At lunchtime she found Marty and they headed for the mess hall. She remembered a potato and egg hero from her last trip but thought she'd lay off the potatoes and look for something lighter on the starch side. They found a table and Marty pulled a bag out of his duffle and put it on the table.

"Oh you lucky married guys," Jane said as he placed sandwiches and salads on the table. "I'm getting a hero. Want anything?"

"Sit down. Beth packed stuff for you too."

"You guys," she said, patting his shoulder. "You are so good to me."

"She's still happy you never came on to me when we were partners, like the one I rode with when I was still in the bag. I practically had to punch her to get her off me."

Jane had heard the story before. "I told you, Marty, you're cute, but you're too young. I like 'em old and experienced. And not married."

He pushed the packages of food to the middle of the table. "Take your choice."

She picked chicken salad on rye and a bunch of raw vegetables and salad with dressing on the side. Cookies and fudge were wrapped in plastic. Beth had even packed cans of tomato juice and a bunch of straws. "I could never compete with this anyway. If you lived with me, you'd starve."

They talked about old times while they ate, then about Jane's new case. He listened, as he always did, with interest, especially curious about the questionable suicide.

"I'm starting to think, with what I've learned in the last couple of days, that she may have been as depressed as that idiot detective who caught the case said she was and maybe she just did it to herself."

"But you're not sure."

"I'm not sure of—"

"Detective Bauer."

She looked up at the sound of the familiar voice. Along with all the bosses of rank, inspector and above, he was in the bag. This let the range officers know who they were so they could be accorded special handling, which allowed them to get placed at once and complete the exercises quickly. If he had come this morning, he would be ready to leave about now.

"Yes, sir," she said, standing up.

"Inspector Hackett. Glad to meet you. I recognize your face. It was on the cover of the *Daily News* last month."

She nodded, smiling. He was doing a beautiful job, looking gorgeous in his blues. "This is my former partner, Marty Hoagland. Uh, Inspector Hackett."

"Nice to meet you, Detective. You ever expect your partner would be a hero?" He shook Marty's hand.

"Every day I worked with her, sir."

Shit. She hated that word. It had been overused to the point of meaninglessness. "I wasn't a hero," she said firmly. "I didn't save anyone, including myself. I got myself in trouble and it took half the Five to get me out."

"You did a good job." He walked around the table to face her, his back to Marty. He offered his hand, and as they shook, he said in a low voice, "I want to jump your bones."

She felt her cheeks color and she suppressed the smile, or almost did. "Thank you, sir. Me too."

He gave her hand a firm squeeze, let go, bade Marty good-bye and walked off to a group of other uniformed bosses.

"I heard he was a hardass," Marty said when they sat down again.

She shrugged. "I knew a guy in his command in the

early nineties who said he'd walk off a roof for him. Pass me the fudge."

The afternoon was the shooting. It was divided into several parts: timed exercises, live action, and a clever video game that tested judgment as well as marksmanship. The live action took place on a range and required moving from barrier to barrier and using cover and concealment. Cover meant a protected firing position, like a mailbox, and concealment was just that, a hiding place like a tree or a bush, which offered no protection from bullets. Moving around she used a few muscles that hadn't gotten much play lately and knew she would feel them tomorrow. But mostly she concentrated on the targets. This was serious business.

The timed exercises measured how quickly the shooter emptied the chambers or, with the newer weapons, the clip, and still maintained a good degree of accuracy. She and Marty had positions next to each other. Marty was a good shot, another reason she had always been happy to have him cover her. She fired the Glock 9mm, with fifteen rounds in the clip plus one under the hammer, first, then her off-duty Smith & Wesson .38, a five-shot. As she finished, a cute young range officer sidled over.

"Hey, Detective Bauer. You still carrying an antique for backup? You dinosaurs and your wheel guns. Jeez."

She grinned at him but it was all on the surface. She was ticked. Forty and she was a dinosaur.

"What was that about?" Marty said when he took the sound barrier earmuffs off.

"Just a kid sucking up to a first-grade. I told you, Marty, I don't like 'em young."

The last thing they did was the cop video game called the FATS machine, Firearm and Tactics System. On the screen, life-sized figures reenact real situations, requiring life-and-death decisions. Is the object in the little girl's hand a hairbrush or a gun handle? Do I shoot, use Mace, back away, or charge? Is the perp really giving up or is he reaching under his jacket for a weapon—or maybe an ID?

Is the hostage a hostage or another perp? Is my partner moving into the line of fire?

Whenever a shot is fired, the computer makes a record of it for later analysis. Jane shot twice, once in error. She felt the beginnings of a headache. Someone had died and she was responsible. In a real situation, she would have taken a life. The image of Maria Brusca lying on the floor of her bedroom dying had not faded. If Jane had not gone to see her that night, Maria would be alive. No suspects had turned up and the search for Bill Fletcher had gone nowhere.

"Detective Bauer?"

"Sorry. I'm done." Just daydreaming, not a good thing to do with a gun in your hand.

She cleaned her weapons under supervision and then found Marty, who was just finishing up too.

"Ready?" he said, looking up from the gear he was stuffing in his bag.

"Ready and tired. I want to go home and sleep."

"I gotta clean my guns when I get home. This place always puts the fear of God in me. And I think we're going out tonight. Just what I need."

They drove back the way they had come. Jane told him about Maria and he said all the right things, that it wasn't her fault, that Brusca shouldn't have opened the door the second time, that Jane couldn't have known someone followed her into the building.

"I could have gone with Defino."

"You think he would've gone up the stairs another flight to see if someone was waiting for you to leave?"

Probably not, she thought. She moved her shoulders, feeling the muscles tighten.

"Answer me."

She elbowed him. "You got all the answers, partner. You don't need another one from me."

He laid off then and they talked about people they knew on the job—who had transferred, who had fucked up, who was pulling the pin. At the curb in front of her building they gathered her paraphernalia and she gave him a kiss on the cheek.

"If I lean over to hug you, I'll fall flat on my face," she said. "Tell Beth I love her and her cooking."

"Come and see us."

"I will."

An old man she had not seen before rode the elevator with her, eyeing her nightstick and the loaded duffle bag. He seemed glad to get out on the floor below hers.

She walked down the hall and set some of the stuff on the floor. She had forgotten to take her key out. Pushing the door open she smelled food cooking. "Hey," she called. "Do I have company?"

"Company and dinner. Give me some of that crap." He came out of the kitchen in jeans and a sweatshirt, took the nightstick and the duffle and dumped them in the bedroom, then came back for a kiss and hug.

"I wasn't expecting you."

"I got rid of the other guy. How'd it go?"

"Fine. What'd you do with your uniform?"

"It's in the trunk of the car. I found a parking space."

"Where's—?"

"Visiting. You know I take care of details. Maybe we'll go for a ride tomorrow."

"You staying overnight?" Her voice was that of a teenager, eager and high-pitched.

"Maybe till Monday morning."

"That's great, Hack. Now I have someone to bitch to. Can you believe a range officer called me a dinosaur?"

32

HE STAYED UNTIL Monday morning. She talked to him about Maria Brusca and Bill Fletcher and what happened to Defino's daughter. At one point he found the memo book he usually kept in his jacket pocket and made some notes. She knew he kept tabs on her cases. His office had a steady flow of information, as accurate and up to date as any in the city. He rarely interfered and then only to protect her.

"What about those baby beads?" he asked.

"Bracelets like that are history. I went to the maternity ward at Bellevue the other night to check. They use plastic bands now that close with Velcro. Nothing you'd want to put away in a memory book."

"So those beads of yours weren't baby beads."

"Actually, I think they were. It turns out Rinzler strung her own necklaces. I went up to the store where she bought some of her beads. The woman recognized the beads I had and remembered Rinzler. Rinzler was selling babies, Hack. I think she made the bracelets herself. Sort of a personal touch."

"You know that for sure, about the baby-selling?"

"Pretty sure. She disappointed two birth mothers that we know about and reneged on most of the fee they expected. It's even possible she was depressed enough to commit suicide, except—"

He waited.

"The remaining bullets in the gun had no prints. Do you clean your bullets or your clip before you use them?"

He shook his head. "Sounds like you've learned a lot."

"Not enough. I want this guy Fletcher so bad I can taste it."

"Keep your eye on Defino."

"I know." Defino would kill him if he got the chance. Not a big loss, but Gordon's job might be on the line.

They drove to Connecticut on Sunday and ate in a good restaurant. Connecticut was a fairly safe place for them to be seen in public. NYPD cops had to live no farther than a contiguous county and that didn't include out of state.

Monday morning the alarm woke them and Hack reached for her.

"Get your ass out of bed, Hackett. You'll be late."

"Five minutes." He had one of those crack of dawn hard-ons and he wasn't going anywhere.

"Hack."

"Four minutes."

She made a small sound and relented.

"I remember. You're not a morning person."

Not with the clock running. Shit. It wasn't going to work.

He licked his index finger and touched her, and for a minute or so, the clock stopped running.

They lay beside each other, holding hands, breathing hard.

"That turns me on," she said, "when you lick your finger."

"I'll remember that. Get your ass out of bed, Bauer. It's Monday morning and we're ten minutes late."

He drank the last of his coffee while Jane cleared the table. He would leave first and she would put her lipstick on and run. She put the shoulder holster on, waiting to say good-bye.

"You know," he said in a conversational tone that he might have used to tell her what the weather was or that the *Times* had an interesting article on the front page, "if we lived together, we could have fun more than once every week or two."

She leaned against the sink, facing him. "I'm told people who live together get bored and after a while it's not so good anymore."

"But we love each other."

Tears stung. Five words and he could get to her. She swallowed and walked toward him. The tears embarrassed her. She saw herself as the person who shouted at that prick Larry Vale, almost kneed him in her anger. This was the other Jane, the one no one knew but hard-assed Inspector Hackett.

She sat on his lap and put her arms around him. Her Glock pressed against his chest, his against her breast. "You cut to the quick, don't you?"

"I have to with you. You're that important to me."

"When will I see you again?"

"In something, lightning and rain," he said, misquoting Shakespeare.

"You'd better go." She got up, brushed at her eyes. She felt tender where the gun had been.

"Put that in your coat pocket till you get to work," he warned. He put on his jacket. "I was thinking we might try for a long weekend in Paris."

"Paris?"

"It's better than Connecticut." He kissed her, buttoned his jacket, picked up his briefcase, and went to the door. "Get a passport."

They had a long meeting with Graves and McElroy at nine-fifteen. The captain was bothered that nothing had come of the search for both Fletcher and the killer of Maria Brusca. Nothing concrete linked Fletcher to the killing.

"Anything going on with the Chinese laundry?"

"I'm going to call Rose, the daughter, today," Jane said, "find out if she ever heard a baby crying there."

"You think that was a transfer point. Give it a try."

She told him about her conversation with Judy Weissman, how she knew the spiral notebook needed to be hidden.

"Lucky for us she didn't burn it." Graves turned pages. "The baby beads didn't check out."

She explained about the bead store and Rinzler's hobby.

"So it's still viable. My aunt used to string beads. She did nice work." He went back to the paper in front of him. "We'll have that pound of paper," he said. "It just won't be in the Stratton file. Anybody want to add anything?"

No one did.

"Keep after those welfare mothers. One of them may tell you something conclusive."

They went back to the office. Crossing the briefing area, MacHovec said, "You're lookin' good this morning. Must have had a helluva weekend."

Shit. "I did. Polished up my shooting at Rodman's Neck. Used a few muscles. Felt good."

He grinned and dropped it. Working with men had changed over the last twenty years, but not enough.

At her desk, she dialed Rose's number and left a message. Then she turned to Defino. "I want to know more from Jackie Warren."

"She already told us she was cheating the system. What do you think she has left?"

"We talked to her before we knew Rinzler was selling babies. I want to know if she got her five thou or if Rinzler gave her the same song and dance and kept the money. Jackie's in the right place on the time line."

"Let's do it."

Jackie Warren dropped her head theatrically as she saw the two detectives at her door. "Don't tell me you got more questions. I already told you everything I know."

"Just a few," Jane said. "May we come in?"

"Sure, why not? Bring the whole force if you want."

Seated in the living room, Jane said, "You told us you

gave your baby up for adoption but you didn't tell Social Services."

"And that's still true, OK? Everything I told you was true."

"Fine with me. Who arranged the adoption?"

Jackie Warren twisted her face. "Some lawyer or other."

"Got a name?" Defino asked.

"I can't remember."

"Think," Jane said. "Was it a man or a woman?"

"Man, I think. Look, I'll never remember. It was a long time ago and I moved on, OK?"

"How much were you paid for the baby?"

"Uh—"

"We need a number, Jackie."

"Five thousand."

"How was it paid, one lump sum or installments?"

Jackie had started to look uncomfortable. "Installments."

"How much each time?"

"I think . . . something like five hundred before I gave birth, then the rest."

"Who delivered the money?"

"Miss Rinzler did. I mean—"

"Miss Rinzler handled the adoption, didn't she?"

"Yeah, OK, she did."

"There wasn't any lawyer, was there?"

"Not that I ever met."

"Now that we understand each other, let's go back. Who arranged the adoption?"

"She did."

"Rinzler."

"Yeah."

"And how much did she give you?"

"Five thousand. Am I gonna get in trouble over this? It was a long time ago."

"You're not in trouble. We're investigating Rinzler. How did she pay you?"

"Five hundred when I was in my last month. Then forty-five hundred after I came home from the hospital."

Jane looked down at the time line. "You got the forty-five hundred from her?"

Jackie blew air through her lips. "I hadda fight for it."

"What happened?"

"Something went wrong, I don't know what. She gave me the five hundred, then I went into labor. She saw me in the hospital. It was a boy. He weighed almost eight pounds and the doctor said he was very healthy. She brought blankets and everything to wrap him in when I left the hospital and she took him from me outside after I checked out. I went home and she called to see how I was. Then she came to my apartment and said there was a problem and she couldn't get the money right away."

"What was the date of birth again?" Defino asked.

"October twentieth."

That made two on the same date. "What kind of problem?" Jane said.

"She said the baby got sick and the new parents decided they didn't want him so they didn't pay her anything."

"What did you do?"

"I said you fucking well better give me that money."

"And she did?"

"Not exactly. We had a big fight about it. She said she didn't have any money because they hadn't paid her and I said she better get it because if I didn't get the whole five thousand, I was going to the police."

"Sounds good," Defino said.

"Well, I figured I had nothing to lose. I gave her a healthy baby and my mother was the witness. That was a cute baby too, I can tell you. Looked like his asshole father. She wasn't gonna leave me with five hundred bucks after all I went through."

"Did she come up with the money?"

"Yeah, eventually. It took maybe a week and she never told me if the baby got well or if they took him or what.

But she came to the apartment with a lot of hundred-dollar bills and my mother counted them twice."

"Was that it?" Jane asked.

"There was something else. Now you ask, it comes back to me. A coupla days later, after she came with the money, a guy came to the apartment, a young guy, hunky. He said if I ever went to the police I was dead. That was it. He said you got your money, now just forget what happened."

"Could you sit with a police artist and do a sketch of him?" Defino asked.

"It was so long ago, I don't think so. He was tall and good-looking, lots of hair, dark, and dark eyes."

Defino pulled out the folded sketch of Bill Fletcher and opened it in front of Jackie Warren.

"That could be him," she said. "Yeah. He was younger than that and his hair was longer. Here he looks like he's more uptight, more establishment. Know what I mean?"

Defino folded the paper. "Tell us again what he said to you."

"He threatened me. He said I'd be killed if I went to the police. I never said a word about it till you came last week. Rinzler never came again—no one came for a couple of weeks—and then when the new caseworker came, I borrowed a baby for her to see. And I been doing that for eight years."

Jane looked at Defino and he shook his head. She thanked Jackie for her story. As they walked to the door, Defino said under his breath, "Get a life."

Rose had left a message while they were out and Jane called her back.

"Hi, Detective Bauer." Her voice was upbeat, a happy girl.

"Rose, I want to ask you a funny question. During that time when you were delivering Mr. Stratton's shirts, was there ever a baby in the laundry?"

"Uh, sure, sometimes. Once in a while a neighbor

would leave a baby so she could go shopping. My mother would watch it or my grandmother."

"Did that happen very often?"

"No, just now and then. There was a little folding crib in the back and the baby would sleep there. My mother kept me away from them so they wouldn't wake up."

"Thanks, Rose." She turned toward Defino.

"Babies in the laundry?"

"Now and then. They had a folding crib they used."

Graves liked it. "Quite a business she was running. The Chinese folks must have gotten a cut, a few bucks for every baby, off the books. Helped put the girl through college eventually. This guy Fletcher must have kept a very low profile for a very long time. But at least we're getting confirmation that Rinzler was selling babies. She must have kept a list of adoptive parents."

"They're not in the spiral notebook," Defino said.

"What else have you got?"

"Her address book, but that looks personal."

"Maybe it was a combination. Call every number till you find something."

"I love police work," Defino said under his breath and Jane laughed.

"I'll go through the address book again," MacHovec said when Graves had left. "Let's divide it up. It's loose-leaf so it'll be easy."

"And it would have been easy for Rinzler to put the adoptive parents on separate pages and pull them out when she was finished with them," Jane said. "I'd like to talk to just one of them." She sat at her desk with her forehead resting on one hand. Judy Weissman could have tossed those pages or Rinzler could have put them out with the garbage. They had gone through so much paper and not found anything that looked meaningful.

"Gordon." She pushed back from her desk. "Where's the carton Judy Weissman gave me and the rest of the stuff from the storage place?"

He got up and pulled the carton out from under the wing of the typewriter table. "It's just shit," he said. "I've gone over every piece of paper. There's tax returns, notes for her taxes, internal memos from Social Services, the kind of crap we get."

"What about the stuff we picked up in Queens?"

"Same kind of thing. Have a look. Maybe you'll find something. I'm calling the *A*'s."

Defino was a good cop, a sharp detective. She didn't expect to find that he had overlooked anything, but she went through the items in the carton anyway. A cookbook for singles had several torn strips of paper as bookmarks. She checked each one and leafed through the book. A recipe for pepper-crusted rare tuna caught her attention and she wrote it down, thinking it might offer some diversion in her boring culinary routine. The papers were just what Defino had described and they were worthless. She flipped each one over to make sure there wasn't anything written on the back.

Finally, she emptied the bag of material they had taken with the warrant and repeated the process. Taxes. Rinzler owned stocks and bonds that paid dividends and she had to list them on her return and pay taxes on them. Otherwise, it was straightforward. She was salaried, as cops were, and owned no real estate, had no mortgage, no moonlighting job that she reported.

The stocks had familiar names: AT&T, IBM, GE. It was an area in which Jane had no expertise but she recognized them. One of the older detectives she had known along the way had once told her to buy Campbell's soup; she would become rich. She hadn't, and she hadn't, but he had retired early and moved to Florida, presumably thanks to his liquid diet.

Rinzler had noted when each of the stocks paid its dividend and how much it was. The money wasn't big but it was four times a year and it added up. A separate sheet listed bonds. These also paid dividends and were identified by long numbers. Unlike stocks, which were traded, the bonds came due, presumably paying back the principal, which could be reinvested. Each one was marked with a yield in the form of a percent. Compared to what banks were paying today, the yields of eight years ago weren't bad, Jane thought: 7.14 percent, 6.9 percent, even 8 percent on one. Surprisingly, the bonds weren't marked with prices. Probably Rinzler cared only about the dividend. Eight percent was 8 percent whether you paid a thousand for the bond or ten thousand.

She was about to turn to the next page when something caught her eye, the dates the bonds came due. They were scattered throughout the year but two of them were labeled 10/20. October 20. Jane could feel her heart pick up its beat.

"Guys," she said. "I think we've got something."

33

GRAVES HAD THAT little smile that he wore when he was listening to something that made him happy. "Go on, go on," he encouraged Jane, who had paused in her less than coherent narration.

"The dates the bonds were due were the dates the babies were born. The spiral notebook is before; the bonds are after. She kept records of pregnancies in the notebook, when the girls were due. When she found an adoptive couple, she made an entry for a bond. She kept the pregnancies separate from the deliveries. I suspect she filed them in different places so no one going through her records would put them together. But Judy Weissman had to decide what to keep and what to toss and these things all ended up in the same place, the storage box in Queens."

"Do we have names for the adoptive parents?" Graves asked.

"Not that I've found so far, but we have phone numbers. See the numbers of the bonds? Here's one that starts with 201. That's New Jersey. Here's 617. Sean says that's Boston. All the numbers are ten digits long and they end with two or three letters. Those could be the initials of the parents, or some other identifier."

"How did she keep together which birth mother and which adoptive parents were a match?"

"I'm not sure yet, but the dividend may be the baby's birth weight. Gordon, didn't Jackie Warren say this morning that her son weighed almost eight pounds?"

"Yeah."

"Well, here's an eight and here's a seven-fourteen. That's close to eight if we figure the number to the right of the decimal point is ounces. And that bond came due on October twentieth, the day Jackie gave birth. The number of the bond starts with 609. That's somewhere in New Jersey."

"Fletcher may have the names. They may have divvied things up so no one would be caught with everything."

"Well, let's use Cole's," Graves said, "and see if those numbers are still viable and whose names are attached."

"I'm on it," MacHovec said, standing.

"Nice going," Graves said.

"Thanks, Cap."

"How'd you do at Rodman's Neck?"

"I qualified."

"Keep that Glock in your pocket."

First MacHovec checked the numbers in the newest Cole's, the directory that listed numbers and gave associated names and addresses. Then he checked the numbers for the year of the adoptions. The one in south Jersey was still the same name and address and one in California also. He handed the sheet of information to Jane, suggesting a woman's voice might be better in this circumstance.

She called the New Jersey number and got no answer.

"I'll take it home. I'll take them all home. Easier to get people at night. Meanwhile, let me go through all that stuff from the storage box and see if I can dig anything else out of it."

"Good job," Defino said. "Shit, I really thought those were her tax notes."

She liked him for not being jealous, or at least keeping it to himself. She doubted she would have figured it out the day they came from the storage, considering how little they knew at the time. It showed the necessity of continued review, even when it seemed that the last drop of information had been squeezed out of the material.

On her way home, she stopped at a post office and got an application for a passport.

After a dinner of Hack's fabulous leftovers, she called the number in south Jersey. The name was McCall, Douglas and Amy. A woman answered and identified herself as Mrs. McCall.

"This is Detective Jane Bauer of the New York Police Department, Mrs. McCall. Nothing's wrong. I'm part of an investigation of a woman you had some dealings with about eight years ago."

"Oh."

That meant she knew what Jane was calling about. "We're not investigating you, ma'am. We'd just like some information. Did you and your husband attempt to adopt a baby around that time?"

"Yes, but I don't know if I should talk about it."

"You're not in any trouble and you won't be. We're investigating a woman named Erica Rinzler who may have arranged the adoption."

"That name doesn't ring a bell."

"Was it a woman you worked with?"

"Yes, but she called herself Alice Jacobs. A dark-haired woman in her thirties. She was no fashion plate but she wore gorgeous beads."

"I think we're talking about the same woman. How did you find her?"

"Through a friend."

"Did the Jacobs woman give you a phone number?"

"Yes, but I don't have it anymore. She worked for the city, I think. I could call her there but I couldn't leave a message except to say Amy called."

"Did you ever meet the birth mother?"

"No. That wasn't how it worked."

"May I ask why you opted to adopt a baby through this woman instead of going through a lawyer or an adoption service?"

"This was faster and easier. She had access to several pregnant women. It worked for my friend."

"What did you pay her for her services?"

"Ten thousand dollars. But there was a problem."

"Tell me about it."

"We paid five thousand up-front. That was to cover expenses. The second five was to be paid when we got the baby, but we never did."

"What happened?"

"Ms. Jacobs called and said he had been born, that he was healthy and beautiful and we could pick him up in a few days, after he left the hospital."

"Where were you going to pick him up?"

"At an apartment in Manhattan. I don't remember the address but my husband might. It was down in the Village. We would meet at noon and we would take possession of the baby and give her five thousand in cash. I made a withdrawal all in hundreds and I had it in an envelope. I had bought a layette and we had a deposit on a crib and furniture. We were going to drive up to New York that morning." She stopped. "I'm sorry," she said, her voice thick. "It's a terrible memory. It's so painful to remember, even now, that darling little boy."

"What happened?" Jane asked softly.

"She called while we were having breakfast. We were so excited. I could feel my heart thumping. We'd wanted a baby for so long." She stopped and Jane waited. "She called. She said a tragedy had occurred. The baby had died of crib death. I just— I nearly collapsed."

"I apologize for making you relive such a terrible situation, Mrs. McCall. Did anything else happen? And what about the money you'd paid?"

"My husband grabbed the phone from me. He said I turned white as a sheet. All I remember is that he started asking her questions and after a minute or so he was shouting at her. I think in distress I become numb and he becomes angry."

"Did you get your money back?"

"Eventually I think we got most of it. She sent it in bills in a registered envelope."

"Do you recall the date that you were to meet her?"

"I know the baby was born October twentieth. I'm not sure how long after that we were supposed to pick him up. Maybe six or seven days later."

"Did you ever see her again, Mrs. McCall?"

"Never. It was too upsetting. You know what, Detective Bauer? I did some reading on crib death after that happened. That kind of thing doesn't usually happen till a baby is a month or more old. I've wondered all these years if she lied to us, if she found another couple who were willing to pay more and she gave our baby to them."

"I don't know the answer to that," Jane said.

"Would that have been against the law, for her to do that?"

"I'm not an expert, but it may be a gray area. I couldn't give you an opinion. Is your husband around? I'd like to know where that apartment was."

"He's not home yet. This is a late night for him. I'll ask him when he gets back. Shall I call you?"

Jane gave her the number. "Were you able to adopt another baby?"

"We didn't have to." The voice changed, becoming upbeat. "I got pregnant. After all those years, I got pregnant, right around the time of the disaster. I gave birth nine months later, almost to the day."

Jane poured some Stoli over ice and sipped it. Probably Jackie Warren's baby had been designated for the McCalls. If Amy McCall's theory was correct, that Rinzler had switched to another couple to make more money, Rinzler had made no record of having done that. A copy of the "bonds" sheet lay on her lap. The letters at the end of the phone number were ADM, Amy and Douglas McCall.

The vodka relaxed her, or at least she relaxed as she sipped it. Hack had given it up when he was a captain. He drank Scotch now and wine with dinner. Jane would never be a captain or a lieutenant or a sergeant. She had her college degree; she didn't want to study for another test, wait in line to be selected while others were placed ahead of her to even out perceived injustices. She had jumped from third grade to first grade after the last case, making the money better, although not as good as the job she had been offered with an insurance company, but she could live on it. And she loved what she was doing.

34

THE SECOND NUMBER on MacHovec's sheet was in California. It was probably too early to call but she gave it a try. The name Sean had come up with was Frank DiLiberto. Mrs. Brusca had made a point of saying they didn't want the baby going to Irish Catholics; it had to be Italian. She dialed the number.

A woman answered, immediately sounding guarded at Jane's introduction. "Where did you get my name?" she asked.

Jane explained it had come up in the investigation of a woman who had placed babies for adoption.

"I thought that was all private."

"Some documents were obtained with a warrant. We were able to locate you through that information. Did you and your husband try to adopt a baby about eight years ago?"

"Why do you want to know?"

"We're looking into the activities of the person who was placing the baby."

"Ask me your questions."

"Who was that person?"

"Her name was Erica Rinzler."

Interesting, Jane thought. Rinzler had used her own name for this one. "Can you tell me what happened?"

She related a story similar to the McCalls', half the payment up front, the birth of the baby girl on October 19, a flight to New York several days later, and then the call at their hotel.

"She said a terrible thing had happened, that the baby died of crib death, you know, SIDS. We were devastated. We had waited months for this baby, we had cried when we heard she was born, and then we flew across the country to pick her up and this happened."

"I'm sorry for your loss, Mrs. DiLiberto. What were the arrangements to pick up the baby when you arrived in New York?"

"She said she'd bring her to the hotel in the afternoon. We sat in the room all morning waiting for her call or for her to show up and then she called to say the baby had died. I was beside myself. I couldn't believe such a thing could happen. My husband was a basket case. It was the worst moment of our lives."

"Mrs. DiLiberto, did Ms. Rinzler pay you back what you had already paid her?"

"She did, every cent. The envelope came about a week later."

"Who made the connection between you and Ms. Rinzler?"

"I'd rather not say."

"I promise you no one is going to get in trouble. You and your friend are not the focus of our investigation."

"It's a woman I've worked with for many years. She was just as devastated as I was when this happened."

"I need a name, Mrs. DiLiberto."

"Her name is Ellie Raymond."

Had to be, Jane thought. That's why Rinzler used her real name; she was Ellie's friend. Raymond lied about everything and I made the mistake of believing her. "Thank you, Mrs. DiLiberto. I appreciate your help."

Jane hung up. She hadn't bothered to get the woman's first name, but it didn't matter. The letters at the end of the phone number on the "bond" sheet were JFD. Maybe another Jane, or a Jennifer, or a Jamie.

She was tired and angry. Ellie Raymond had known what was going on and eight years after her friend's death, she hung on to the secrecy to protect her memory. The babies had died; Jane was sure of that now. It wasn't a bait and switch to make more money. They were dead and that was why Rinzler stopped visiting Stratton and her pregnant clients. She didn't want to be seen in Alphabet City and she wanted out of the baby-selling business.

Jane found Ellie Raymond's phone number and dialed it.

"Hi," the pleasant voice said when Jane identified herself. "What's up?"

"Plenty," Jane said tartly. "I have just talked to Mrs. DiLiberto."

"Oh shit."

"Exactly. I need some answers from you and there are a couple of ways we can go. You can give them to me over the telephone or I can fly—"

"OK. I get the picture. Ask your questions. I'll answer as truthfully as I can."

"What was Erica Rinzler's job on the side?"

A sigh. "There were girls in New York who got pregnant and didn't know if they wanted abortions or wanted to keep the babies or wanted to give them up for adoption. She intervened in some of those cases and—"

"Which cases did she intervene in?"

"What difference does that make?"

"It makes a difference." She wanted Raymond to say it out loud.

"White girls, Asian girls. White and Asian babies are the ones in greatest demand. She talked to them—she was an expert counselor; I can tell you that from personal experience—and if they said they'd like to give their babies up for adoption, she arranged it."

"With whom? Who did she work with?"

"She never told me. She came out here once to visit—that's when she met Jennifer DiLiberto—and we talked about it. It sounded very benign, Detective Bauer. All Erica was doing was putting people who needed each other together. What's so wrong with that?"

"Nothing. But it didn't end there. I want every name you can give me."

"I can't give you any names. She didn't tell me. She just outlined what she was doing. I knew Jen had wanted to conceive for years and I introduced her to Erica. Those are the only two names I know."

"What did Erica tell you happened to the baby designated for the DiLibertos?"

"She said it died the night before Jen and Frank were to pick it up. She said the person caring for the baby woke up and found it dead and called Erica. Erica was almost in tears when she talked to Jen."

"How did it die?"

"She said crib death. That's all I know. You can make me swear under oath but I can't tell you what I don't know."

"How long was Rinzler involved in this business?"

"A couple of years. She didn't make much. The birth mother got most of it and she had to pay the nurse who watched the babies between the time they got out of the hospital and the new parents took them. And there were legal costs too. Erica did it because she was able to make people happy."

You believe that, you believe in the tooth fairy, Jane

thought. "And you think that Erica didn't commit suicide?"

"I know she was very down because that little baby died. But Erica was a survivor. It seemed out of character for her to go to a hotel and shoot herself. And where would she get a gun? She didn't move in those circles."

"Did you tell Mrs. Weissman what you know?"

"Not a word. I don't know what she knows, but she didn't hear it from me. I talked to her, yes, but just to give my condolences."

"Did she tell you anything?"

"No. She asked me if there was anything of Erica's I wanted and I said, 'Give me a string of beads, any beads. Just to remember her by.' "

"Thank you, Mrs. Raymond. We may be in touch again."

The ice had melted in the glass. She drank the rest and pushed it out of the way. The conflict she had placed Ellie Raymond in was one she had gone through herself many times. Would she lie to protect her mother? Her father? Hack? Of the three of them only Hack did the kind of work that might lead to indiscretions. If her father had taken a couple of pencils from his workplace, that was the extent of his dishonesty. Her mother had stayed at home, occasionally working part-time when it suited her, never earning very much. But Hack, by virtue of his connections and rank, was placed in situations that required regular doses of integrity and offered opportunities that might enrich him illegally. She knew she would leave him if she found out he had done such a thing. But would she lie to save him? It was one of several unanswerable questions in her life and she knew that that question would never arise.

This evening had worn her out. By the time Douglas McCall telephoned at ten-thirty, she had almost forgotten who he was and why he was calling. An affable man, he gave an account of the events of the aborted adoption that almost matched his wife's. He described Alice Jacobs, including her clothing and hairstyle, so clearly that Jane was convinced the woman was Erica Rinzler.

"Do you recall the address where you were supposed to pick up the baby?" she asked.

"It was Horatio Street in the Village." He gave her the number. "I went over there one day."

"Tell me about it." This was an unexpected dividend.

"Yeah, I was in the city on business one day about a month or two after . . . what happened. I took a cab down to Horatio Street and walked around. There are a lot of old buildings in that part of town but this one had been well-maintained. It was apartment three-C and I managed to get inside the front door when someone came out. There was no name on the bell downstairs, just some letters. I went upstairs and rang the bell. A guy came to the door, a young guy, early twenties. It was noon when I got there but he'd been sleeping, looked like he'd had a hard night. I asked him if he worked with Alice Jacobs and he said I must have the wrong address. That was it. I don't know why I did it, I just felt something had been left unfinished. Amy didn't believe the baby died, and the more I thought about it, the more I agreed with her. There was something sleazy about that whole operation, although if it had gone through and we'd gotten the baby, I wouldn't have noticed it."

"Thank you for your recollections, Mr. McCall, and your candidness. I appreciate it."

"No trouble. You trying to make a case against the Jacobs woman?"

"We're investigating her activities. At this point, I can't say more than that."

Like the DiLibertos, the McCalls presented a concrete case. Almost certainly, they had contracted to adopt Jackie Warren's baby. Exhausted, Jane left the glass and the papers where they lay. Muttering a few obscenities, she went to bed.

35

"SO WE GOT two recipients for sure and three babies born around the same time," Defino said after Jane had briefed them on the phone calls. "And your pal Ellie Raymond was holding back on you."

"Yeah. I liked her, that was the problem. It made me believe her. I should go back to second grade for that one."

Defino chuckled. He had lightened up in the last day or so. "So we going to Horatio Street or what?"

When they climbed up out of the subway in the Village, Defino looked around and lit up, his mood easy. "I used to have a girlfriend around here," he said, sounding nostalgic. "A long time ago. She was something."

"That sounds interesting."

"Yeah." He blew smoke. "What a body on that girl. She was gorgeous. We used to go dancing."

"And then back to her apartment."

"Yeah, that too."

"What happened?"

"What usually happens. She went this way I went that way. Ran into her once when I was engaged to Toni. She didn't look as good anymore."

"I'm glad to hear it."

"I was too." He grinned and dropped the cigarette on the pavement, rubbing it out. "This looks like the place."

The name next to the bell for 3C was B. White. Defino

pressed it but no one answered. Then he pressed a bunch of buttons and the door was buzzed open. New Yorkers never learned. Upstairs they rang the doorbell and a young black woman with a towel around her head opened up. She looked scared when she saw the shields but she backed up and let them in, tightening the belt on her terry-cloth robe.

She had lived there two years and with relief she directed them to the super, who was in the building next door.

The super for both buildings was a fortyish Hispanic man named Sanchez. He was stocky and wore denim overalls with tools poking out of several pockets. He wiped his hands on his clothes as he let them in.

"How long have you been super here?" Defino asked.

"Ten years, almost eleven."

"Can you tell us who lived in apartment three-C in the next building eight years ago?"

"I can look." He took a thick book off a shelf and flipped pages. "Three-C?"

"Right."

"Guy named Lefferts. I kinda remember him. He moved out and we had a coupla others there."

Defino took out the sketch of Fletcher and showed it to Sanchez.

"Yeah, that could be him. He was younger, had longer hair. He had hair all over the place."

"You know where he went?"

"Nope."

"He didn't leave a forwarding address for the security?"

"It ain't in the book. Sometimes they come back, pick up the check themselves."

Because they didn't want to leave a trail, Jane thought. MacHovec might be able to trace him.

Out on the street Defino said, "Hang on."

"What's up?"

Defino's hand was moving toward the gun against his

chest. Jane felt her heartbeat rise. She put her hand in her pocket where the Glock was and grasped it.

"Across the street. Guy ducked into a storefront when he saw us come down the stairs. I'm going over to look." He glanced both ways and sprinted across the street with the agility of a man half his age, Jane behind him. Defino had removed his gun from his shoulder holster and now he held it along the side of his coat, barely visible to anyone approaching him. He stopped on the far sidewalk, looked back at her, and moved slowly to his right.

Jane felt adrenaline pumping, right on schedule. She didn't know which storefront he was aiming for so she kept behind him, her eyes seeking any movement. He stopped suddenly at the second store and edged forward, then into the recessed entrance. She ran a few paces to catch up, grabbing her shield.

Defino had opened the door to the dry cleaner and was inside. She followed.

"Anyone come in here a minute ago?" he asked the gum-chewing plump girl behind the counter.

"Uh-uh."

"A man, taller than me, dark hair?"

"Didn'tcha hear me? I said no." Her right hand was curled tightly around a bill. Maybe he had tossed it at her as he told her to shut up about him and then vaulted the counter.

Defino went over it, his shield in his left hand so the girl could see it. Jane followed, her shield also visible, some of Saturday's muscles rebelling. Ahead of her she could hear Defino asking questions rapidly about the man who had come through. When she looked at the faces, she saw a lot of blank stares. The people working there were Hispanic; they could use language as an excuse for silence.

Defino pushed open a back door and Jane joined him outside. No one was visible. Nothing stirred except weeds in cracks between concrete blocks and litter. Buildings surrounded them and an occasional alley that led to Gansevoort Street, the next street north of Horatio.

"Shit," he said. "I saw him go in."

"Fletcher?"

"Could have been. Son of a bitch. He followed us over here."

"Well he knows we're onto him now. And he can't know from whom. They must have used the Horatio Street address for more than one baby pickup."

"Let's go back and give that pudgy broad a hard time."

The girl was still there, this time looking nervous, both her hands empty.

"Who was the guy who came in here just before us?" Defino asked in an icy voice.

"There wasn't anybody. You got it wrong."

"Listen you, I find that guy and he tells me he was in here, you're in big trouble."

"I don't know what you're talkin' about."

"We're talking about you lying to us," Jane said. "Lying. Got it?"

"Lea' me alone." The girl was on the verge of tears.

Defino muttered something unintelligible, then said, "Let's go."

They left.

"You think it was Fletcher." Lieutenant McElroy's face was clouded.

"I saw him for maybe three seconds," Defino said, "but it looked like the sketch. We were coming down the stairs and I spotted him. He was looking right at us. Then he disappeared in the storefront." He told McElroy about the girl with the bill in her hand. "She was scared shitless but I didn't want to push it."

"Good thinking. Write it up." And to both of them. "Clean your guns."

Jane and Hack had spent a couple of hours after breakfast on Sunday doing just that. It was a tradition after a day at Rodman's Neck. All her ammo was new. She would do some running on the way home tonight, just to loosen up her joints.

McElroy left and Jane turned to Defino. "We need to talk. You too, Sean. Two things happened that October.

One: two babies died. Rinzler didn't just decide to turn a better deal. She wouldn't have done that to Ellie Raymond's friend. And the second thing is: Rinzler stopped seeing Stratton right around the time of these events. And she stopped seeing other clients, some of whom were pissed at her. None of this gives us a reason why Fletcher is watching us, or why he did what he did to Gordon's daughter. If a baby dies, so what? You get rid of the body and no one knows any different."

MacHovec moved some papers on his desk, but said nothing.

"So what's the reason Fletcher—or Lefferts, if that's his real name—is threatening us?"

"Because he killed Rinzler," Defino said.

"That's what I think. If she committed suicide, he's off the hook."

"And if he did it, he'll never be off the hook for it. So how did he know we were reopening the case?" He shrugged. "Vale."

"Vale. But I don't know how to crack him, Gordon."

"We have to get together with Bobby Chen and the laundry folks. With Rose there to soften the impact. But we have to work it out pretty good beforehand. We only get one shot and then we're done. Any more and we'll all be up on charges."

"I'll write a list of questions, we'll talk about them, and then we'll see what a good time would be." No time would be good, she knew that, but they'd have to try. If a baby was left periodically at the laundry, maybe Rose's family would admit it. What could be wrong with taking care of an infant for an afternoon?

"I got something," MacHovec said. "This morning while you were jumping counters at the dry cleaner's. I been calling around to see if any dead babies were found around that date in October. So far there's nothing for October or November, but some body parts turned up in the Bronx at the end of December."

"Parts?" Jane said.

"It was a very young infant and it had dried out and

there wasn't much left. A guy found a split plastic bag at a landfill in the Bronx. They kept it out of the papers but the guy brought the bag to the station house. There wasn't enough for a whole autopsy and the ME couldn't give a definitive cause of death. Some babies are born dead. This was a girl." He passed a two-page fax to Jane. "That's the long and short of it."

It said approximately what MacHovec had just told them. "It could be Brusca's baby. Means someone made a trip to the Bronx carrying a dead baby. I don't know if I want to ask the mother for a DNA sample." The thought of it made her feel a little sick.

"Let's hold off," Defino said. "Did the ME say how long it had been dead?"

"A guess. A couple of months. That puts it in the ballpark, but he says it's a tentative estimate."

"Everything's tentative in this one."

"You still looking for bodies?" Jane asked MacHovec.

"I got calls out. And I'm trying to find where this guy Lefferts went after he left Horatio Street. I'm not sure we'll get anything on that."

While he did his thing, Jane put together a list of questions for the family at the Chinese laundry. Confronting these people was going to be the toughest thing they had done. Rose would consider it a betrayal. Bobby Chen would be put to the test. And if the three older people simply sat impassively after saying they knew nothing, they had nowhere to go.

By late afternoon MacHovec had heard from no other precincts and Defino had his paperwork done. She sat with him in the coffee room and he looked over the questions, simple ones about babysitting, whose babies they were, how old they were, how long they stayed in the laundry, who took care of them. Did they change diapers and feed them? Who paid for that? The last question she had crossed out.

"We gotta hope they answer question one," Defino said.

"Let's run it by McElroy and then give Rose a call."

McElroy was edgy. He didn't often pass the buck to Graves, but he did this time.

Graves listened, frowned, and looked carefully at the sheets of paper. He had a reputation for making quick decisions and he didn't disappoint. "I don't know what else we can do. You've made about every contact you can. Can you arrange a meet through the daughter?" He looked at Jane.

"I'll give her a call."

"I heard what happened this morning. I lose my best two detectives, I'm not going to be a happy man. Watch yourselves."

Rose answered the phone, listened to Jane's request, and promised to get back to her after talking to her parents.

"Your grandmother should be there too," Jane said.

"Is that necessary?"

"It would be helpful."

"I'll try."

MacHovec had answered his phone while Jane was talking to Rose. "Got another dead baby," he said when she hung up.

"Where?"

"Staten Island landfill. Same story, remains in a plastic bag. This was a girl too."

"So there were three babies," Defino said. "One of the adoptive mothers was supposed to get a boy."

"Looks like it. This one's another partial too. ME thinks dogs got to it, maybe rats, didn't leave much. Time of death indeterminate. Ditto the cause."

"When was it found?" Jane asked.

"Oh yeah." He checked his notes. "March, after the thaw. I won't give you the details. You're not lookin' good."

"I'm not feeling good. What the hell happened to those babies?"

"Maybe Mama Tsao'll tell us," Defino said wryly.

Fat chance.

Rose called after dinner. She sounded less assured than

earlier. "My parents want to know what this is all about," she said. "They're nervous and so am I, Detective Bauer."

"Rose, we're not investigating them. We think they got involved in something that they didn't understand and what they tell us should lead us to a person we've been looking for."

"I'm afraid for them, Detective Bauer. They have very little and they don't need trouble. Should I get a lawyer?"

"If the time comes that they need a lawyer, we will stop the questioning. That's not going to happen."

"Let me call you back."

The wait was over an hour. If this didn't work, it meant reinterviewing all of Rinzler's clients.

Jane paced, then did a bunch of push-ups, noticing that they were harder to do every year. Watching Defino fairly fly over the counter that morning had given her pause. She needed to lose a few pounds and walk to work more often.

Finally the phone rang and Rose said hello.

"How's it going?" Jane asked.

"They'll see you. Not tomorrow night because something is happening at the church. Can you make it on Thursday?"

"Just tell me where."

Rose gave an address in Chinatown and a chill passed over Jane's shoulders. She hadn't been there since the end of her last case and the memories still disturbed her sleep.

"Are you coming alone?" Rose asked.

"Detective Defino will join me. He's part of the investigation. And I believe Officer Chen will join us." As she spoke, she hoped it didn't sound like a crowd.

"All right. Is seven o'clock good for you?"

"Whatever is good for your family, Rose."

"We'll see you at seven then."

Jane called McElroy to tell him.

"I might just sit in on this myself. How many are coming?"

"Defino, Officer Chen, and me."

"That's enough. We don't want to outnumber them."

Good thinking. Defino said he'd be there. They could get dinner and then walk over. It took a while to reach Bobby Chen, but she was agreeable even though she would miss a night of law school.

Tomorrow they would all sit down together and work out the script, as though they were talking to a head of government and didn't want to provoke a war. Wars were always disastrous.

36

JANE TOOK SPECIAL pains on Wednesday morning to watch her back. In this part of New York, as in most others, finding a place to park was nearly impossible, even illegally. If someone wanted to tail you, he had to do it on foot or risk having his car ticketed or towed. On days when no street cleaning was scheduled or at night, cars lined both curbs, generally parked so close together that it took skill and patience to extricate them. Unless someone had found a spot last night and spent the night in the car, he would be on foot.

It was mild enough for her to walk and jog to Centre Street. When she arrived, her cheeks were pink and cold and she felt good health oozing out of her pores. McElroy had scheduled their conference for one P.M. and MacHovec had already put in a call to Bobby Chen to see if she could make it. She called back at twenty after nine and said she would be there.

McElroy also had a comment on the dead babies Mac-

Hovec had figuratively dug up. "I expect that happens more than you think, certainly more than gets reported. Girls give birth, strangle the baby and toss it, or just toss it. If we can get DNA from those remains, maybe we can make a case."

"We'll need to go back to Jackie Warren and Maria Brusca's mother," Defino said. "And maybe some of the others we've talked to."

"A little spit'll do it," McElroy said.

At nine-forty Jane's phone rang. "Can I see you tonight?"

"Sure."

"I've got something to tell you. Don't wait dinner. I'll get there when I get there."

"OK."

MacHovec looked her way as she hung up. "You have the shortest phone calls in the history of the telephone."

Jane laughed. "Shorthand between friends."

She suspected he was going to tell her about his plans for Paris. They hadn't talked about it since he told her to get a passport, but she had daydreamed about it on her own. The more she thought about it, the better she liked the idea. She had planned to take accumulated vacation time in December but had ended up using medical leave, and the vacation was still there for the taking. The application was filled out, and all she needed now was a photo. She would stop in a camera shop on the way home and get them instantly. Instantly was starting to sound like a good idea.

Bobby Chen showed up a little before one. Jane and Defino had eaten early to be ready and they all went into the conference room. McElroy had said he would attend and he sat down at the table while they were talking about nothing in particular and introduced himself to Bobby.

"Glad to meet you, Lieutenant," she said.

"What's your opinion of how successful this meeting will be tomorrow night?"

"Honestly? Unless something unforeseen happens, we'll

end up with nothing. I talked to them a couple of weeks ago at the laundry and they're not going to give us anything. Maybe we can move in from left field and get them to say something before they know what they're doing."

"Kinda the way I feel. But the less they tell us, the more I feel they know something we should know."

"Like what?"

"Like how many babies they watched for the Rinzler woman and over what period of time. Like who picked them up from the laundry. Like did they deliver babies to some other location?"

"I'll do my best."

They batted it around for two hours, Bobby suggesting polite ways to phrase questions and making notes in Chinese on a pad she had brought with her.

"I'll talk to my mother tonight," she said, "and ask her advice. She's very sensible. And I'll bring them flowers."

Before they left Centre Street, Defino made fresh copies of the sketches of Rinzler and Fletcher and MacHovec added color to the beads Rinzler was wearing. Defino laid the sketches in a file folder to keep them flat and left them on his desk. They would take them tomorrow night.

MacHovec's connection at the post office had no leads on Fletcher/Lefferts. When he left the Horatio Street address, nothing was forwarded. Junk mail was discarded and bills, if any had been sent, were held the required length of time and either picked up or sent back to the point of origin.

Before Jane left for the day, Rose called, sounding anxious. She wanted to know if everything was set for tomorrow night. Jane assured her they would be there on time and everything was fine.

"Getting a case of nerves?" Defino asked.

"Sounds like it. Bobby was pretty negative this afternoon. I hope we get something."

"Well, Friday morning we can go back to the other clients and pick up spit."

"Nice to know it's come down to that."

MacHovec left. He had prettied up the time line and Jane Xeroxed it piece by piece. Like everything else in this case, she was tired of looking at it.

She started home just after Defino, stopping at the camera shop to have her picture taken. The results weren't bad. As the camera clicked, she had imagined holding Hack's hand and looking up at the Eiffel Tower. It worked. She looked happy.

She stood at the door of the shop and looked left and right. If Fletcher was tailing her, he wasn't visible. Her right hand grasped the Glock in her coat pocket. She had decided that if he touched her, she would shoot him and worry about a story afterward.

Safely in the apartment, she had begun putting dinner together when the phone rang.

"I'm in a foul mood," Hack's voice said. "Let's cancel tonight."

"Fine."

"What does that mean?"

Shit. That was unlike him. "It means you're in a foul mood and you don't want to come over and whatever I say is wrong."

"Right." He hung up.

I don't need this, she thought. I'm in the middle of a case we're never going to close and the man I love is acting like a pigheaded boor. Even dinner wasn't going well. Salad, grapefruit, what was that thing in the freezer? She took it out and inspected it. Why didn't she label things? Why did she think she would remember two weeks later what she had bought and put away for a future meal?

I'm thinking the way he sounds, she thought, pigheaded. That's what happens when you love a man. You can't live with him, you can't live without him, and you can't change things. Let him go home and bitch to his wife. She put the steak under the broiler, knowing it would be raw in the middle no matter how long she cooked it. Why couldn't she remember to take it out the night before or even in the morning?

She was furious with him, not because he had canceled—

that had happened before—but why and how he had done it. Paris would have to wait, or whatever he wanted to talk to her about. Maybe he would forget what it was.

She finished eating and found the passport application where she had left it on the table in the living room. Should she even bother now? She took the pictures out of her bag and looked at them. Shit. She dropped them on top of the application and left them there, picking up the book she was reading. As she opened it at the bookmark, the doorbell rang.

She got up and opened the door. Hack had his key in his hand.

"You open the door without checking?"

"You coming or going?" she said icily.

He walked inside and she locked the door. "I have some calls to make," he said.

"Make them."

He hung up his coat and sat on the sofa, spreading some papers from his briefcase on the table where she had left her book and the passport application, and taking his phone out of his pocket. He dialed a number and started talking without introduction.

"Here's the way it's going to be," he said. "This is the second time and I want the guy's shield jerked so fast the wind will knock him over. This dummy is on a one-way track to the Trial Room." The Trial Room was a courtlike room at One PP where members of the department were actually tried for rules and regulations violations. He listened briefly. "Fuck him. And fuck you too. There are no third chances, you got that? He shouldn't have had a second but he's your boy and you intervened. I want this taken care of tonight."

Jane went into the second bedroom, her office, closed the door, and called her father. They talked for ten minutes and she answered all his questions about the case. When she hung up, she opened the door and heard the tirade continuing.

"Yeah? Well wait till it's on the front page tomorrow. Then tell me you can live with it."

She got her coat, slipped the Glock into the pocket, and took her keys. A walk in the night air would calm her down and help her deal with him. For all she knew, he might be gone when she got back. He had been on the phone, one call or another, for half an hour.

As she passed the living room he said, "Hang on," covered the mouthpiece, and said to her, "Don't go. I'm almost finished."

She stopped and looked at him, undecided. He was back chewing out the guy at the other end. Shit. She dropped her keys next to her bag, put the Glock on top of the refrigerator, and hung up her coat. Five minutes, she thought. Then I find a good movie and sit there for two hours.

"I'm done."

"Maybe this isn't the time for a conversation."

"A shithead uniform in the office of the chief of personnel leaked a story to his buddy at the *Post* that we've been keeping under wraps for months and it landed on my desk. This bonehead did it once before and got away with it. He's not getting away with it this time."

She considered her response. "You acted like a pig."

"I was angry."

"Not at me you weren't." She was surprised at her own anger.

"I expect you to understand."

Son of a bitch. He wasn't going to apologize.

"Jane—"

She backed away a step. If he touched her, she wasn't sure whether she would melt in his arms or slap him, and she thought it might be the latter.

"I've had a hard day," he said. "I don't need—"

"Don't need what?"

"A fight with you."

"That's all you can say?"

"I love you. You know I love you. Isn't that enough?"

"No." She wished she had gone out the door when she had the chance. This was ridiculous; it was awful. She was standing in her goddamn kitchen, fighting with the person she loved more than anyone else on earth, and they were at a standoff. Worse, he wasn't going to budge. All he would do was justify himself. He deserved a pummeling, anything to get him to accept responsibility for his words.

Abruptly, he left the kitchen, returning in a few seconds with his briefcase, which he put on the table. "I came here to— I wanted to tell you something. You. First."

Apologize, her inner voice shouted, but he was done. It had passed. He was on to something new. She watched him as he reached to the bottom of the briefcase and hauled out a tall, thin bag that held a bottle. He took it out. There was no mistaking champagne. She moved her eyes from the bottle to his face.

"I got the word this morning. I'm trading in my eagle for a star." An eagle was inspector; a star was deputy chief.

"Hack. That's wonderful."

"I forgot to put it on ice."

"Give it half an hour in the freezer." She took it from him and stashed it near an unopened quart of ice cream she kept there in case he showed up without any. Deputy chief. It couldn't have been better news.

"May I touch you?"

"I don't know."

"I've never seen you so angry."

"You're a son of a bitch, Hackett."

He touched her arm, so tentatively she hardly felt it. "You're the only one on the job who didn't know it."

He stayed till morning, his wife still away. His cell phone rang several times at inconvenient moments and he dealt with the calls irritably. "Yeah," he said at one point, "I believe in freedom of the press. I just don't want traitors in my units. If he gave it away for a meal in midtown, what would he do for real money? Sell his shield?"

She was worried about a tail in the street seeing him leave her building and she told him how to go out the delivery door and through an alley to the next street.

He had corked the remainder of the champagne, a good French label, and left it for her to finish. The spare ice cream was gone. He had not apologized.

Ten minutes after he left, she set off on foot, thinking more of Hack's news than anything else. The highest civil service rank in the department was captain, two gold bars, and after that, every promotion was an appointment. He had reached deputy inspector in his mid-forties, the gold leaf, and inspector, the eagle, only two years ago. His career had given him a wide range of experience. He had started the job fresh out of NYU. Not long after he got his gold shield, the detective's shield, he had passed the sergeant's test and begun studying for the lieutenant's test while he was in law school. He had been a lieutenant when he met her and moved on to captain not long after. As lieutenant, he had worked as a second whip, McElroy's job at Centre Street, in a detective squad; she forgot where.

When he became captain, he moved over to the Intelligence Division on Hudson Street. He had liked Intel, he told her, in one of a thousand conversations over the last ten years. That had gotten him the gold leaf. He had moved in and out of Uniformed Police Commands and Headquarters units, giving him good exposure. Roughly twenty-five thousand people were on the job; if you wanted to move up, you had to be visible. Cops his age were walking beats and sitting behind counters in station houses, where they would spend the rest of their days on the job. Hack had had most of his tickets punched and had earned this recognition. To achieve a top position, chief, he had to move carefully now. Not a single mistake would be tolerated. His sensitivity for department politics would be his best weapon.

This appointment had not come as a complete surprise. He had been interviewed at the commissioner's office several weeks ago, and he knew what slot was opening up, but he hadn't been the only candidate and he hadn't told her anything further. He must have known for the last week or two that he was on the short list, but he wasn't a man to talk about what was possible until it was a sure thing. And if it hadn't happened, he wouldn't have moaned and groaned or spent hours trying to second-guess what went wrong. He was a realist in all aspects of his life.

After the star was pinned to his uniform, he would be expected to throw a party in his present command to wet down his new shield. Not much chance Jane would be invited, but he would see her later or the next day. It was the way they lived.

She stopped at a red light and made a complete turn, checking for Fletcher, then hopped off the curb at the green. Fletcher didn't want to kill her, she decided, at least not until he knew everything the team had learned. Then he would deal with it. He was giving them rope. She just hoped it would end up around his neck, not theirs.

37

SHE GRABBED A copy of the *Post* from a newsstand near 137 Centre Street and took it upstairs without reading it. The cover had a heartrending picture of a woman in grief, not likely the source of Hack's agitation but the kind of thing that sold papers.

It was eight forty-seven when she sat down at her desk. Drinking her coffee, she and Defino talked about getting DNA samples from the women who had given birth at the end of October, and Defino made a list of candidates.

At nine, Jane became aware that MacHovec's desk was still empty. "Where's Sean?" she asked.

"It's not my day to babysit him."

Jane got up and went back to Annie's office. She shrugged. "What else is new?"

"He's always here on time. Do you have his home phone number?"

Annie flipped her Rolodex, wrote a number on a slip of paper, and handed it to Jane. "He's probably having a morning drink." Her feelings about MacHovec were no secret and anything that reinforced them gave her satisfaction.

At her desk, Jane dialed the number. "Mrs. MacHovec?" she asked when a woman answered.

"She can't come to the phone right now. Can I help you?"

"This is Detective Bauer at Centre Street. Detective MacHovec hasn't come in yet and he's always on time. I wondered—"

"He left at the usual time. Maybe the subway was delayed."

"That's probably it. Thank you."

"He on his way?" Defino asked.

"So she says."

"Don't sweat it. He stopped for coffee."

"Something's wrong, Gordon." It had happened once before, in the fall, not exactly this way. After doing a search at One PP, MacHovec had stopped off for a couple of beers, neglected to make his rings, antagonized Annie, and shuffled in half crocked. "He doesn't buy coffee and he doesn't drink this early." MacHovec didn't spend a dime he didn't have to.

"A drinker drinks when he feels like it, when the opportunity is there."

She looked at her watch. Nine-twenty. Everyone gets caught in a subway backup once in a while, but he had never been more than five or ten minutes late. Defino tossed his list of women needing DNA tests on her desk. She glanced at it, nodded, and tossed it back. Nine-thirty. The phones in the office were all still. If MacHovec didn't want to talk to Annie, he knew he could reach Jane and she would smooth things over for him. She had done it before. Something was wrong. She was feeling it in her stomach. She took the *Post* out of the drawer where she kept her bag and opened it to page two.

An entire police unit was being dissolved after an internal affairs investigation. The description of what they had done was mind-blowing. The top of the command structure was being flopped back to the bag; two mid-level supervisors were being formally charged and fired on orders from the commissioner. The fallout would have the job in turmoil for months. It was exactly the kind of story the department kept under wraps until they were ready to act.

As Jane moved down to the details, Annie knocked on the open door. Her face was ashen.

"What is it?" Jane said.

"I just got a call. Detective MacHovec phoned in a ten-thirteen."

Ten-thirteen was the code for "officer needs assistance," the signal for a major event or life-threatening situation including a wounded cop or a shootout. When it was broadcast on department radios, all department personnel in the area responded as quickly as possible. "Where did he call in from?"

"Centre Street near Canal." She looked as though she were about to cry. "He must have gotten off the subway there."

Defino was out of his chair and running for the stairs in seconds.

"Tell Lieutenant McElroy, Annie, and tell him we're on our way."

On the street they turned north. Sirens sounded, but this was New York, the city of unending emergencies; sirens were always sounding. It wasn't far, and at their pace less than two minutes to the southwest corner. They could see a crowd pushing to get the best view they could of another New York crime scene. A van from a cable station was edging toward the curb, a reporter already out and weaving into the crowd; this was news.

"Let us through," Defino ordered. He held his shield high and elbowed civilians out of the way, ignoring curses and catcalls. They only love you when you're doing them a favor.

Radio cars were parked all over the intersection, lights rotating on roofs. A couple of cops in uniform were trying to redirect the traffic away from the scene.

"Gordon," Jane said, her voice shaky. She put her hand on his arm. On the sidewalk, covered by a disposable department sheet, was a body. The crime scene detectives hadn't arrived yet—they had a long trip from Queens—but the still-arriving radio cars were bringing brass of all ranks. A shooting involving a cop occurs this close to headquarters, every boss not chained to a desk at One PP would be there in minutes. The commissioner was not yet on the scene. Before appearing, he would have to be fully briefed by phone.

"Calm down," Defino said. "He's over there."

"Who?"

It was MacHovec, standing outside a radio car, talking to two men in plainclothes.

"Thank God."

They moved quickly across the sidewalk and into the street now fully blocked with radio cars.

"Howdy, partners," he said. His voice was calm but his face looked a wreck. The men talking to him moved away and eyed the newcomers.

Jane opened her hands in a what-happened gesture, not wanting to ask a question that could get him in trouble.

"He went for my gun in the subway stairwell," he said, nodding toward the body. "Take a look."

They walked over, keeping their shields visible. Defino knelt and pulled the sheet down to reveal the face. "Holy shit," he said.

It was Fletcher, the handsome face pale and peaceful. Standing, Defino kicked the body angrily around the buttocks, his mouth set in hatred.

"Gordon," Jane said, pulling him away as a uniformed

sergeant dashed over. "It's OK," she told him. "We're fine. We're leaving."

The sergeant gave Defino a look that should have reduced him to ashes. Then he said, "Get out of here, both of you."

Hack got out of a radio car as they went back to MacHovec, who was smiling now. He had enjoyed the small drama. "I got rid of him, partner," MacHovec said. "He won't touch your kid anymore."

The two men stood for a moment, their eyes locked. Then Defino turned away.

"Anyone we can call?" Jane asked MacHovec.

"All taken care of. I'll see you later, minus my weapon." It was standard procedure to take a cop's gun after it had been used in a shooting.

"Let's get a cup of coffee," Jane said to Defino.

"Fucking rapist," he said under his breath. "I wanted that guy so bad—"

"I know."

They passed a pair of uniforms who were rolling out the yellow crime scene tape, turned a corner, and found a coffee shop.

"Anyone know what happened?" Graves had come into their office when they returned after lunch. "I already called the Detectives Endowment Association and had them send over a union trustee to talk to MacHovec and their lawyer is responding ASAP. The deceased didn't have a weapon on him."

"He went for MacHovec's gun when he came up from the subway," Jane said. "Sean wasn't just walking down the street when he decided to kill Fletcher."

"Anything else?"

"Nothing," Defino said, "except that it was Fletcher."

"Well, your family should rest a lot better tonight. Where does this leave us?"

"We still don't know why Stratton died," Jane said, "if anyone here remembers Stratton."

"His sister does. She's called me twice. And you don't

know if Rinzler was a homicide or a suicide. And you don't know what the Chinese laundry connection was. So the case isn't closed. You seeing the Chinese family tonight?"

They both said yes.

"You feeling up to it?"

"We're fine, Cap." Jane waited to see if he had gotten a complaint about Defino.

"I got a phone call, Gordon."

"I'm sorry. I was out of line."

"Consider this your chewing out."

"Thank you, sir."

MacHovec didn't turn up for the rest of the day. Defino called his wife and gave her the good news.

Then Flora called. "You want to tell me what happened on Centre Street and Canal this morning? That was your partner, I'm told."

"Hi, Flora. How are you today?"

"Don't give me hi Flora. Give me the truth."

She told Flora what she knew, which was little.

"Who was following whom?"

"If I knew, I would tell you."

"There'll be one hell of an investigation on this one, you know."

"He's a good cop. He'll come through it."

"You know the deceased?"

"We were looking for him."

"And your partner found him."

"Other way around, I think."

"Let's hope so."

38

JANE AND DEFINO had dinner out, drinking coffee leisurely at the end. Defino was feeling a lot better. He had talked to his daughter when she got home from school. He could call off the cops who were watching her morning and afternoon on their own time, keeping her safe. His family could start living normally again.

At a quarter to seven they left the restaurant and Defino hailed a cab. They were close to Chinatown but he didn't want to walk, out of deference, Jane thought, to her. It was her first time back in the Five since her ordeal. The taxi passed the building where it had happened and she swallowed and said nothing.

Defino paid the cabbie and they entered the hallway of the Tsao family's building. It was still before seven and they waited there. A moment later, Bobby Chen showed up, holding a bouquet of flowers. They went upstairs together and Bobby knocked and called through the door, announcing herself.

Inside, the apartment reflected a middle-class family with Eastern taste. The decrepit appearance of the building ended at the door. Rose took their coats. Jane had moved her Glock to her pants pocket and Defino's was inside his jacket. They could have been a New York couple visiting their Chinese friends.

Rose's mother served tea and desserts. Jane had eaten them before during her tour in the Five. She didn't like them much, but she ate and gave compliments to the hostess.

Finally they got started, Bobby doing the talking and translating into English, although the meanings of the responses were often clear from the tone of voice and the facial movements. Bobby started off with innocuous questions she had made up on her own to soften them up, and there were smiles and agreement. That ended when she asked about the babysitting.

"They say there were no babies," Bobby reported as Rose picked up the conversation, perhaps reminding them of the crib she remembered from her childhood.

Her mother responded coldly, waving her husband off.

"No babies," Bobby said again. She leaned forward and said something. After Rose's mother, shaking her head, commented, Bobby said, "She doesn't understand why I'm repeating a question she has already answered." Bobby opened the file folder Defino had given her and took out the sketch of Rinzler. Passing it to Rose's mother, she asked a question.

The woman shook her head and Bobby showed it to the husband, who refused to touch it. Bobby turned to the grandmother, who acted as though she were the only person in the room. Her eyes never moved toward the picture.

Bobby repeated her actions with the sketch of Fletcher, with the same results.

"Tell her we know a baby was there," Defino said quietly and Rose turned to look at him. "Otherwise we'll be here all night and get nothing."

As Bobby began to speak, Rose put her hand up to stop her. Then Rose, looking from one family member to the other, asked her own question.

There was silence for a moment. Then Rose's mother whispered to her husband.

Jane glanced over at the grandmother and touched Bobby's arm. "Look."

Bobby turned toward the old woman. Tears were coursing down her gnarled face. She stared stoically ahead, as though unaware of them.

Bobby leaned toward her and whispered something. The old woman began to cry loudly, wailing and speaking. Rose said, "Oh no," as she listened and then Rose's mother stood and began to shout and wave her hands, apparently trying to interfere with whatever her mother was saying.

Through the chaos, Bobby, who had moved toward the old woman, knelt in front of her, holding one hand and listening to the sounds that poured from her lips as fast as the tears poured from her eyes.

Jane and Defino sat quietly, observing, Jane hoping that something useful was developing. Rose watched her grandmother, wide-eyed, then began to cry herself. The scene lasted several minutes. Then Bobby Chen patted the old woman's hand, gave her a tissue, and backed away.

"We can go now," she said in a low voice, "or I can tell you what she said and maybe you have a question."

"Tell us," Defino said.

She spoke softly, as though the older people might hear and understand. "The woman in the picture had an agreement with them. Once in a while she would bring a baby to the laundry, a newborn. Each one had a little bracelet of tiny beads and one big bead that had a letter or a number on it. She provided the crib and the diapers and the bottles of milk. All they had to do was keep the baby there.

"She usually brought the baby around lunchtime and she always came in the back door of the laundry. She apparently used Stratton to send messages about when they could expect her to bring a baby. Rose delivered Mr. Stratton's laundry and he would pay for it by putting money in an envelope. The woman would then add a note with a day of the week written on it. That was when the next baby would come.

"After she dropped off a baby, if she didn't pick it up later that day, the grandmother would take it home with some bottles of milk and the woman, Rinzler, would come the next day and take it."

"What about the man?" Defino asked, referring to Fletcher.

"Sometimes he picked up the baby, but not often. The last time Rinzler came—it may have been two days in a row; she wasn't completely coherent—she brought four babies, not all at once. They stuffed two in the little crib and put two on a table where they did the ironing. The Rinzler woman brought extra bottles and diapers. They had never had more than one baby at a time and they didn't have enough milk for all of them.

"They fed the babies before they left for the evening. The grandmother intended to come back in the middle of the night and feed them again, but she was very tired and she slept through the night.

"She remembers that it was very cold, unusually cold for the end of October. So when they left for home, they lit a kerosene stove to keep the place warm. The landlord didn't supply heat after business hours in the stores." Bobby stopped.

The ranting had subsided too, and the old woman sat with her head in her hands, Rose beside her, patting her back. Rose's mother was walking around, muttering to herself.

"A tragedy happened," Bobby Chen said, her face distraught as she related it. "There must have been fumes from the stove because when the family came in in the morning, all the babies were dead."

"Oh shit," Defino said.

Jane took a deep breath. "What did they do?"

"They had a number for Rinzler. They called her and left a message. I think they have more English than they let on, at least Rose's parents. In any case, Rinzler showed up an hour or so later with the man in the other picture." She meant Fletcher. "Rinzler was terribly upset. They put the babies in laundry bags and took them away. That was the end. They never saw her again."

"Rinzler pay them?" Defino asked.

"Yes. I think she said a few hundred, but I don't remember exactly. It was enough to make it worth their while. You can see how upset she is. The three of them decided they would admit nothing, but Grandma lost control when the babies came up. She blames herself."

"It wasn't her fault," Jane said.

"I told her that. It's not always easy to rid yourself of blame. It happened a long time ago but she'll never forget it."

They got up to go. Bobby said their good-byes and Jane and Defino added their own in English. Rose walked out into the hallway with them.

"I didn't know," she said. "I remembered that Mr. Stratton sent money back to my parents for his laundry, but I didn't know anything else was in the envelope. I just gave the envelope to my mother. I'm so sorry. Will my parents get into trouble?"

"It was an accident," Defino said. "Tell them not to worry. We're glad they told us the truth."

"Thank you. Good night." She smiled and went back inside the apartment.

Out on the street, they walked a block to find a taxi. Jane and Defino went as far as the parking lot where Defino's car waited and Bobby took the taxi home.

"Didn't expect that," Defino said as they walked to his car.

"Four dead babies. Rinzler must have been on the verge of collapse. How are we going to determine if Fletcher killed her?"

"I'll think about it tomorrow."

He dropped her at her building and took off. Inside, she emptied the mailbox and went upstairs, leafing through the envelopes on the elevator. At her door, she stopped. A piece of yellow paper was taped under the peephole: See the super.

She pulled it off, went inside, and left her bag and coat, then went downstairs again and rang his bell.

"Oh, Miss Bauer. Hi. You got a delivery this afternoon. I'll get it for you."

She felt uneasy. She hadn't ordered anything for weeks and wasn't expecting anything. The super came back in half a minute carrying a glass vase filled with red roses.

She saw them and said, "Oh."

"Guess someone thought it was Valentine's Day."

"I guess so." She thanked him and went up to her apartment, carrying the vase carefully. The round bottom was filled with water. In the kitchen she removed the tiny envelope and pulled out the card. It had flowers across the top and no printed message and no written message. A familiar hand had written the letter *H* in black ink.

She smiled, breathed in their essence, and placed the vase in the living room on the table where the passport application still lay. He still hadn't said he was sorry.

39

IT WAS TIME to wrap up the case. Captain Graves had his pound of paper, if not his pound of flesh. Since he was dealing with Mrs. C., he could work out what to say. Jane jogged to work Friday morning, her gun in her shoulder bag once again, and her off-duty left in the apartment. It was a hell of a lot easier to run without the damn weight on her right ankle.

She had telephoned McElroy last night after tending to the flowers, telling him the bottom line of their evening meeting with the Chinese family. By the time she arrived at Centre Street, Graves would know what happened but he would want to hear it in detail from her and Defino. It was MacHovec she was worried about. If Fletcher was unarmed, MacHovec would have to come up with a good story for the shooting. The fact that Angela Defino had nearly been raped by the guy would go a long way. And all of them had studied the sketch of Fletcher to the point where any one of them would recognize him. He was a threat. Although all of this was logical and convincing to a cop, Internal Affairs would look at it differently, and MacHovec would be given a hard time at the very least.

Annie gave her a smile and a big hello when she got to the second floor. Hurrying across the briefing area, Jane looked inside the office and was cheered to see MacHovec sitting in his usual place.

"How are you?" she said.

"On the job. How are you?"

"Can you say anything?"

"They've got my weapon and the DEA sent a lawyer over. I had a heart-to-heart with the whip and he's OK with the shooting."

She wondered what had passed between the two men before her arrival, but that was between them. A note on her desk told her a meeting had been scheduled in the whip's office at nine-thirty. Time for coffee and a brief phone call.

She dialed Hack's number, possibly, she thought, for the last time. He would assume his new command in a short time, perhaps as soon as Monday.

"Hackett."

"Thank you."

"You know why I sent them?"

"Guilt."

He laughed. "How 'bout love?"

"How 'bout it?" she said with a grin.

"Your partner's got a problem."

"I know."

"We can talk about it later. Meanwhile, think Paris."

"I will."

"That's a great passport picture."

When she hung up, she pressed the key that dialed her

father's number and hung up before it rang, a security procedure.

MacHovec was laughing again. "If I had conversations like that, I'd be in more trouble than I am right now."

"I'm not in trouble, Sean. Can I buy you guys coffee?"

Two syllables of agreement sent her on her way. She had a thing about not getting coffee for men. She hadn't needed Flora to point out it was demeaning. But after being on the receiving end so often, she didn't mind.

They carried coffee and files into Graves's office. He was looking a lot better this morning, and so was McElroy. Annie sat apart from them, her notebook open. She glanced at MacHovec with a less than benign expression.

They started off with a recap of last night.

"Four," MacHovec said when the number of dead babies came up. "What happened nine months before that?"

"A cold night in January," McElroy said. "That'll do it every time."

"Let's stick to what happened," Graves said sternly.

When they were done, they talked about Stratton—"Anyone remember Stratton?"—and what Mrs. Constantine should be told.

"I think it's pretty clear Rinzler deserted her client, Cap," Jane said. "It's easy to see why. Whether Mrs. C. thinks so or not, he must have been teetering on the brink of depression. He hadn't seen his shrink for almost two years. The ME said there were no drugs in his body, good or bad, so he hadn't been taking his meds. Rinzler stopped coming, Rose stopped coming, Vale"—Defino inserted an obscenity—"either stopped looking in on him or was told to stop by Rinzler. We'll never know what went through Stratton's head, but he didn't cook, he didn't order food, he stopped drinking water, and he died. He was probably too weak to pick up the phone near the end."

"So we pin this on Rinzler," Graves said.

"Sure."

"Mrs. Constantine'll probably sue Social Services." It was clear the idea didn't appeal to him.

"Maybe not. They'll give her a hard time in court. She bears some of the responsibility. Sean, you got the time line?"

He handed it across the desk, the new updated version with highlights on the third week of October.

"Look at when she left for Paris."

"OK."

"That was October fifteenth, four days before those babies were born. She didn't see him just before she left. She told me the last time I called that she tried to reach him several times but he didn't answer. She just assumed he was OK."

"And you think he wasn't."

"We'll never know. We can't tell from Rinzler's records when she last saw him because she fudged it. Maybe Rinzler was busy with real cases and didn't get to see Stratton around the time Mrs. C. was calling. Then, with four babies at once, she didn't have time. She was calling four sets of adoptive parents and setting up four times and places to present them with their babies. She got the babies from the birth mothers, took them to the laundry, set up the meetings, and got a phone call the next morning that there was trouble. No way was she ever going to set foot in Alphabet City again after she and Fletcher got rid of the bodies."

"I'll handle all further communication with her," Graves said, his intent clearly understood. "This is a case where everyone failed the victim at the same time."

"Looks like it to me," Defino said. "Vale was being paid to check on Stratton. At least he got a Christmas present from Constantine, he told us. I think Vale's taking a walk on this. Fletcher's gone, Rinzler's gone, the laundry folks weren't involved in his welfare. Nobody's left who can give us answers."

"So what do we know about Rinzler's death? We reopened the case. How do we close it?"

"Jane and I have talked about it," Defino said. "If she

didn't kill herself, Fletcher killed her. He was a guy who knew what he was doing. The ME said the time of death was about six the previous evening, the day Rinzler was supposed to meet a friend for lunch. We don't think there was any lunch. We think she went to the hotel and waited for Fletcher to come and talk to her. Maybe they wanted to keep the baby business going and she had some ideas, or he did, on how to do it. Or maybe she borrowed money from him to pay back the adoptive parents and she needed to talk to him about it. Whatever it was, she was trouble for him and he decided to end it.

"He goes to the hotel late afternoon, early evening, when there's lots of activity, people going in and out for dinner, the theater, whatnot. He carries a backpack, not unusual for people in that class of hotel. It wasn't the Waldorf, remember. He's got his Colt fully loaded in the right-hand pocket of his windbreaker and he's wearing a baseball cap and keeps his head down in the elevator. Or he takes the stairs. Less chance of running into anyone. He's also got a cheap white cotton glove in the pocket with the gun.

"Rinzler's expecting him, opens the door, he goes in. If the TV isn't on, he turns it on. There's only the one bed and one chair to sit on so he takes the chair and she sits on the bed to his left while they talk. He sweet-talks her a while—this guy was good at that—and while they're talking he slips on the glove that's in his right pocket and grasps the gun. Maybe puts his left arm around her shoulders. When he's got her calmed down, he takes the gun out in his right hand where she doesn't see it, holds her right hand in his left near the gun, brings the gun up to her right temple, and pulls the trigger. One shot at close range, her body slumps off the bed to the floor. No pulse, so he's done the job. He puts the gun in her right hand, gets the prints where he wants them, job's done. Only her prints are on the gun and Lew Beech says it's a suicide and never asks why there are no prints on the bullets." He looked at Jane. "You want to pick it up? I need a glass of water."

"The rest of it," she said, "is just cleaning up after himself. He's got tissues in his pocket. He rubs the power button on the TV remote, smooths out where maybe he sat on the bed, maybe checks the hall again, then goes to the bathroom where he cleans his face and hands over and over, making sure there's no blood. The used tissues go with him, zipped back in the pocket.

"Then he changes into clothes he's got in his backpack, a jogging suit maybe, a fresh windbreaker just like the first one. The clothes he was wearing get rolled up and packed away. He checks the hall, it's empty, he goes down on the elevator or the stairs, out to Fifty-fourth Street and he's home free."

"And Lew Beech looks at the body, asks a couple of dumb questions, and says it's a suicide," Defino said, returning with a cup of water.

"But you can't prove it," Graves said. "So we have to close the case and say it's a suicide."

They hadn't expected anything else, but at least they had it on the record. Graves would want them to write it up. It was Friday, a good day to clean up loose ends.

"Good work, Detectives," Graves said, his face softening. "On another subject, Inspector Hackett has been promoted to deputy chief. He's giving a party next Wednesday night at a restaurant near One PP and he's invited the whole squad."

"Us?" Defino said. "I don't even know him."

"He's got a reputation as a generous person so yes, all of us. You too, Annie. Bring your best guy and have a good time. I've heard the chief of D is happy with our work. It must have filtered down."

They shuffled out of the office. "You going?" Defino asked.

"Sure. Why not? I've never been to one for a deputy chief."

"You're right. Why not?"

"Sean," she said, "you come too."

"I'll think about it. Free booze?"

"You're ten years out of date," Defino said.

"You bringing your boyfriend?" MacHovec asked Jane.

"I'll go with my partner. It's safer."

A formal invitation to the party was buried in her inbox. Defino called and accepted for both of them. Detectives from the other offices dropped by and asked if they were going. Everyone seemed to think the invitation meant a promotion was in the works. Fat chance.

They spent the day typing up Fives, discarding useless notes, repacking the material Judy Weissman had voluntarily surrendered and the smaller amount that they had taken from the storage place with the warrant. It was a day's work.

MacHovec got several calls during the day, obviously from his lawyer and others involved in the case. In the afternoon Graves dropped by holding the faxed preliminary autopsy on Fletcher, aka Lefferts. If he had used other names in his relatively short life, they were yet to be discovered, but MacHovec was working on it and if anyone could turn up information, he could.

"No surprises," Graves said. He dropped a copy of the report on MacHovec's desk. "This is part of the investigation. Give me my pound of paper when the whole thing comes in next week."

"More than a pound with the pictures," Defino said.

Not that it would matter. Mrs. C. would be unhappy that the investigation had been inconclusive and the team, while relieved, shared that feeling. Nothing compared to the satisfaction of hearing a perp confess or at least finding several upstanding citizens who could turn state's evidence.

MacHovec copied the ME's report and submitted one to the file. The file would be part of his defense, if it came to that, and surely part of his case with Internal Affairs. "Well," he said, locking his desk, "I'll see you folks Monday. Maybe we'll have a new old case to work on. Four weeks this one took."

"Have a good weekend," Jane said.

Defino nodded in MacHovec's direction, his attitude softening, but not enough to elicit a syllable.

Jane stuck around after he was gone and called her father, telling him the case had been resolved if not concluded definitively. He had heard about the shooting, as all New York had by that time, and he wanted Jane's insider's account of it.

"All I know is what you read in the papers, Dad. MacHovec called in a ten-thirteen and Defino and I ran. It wasn't far from the office, but by the time we got there, the street was full of brass and the action was over."

"The brass," he said. "Yeah, I think I heard the commissioner interviewed later on, one of those we-can't-say-anything-at-the-moment statements."

"Internal Affairs will give MacHovec a hard time, but I think he'll make it. I hope so." She asked about his health, about his friend Madeleine, and wound up the conversation. It was time to go home.

40

AS USUAL, SHE was one of the last to leave; both the whip's and the second whip's offices were empty. Outside the weather was glorious, the sometime January thaw having moved in from the south or west or wherever good weather came from. She jogged across Manhattan, sensing that it was working, that her legs were responding, her breathing less labored.

The weekend was before her and her cupboard was bare. She stopped and shopped as night fell, picking up a package of firewood on the way out. It was heavy and she was glad she didn't have far to carry it.

Juggling her bags, she opened the mailbox, tucked the mail in one of the bags, and rode the elevator up. In front of the door she put one bag down and worked the key, vaguely aware of a shadow at the other end of the hall. As she pushed the door open and lifted the second bag, she felt something hard in the middle of her back. She froze.

"Walk inside," a female voice said. "Put the bag down and raise your hands."

She did as she was told, trying unsuccessfully to place the voice. Names ran through her mind: Judy Weissman, Mimi Bruegger, Ellie Raymond, Mrs. Brusca. They all came up zeros.

"Put your purse on the floor. Take your coat off and drop it on the floor. *Don't turn around.*"

She complied. The Glock was in her handbag and her off-duty was in the bedroom closet. She was at the mercy of whoever this was.

"Walk into the kitchen and sit down with your hands on the table."

She walked to a far chair, turned to pull it out, and looked toward the doorway at the figure holding the gun. "Patricia Washington," Jane said, her voice barely audible.

"One and the same. Sit." Still standing, Washington pushed the hood of her black sweatshirt jacket off her head and unzipped it, never changing the direction of the gun.

From where Jane was sitting, it looked like an S&W, much like her off-duty. What kind of double life was this woman involved in that she had a gun? And then, as so often happened, a capsule of speech replayed itself. "I have a brother with a problem." A brother, no doubt, who had access to drugs and guns, who had served time and learned a lot in Rikers and Attica, enough to assist his social worker sister in whatever moneymaking scheme she dreamed up with Erica Rinzler. And they had never looked into his background.

"Patricia," Jane began.

"Don't call me by my first name, Jane. I'm your equal, not your subordinate, and I have the gun." Her eyes flashed as she spoke.

"I apologize. I just wanted to say we should talk." All the work at Rodman's Neck and the gun was in her bag on the floor of the foyer.

"There's been enough talk. Your partner killed my lover yesterday. Someone has to pay for that and you're closer than Queens. Where's your weapon?"

Lover. Fletcher had been her young, gorgeous lover. "In my bag," she managed to say, the view of Washington's living room passing before her eyes, the pipe and the tobacco pouch on the end table. "That was his pipe."

"I knew you saw it. Yes, it was his pipe. Where's your second gun?"

"In a closet."

Washington smiled. "Your partner got rid of the threat to your safety yesterday, right? Stick your legs out and pull up your pants."

Jane pushed her chair back and did as she was told.

Washington observed, but stayed where she was. Then she sat down across the length of the table from Jane, a long enough distance that she was unreachable. The gun remained poised. "It never even occurred to you that it could be me, did it? You were looking for a man and all I was was a boring civil servant living out her mundane life at Human Resources until it was pension time."

The table was old, thick, and heavy. Jane had moved it often enough to know its weight. She wondered if she had the strength to tip it up high enough and fast enough to shield herself from the inevitable bullets, which would almost certainly lodge in the thick wood. "We thought you were her friend."

"I was. We dreamed the scheme up together. It was perfect. We were helping little white and Asian girls out of a pickle they'd gotten themselves into and we were making money besides. Then a group of unlucky events happened all at once and we were in deep shit."

"I don't see why you couldn't have continued," Jane said, speaking conversationally, alternatives racing through her mind. "The babies' bodies were disposed of outside of Alphabet City. No one could connect you to them. The Chinese family would never talk."

Washington eyed her, picking up on what Jane knew. Before she could retort, the phone rang. Both of them froze.

"Don't move," Washington ordered.

It rang three times and Jane's recorded voice came on with the routine message followed by the beep.

"This is Flora. You'll never guess who invited me to a party to wet down his shield. Give me a call when you come home."

"You're not coming home tonight, Jane, and you've made your last call," Washington said. "You wanted to know what happened eight years ago after the babies died and Erica paid off the mothers. She got a bad case of guilt is what happened. Depression. Her sister thought it was because she lost her job. It was the babies, all those lovely little white babies that died in the Chinese laundry. She didn't have the guts for it. She wanted to go to the police and tell them what happened. She wanted to blow our nice little operation wide open."

"*You* shot her," Jane said, her shock audible.

"Someone had to, and the man you call Fletcher was too young and inexperienced to handle it. He was *very* good at some things and almost useless at others. Like I told him to watch you people and find out what you knew. Instead, he moves in on the cop's kid and tries to tough talk her father off the case. Not a smart move. He was too impetuous, but I loved that in him.

"Where was I?" Washington squinted, trying to remember. "Yes, Erica. We were to meet at that hotel, have dinner, and talk about what she intended to do. My brother got me a gun and gave me a lesson in making it look like suicide. It wasn't hard. I needed a change of clothes, some gloves, some clean-up material, and a dose of determination. If that stupid, weak bitch had mentioned my name to the police, that was the end for me. I couldn't let her do it."

That was the scenario Jane and Defino had worked out. Now she wondered how this one would end. If she tilted her chair and dropped to the floor, she might be able to crawl under the table before Washington got down with the gun. Whatever she decided to do, she had to make up her mind fast; Washington was coming to the end of her story and that would coincide with the end of Jane's life.

"So you made it look like suicide. You did a good job; that's how it went down. The detective on the case bought it just the way you planned it."

"I'm not stupid and neither is my brother. There was nothing in that room that would lead to murder."

Think and play for time. There wasn't a chance in hell that Hack would show up and no one else had the key. Saving her life was up to her. "The hotel operator said a man called."

"A man did call." Washington seemed both proud and amused. She had fooled the cops eight years ago and fooled them again this year. "But it wasn't a man who showed up at the hotel."

"Nice going." There were no other alternatives besides tipping the table and dropping to the floor. The table was empty and nothing nearby could be used as a weapon. All those lovely knives on the counter were out of reach. Even the salt and pepper mills were too far away to be of use. That's what came of being neat. Shit. To think neatness might cost her her life.

She began to feel panicky in earnest, her heartbeat increasing, her hands starting to sweat, her mouth drying. "Tell me about Maria Brusca," she said, grabbing for the only other topic she could think of, the last unanswered question.

"I followed you there after you went to where the streetwalkers were, over on the East Side."

"You did that too." Fletcher had been only a lover and

junior partner; sitting across from her was the brains and brawn of the operation, and the hatchet man.

"You were getting too close. I needed to shut her up. I knew if she was dead, her mother would be too scared to talk."

"Her mother did talk."

"Even I make mistakes."

"Vale," Jane said, dragging one final name out of her head. "He told Fletcher to go after my partner's daughter."

"Vale was nothing more than a watchdog and for a while he was Erica's lover. We didn't really need him but Erica brought him in. He was useful for running errands. He had my number and he kept me posted. Vale didn't tell anyone what to do. I made the decisions."

Decisions. Make a choice, Jane, she said to herself as Patricia Washington continued talking and then leveled her weapon at Jane. She pushed the chair to her right and dropped to the floor, then scrambled under the table as a shot was fired. Somebody call 911, she pleaded silently to her unknown neighbors, knowing the chances of that were minimal.

She thrust herself forward the length of the table as Washington pushed back her chair and stood, her knees straightening. She fired a second shot at the table, then sank to the floor as Jane charged toward her ankles, pushing them as hard as she could to destabilize Washington, listening as she did so for the sound of the gun dropping, but Washington must have held on to it.

The effect of the charge was to lift Washington's feet off the ground and tip her body face forward onto the table. Washington landed with a shout of pain and kicked as hard as she could to disengage her feet from Jane's grasp. It was a catfight and Washington still had the gun. Jane pushed the ankles forward, sliding Washington off the table and onto the floor.

They were about the same height, Jane a bit younger and several pounds lighter. But the gun was still in Washington's right hand and she was twisting and kicking to regain her advantage. Jane threw herself on top of Washington and tenaciously attacked the hand holding the weapon. On her back, Washington screamed and writhed as Jane pounded the wrist on the floor with her fist until the fingers released the gun; then she grabbed it.

Washington came after her, her eyes bright with fury, her hands reaching to kill.

"Get back, Washington," Jane shouted, but the assault never wavered. On her back on the floor, Jane tried to kick Washington's torso with both feet, rolling into the woman's body from a fetal position.

Washington dodged, deflecting some of the strength of the attack, and came at her again.

"I'll shoot you," Jane shouted. "Back off."

But backing off was not an option for Washington, her rage carrying her forward. Jane raised her knees again to ward off the onslaught, cocked the gun, pointed it dead in front of her, and squeezed the trigger.

The explosion was followed by silence. Jane slid backward, away from Washington, and breathed deeply twice. Shaking, she moved over to Washington's body, still aiming the gun at her. Quickly running her hand over the woman, she searched carefully for any bulges that might be more weapons. Satisfied that none were there, Jane checked for a pulse and found it weak. Holding her eyes on Washington, she moved to the phone and dialed 911.

"This is Detective Jane Bauer," she heard an unsteady voice say. She added her shield number. "There's been a shooting in my apartment. Send a bus and notify Central that I need a patrol supervisor ASAP." She gave the address and put the phone down, but did not hang it up. She might need an open line again. Then she went back to see if Patricia Washington was still alive.

Before the first sector car and the ambulance arrived, she called McElroy and told him what had happened. She was on the phone with Defino when the first two cops knocked and came through the open door. Seconds later, a sergeant and his driver arrived. "I'll get back to you," she said and hung up.

It was the first time her home had become a crime scene. She had her shield visible and the uniforms were very solicitous, one of them checking Washington and the other asking if there was anything he could do for Jane.

"I'm fine," she said weakly and went to the refrigerator for some ice. "Is she alive?"

"Just barely," the second cop said.

The ambulance took a little longer, the paramedics arriving with a gurney. They got down on the floor and tended to Washington while one of the cops called the Six for a detective.

Jane was glad Washington was alive. It meant they would get her out of the apartment as soon as they stabilized her. If she were already dead, the body would remain for hours on the kitchen floor while the detectives conducted their investigation. She didn't want to leave her home, didn't want to find another place to sleep tonight. She remembered when Maria Brusca's roommate, Darlene, had called, the day after Washington shot Maria, Darlene screaming that her home had become a fucking crime scene. Now it was happening to Jane.

McElroy showed up and Defino drove in from Queens. The lieutenant on duty at the Six arrived with the two detectives who had caught the case. As each succeeding group flowed in, Jane felt increasingly worse. It began to sink in that this woman had come here to kill her and in saving herself, she may have done to Patricia Washington what Washington wanted to do to her.

The phone rang and it was the Detectives Endowment Association trustee saying he was on his way over.

Marty Hoagland called and all she could say was "How did you find out?"

"Got a call. Look, I'm coming to get you. You should stay with us this weekend."

"Thanks, Marty, but I want to stay here."

"You sure?"

It was almost the only thing she was sure of. "Yes. I'll talk to you tomorrow."

Finally, the detective with the notebook sat down with her in the living room. A few feet away, the DEA trustee and the union lawyer took notes. They would interfere only if the investigating detectives or an overzealous boss tried to pressure Jane or make the case something it wasn't.

She pushed away the passport application, then turned it over and covered it with a magazine. Her mind was growing fuzzy, but it was still functioning.

"I'm Harry Jones," the detective said. He was tall and black and looked like he could punch you through the wall to the next apartment if he had a mind to. She liked his looks. "Let's start at the beginning."

"The beginning of tonight or the beginning of the case?"

His face showed confusion. "Let's start with tonight."

"I took the elevator up," Jane said. "I had two bags from the grocery. My key was in my right hand. I think I saw her, like a shadow down the hall. She may have come from the stairwell; I'm not sure. I put my key in the lock, turned it, and pushed the door open. That's when I felt the gun in my back."

She described the whole encounter, hearing her thin voice recount a tale of terror as though it were a recipe or the reading of an article in the paper.

"You want a glass of water?" Jones asked.

"Yeah, I'll get it."

"Stay there. I don't want you in the kitchen."

"Lots of ice," Jane said.

He came back and she drank it all, sucking a piece of ice at the end. She looked up and saw Marty come into the apartment.

"Marty." She went over and hugged him, feeling tears.

"It's OK, honey," he said. "You're gonna be OK."

"Oh Marty. I'm so glad you're here." She introduced him to Defino. "Marty and I were partners for about a hundred years," she said. Then she remembered Harry Jones and went back to the sofa and her story.

Hours passed. She went over the story again. I came up in the elevator. I had two bags of groceries. The key was in my hand . . .

"You want to fill me in on this case you were working on?" Jones asked.

"Give her a break, Detective," Lieutenant McElroy said. "I can tell you about it. Detective Defino here is also on the case. Detective Bauer has been more than cooperative and she may need some medical attention. She looks like she's about to drop."

The phone rang and someone answered it, spoke briefly, hung up. "She's dead," he said and a current charged through Jane's body.

She started shaking, put her hands in front of her face, and willed herself to be calm.

"OK, that settles it," McElroy said. "The interview is over now. You can talk to her tomorrow. She's told you everything she knows."

"Somebody get her out of here," Jones said.

Jane shook her head. "I'm not going anywhere. I live here. I'm staying. I just want to get to sleep."

They backed down but it was another two hours before they left. McElroy, Defino, and Marty all tried to convince her to leave, but she remained firm. She bolted the door after them, took a hot shower, and went to bed.

I came up on the elevator, she heard herself say. I had two bags of groceries. The key was in my hand. I put it in the lock and opened the door. . . .

Over and over the scene played itself out like an old black-and-white movie. She saw them all, Jones and Gordon, Marty and McElroy, the uniforms, the lieutenant from the Six, the other detective, the crime scene detectives. I took the elevator up. I had two bags of groceries. The key was in my hand. . . .

When she finally fell asleep, it was one in the morning or later. When the phone rang, she answered groggily.

"Are you OK?"

Her throat constricted. "I'm fine."

"You don't sound fine. I'll be there in half an hour."

"Don't, Hack. I'm too out of it to hold a conversation."

"Half an hour," he said and hung up.

He let himself in and called to her. She had tried to sleep again but couldn't. She had brushed her teeth, splashed cold water on her face, wrapped herself in a robe, and was sitting in the dark living room, where he found her. He dropped his jacket on a chair, sat down, and drew her to him.

"You want to tell me about it?"

"She came here to kill me."

"OK. OK, baby. Don't talk."

Leaning against him, she fell asleep.

41

BY THE TIME she arrived at Centre Street on Monday morning, they had all been informed. Everyone had something comforting to say. Captain Graves, who had called twice over the weekend, said, "Make an appointment with a shrink."

"Uh—"

"See a shrink," he ordered.

Shit. Hack had said the same thing. "I'll call Psych Evaluation at John Jay and arrange it," she promised. John Jay College of Criminal Justice was a short subway ride uptown.

She went to Annie's office and Annie hugged her and said how glad she was that Jane was OK.

"I need to see a shrink; at least the whip says I have to. Can you make me an appointment?"

"Sure. Man or woman?"

The question stymied her. "Just someone who can sign that I've been there so they don't bother me."

"You need to go right away?"

Jane managed a grin. "Do I look that bad?"

"I didn't mean—"

"I know. Whenever they've got a slow day."

They went into Graves's office at nine-thirty. Annie came in and handed Jane a slip of paper with a name, time, and address.

"Looks like we cleared the Rinzler case a day too soon," Graves said. "We all know what happened?" He looked at MacHovec, who nodded. "I have a little information that's going to be useful for Sean's case as well as the Rinzler case. A buddy of mine in ballistics put in some overtime on Saturday and checked the Smith & Wesson Washington had and the test firings confirm that it's the same gun that fired the bullets that killed Maria Brusca."

Jane said, "Good," and the others nodded. That, coupled with Washington's statement that Fletcher was her partner, should go a long way to clearing MacHovec. And Sean could dig up phone records that would likely include calls between them.

"So we've cleared the Brusca homicide for Midtown North," Graves said, "the Rinzler homicide, the kidnapping of Gordon's daughter, and maybe the legendary Judge Crater's disappearance."

"Only thing we didn't do is clear the Stratton case," Defino said.

"I talked to Mrs. Constantine over the weekend. She's not happy but I think she accepted our resolution of what happened. I referred to Sean's time line and although I didn't say it explicitly, I think she got the idea that she shares a small amount of responsibility for what happened to her brother."

They talked about it for a few minutes, MacHovec expressing the strongest opinions.

"That was some apartment," Defino said of the Park Avenue building. "They don't build 'em that way in Queens."

Graves smiled. "You should take a few days off, Jane," he said. "Just to calm yourself down."

"I'm taking a vacation in March. I don't want to waste any days."

"Where are you going?" Annie asked.

"Haven't decided yet. Somewhere out of range of New York cell phones."

"Good idea," Graves told her. "Well, you folks have paperwork to clean up. I'll see you Wednesday night."

That was Hack's party. Today he was starting as assistant borough commander of the Bronx, not too far from where Jane's father lived. He would have his hands full but he was taking time in March for Paris.

Flora called, Marty called, Detective Jones called twice. Jane made a note to call Judy Weissman, Erica Rinzler's sister, to tell her how the case had been resolved. Then she ducked out and walked to Little Italy and talked to Mrs. Brusca for an hour. When she was done, she felt exhausted and emotionally wrung out. She took a taxi home, locked the apartment door, poured some Stoli over ice, and put her feet up. This time, it was really over.

The party Wednesday evening was in a restaurant within walking distance from One PP and farther from Centre Street. Defino sprang for a cab. MacHovec went home. Apparently, if there was no free booze, he wasn't interested.

Flora arrived just as they did and they went in together. An attractive buffet table had been set up in a large back room. About twenty people were already there, grouped around Hack. Male laughter resounded in the room. A slim, beautiful uniformed woman with a deputy inspector's gold leaf made her way through the crowd of men, grinning, and hugged Hack like an old flame.

"Guess he can get a piece of anything he wants," Defino said, watching.

Jane laughed, feeling good. "Guess he can."

Flora's face made some gyrations of its own. "Think he'd give me a kiss like that?"

"Go for it."

Flora laughed. Then, seeing someone she knew, she excused herself.

Jane hung with Defino. McElroy joined them and they went through the buffet.

"Just needs a glass of champagne," McElroy said. "I guess he'll have that later."

The room had grown crowded. Jane and Defino talked to the other members of the squad, most of whom Jane hadn't said much to in the last month. One original team had left and three new members had come on board at the start of the year. One member was a woman.

"He'll be coming around to say hello," McElroy said. "The captain's with him."

Hack had begun to make the rounds, a daughter on each side of him. If his wife was there, she was invisible. It took twenty minutes for him to get to where most of Graves's squad was milling around. As he stopped to greet each member, he called him by name. Like the good boss he was, he had studied the pictures before the party and committed them to memory. They would still be there ten years from now.

The daughters were glowing, shaking hands with each guest and engaging them in conversation.

"Detective Defino," Hack said as he approached, offering his hand. "Good job on the Stratton case. Or was it the Rinzler case?"

"We aren't sure," Defino said. "Just glad it's behind us."

"So am I. Detective Bauer. That was some ordeal you went through over the weekend. You're lookin' good. My daughters, Susy and Michelle. Detective Bauer was on the front page of the *News* a couple of months ago, girls."

"I remember that," the older daughter said. "Daddy doesn't usually bring the *Daily News* home but he did that day. What a story."

"I'm glad that's behind me too."

Hack shook her hand, holding it that extra second, then moved on.

A few minutes later a group on the other side of the room started chanting, "Speech, speech."

Hack made his way to a lectern that was set up near the buffet table, his hand raised to quiet the crowd. "I actually have a few words I'd like to say," he said, taking some folded sheets from his jacket pocket and smoothing them open on the lectern. His eyes scanned the crowd until he found Jane and, looking directly at her, he licked his right index finger.

The gesture jolted her. She put the fingers of her left hand over her lips to hide the smile. Hack looked down at the papers as though he hadn't noticed and paged to another sheet. Then he began to speak.

"I'll drive you home," Defino said. "I'm parked at the Puzzle Palace."

"Thanks. I'd rather walk. It's a nice night."

"I'd feel better if I dropped you. You know, New York, the mean streets."

"Thanks, Gordon, but they're my mean streets. I'd really like to walk."

They parted outside the restaurant, Defino still concerned. Jane crossed the street and started walking north. She felt good, body and mind, heart and soul. He had done it so she could meet his daughters, invited a whole squad of people he didn't know so she could come with no questions asked. They were lovely girls, the older one about the age of her daughter.

She thought about her daughter and smiled. That was what she shared with Jackie Warren and Maria Brusca and the others; they were all birth mothers who gave up their children. Jane had been only one small step above them economically, and she had had two parents who supported her, the crucial difference in most of the cases.

At Houston Street she turned west. Reaching Broadway, she crossed, sensing at the exact center of the street that she had entered the Six, her spiritual home for ten years and now the place where she lived. It was where she was working when she fell in love with Hack. Hallowed ground, she thought, even though she'd almost died in that precinct five days ago.

She wove through dark streets that had names instead of numbers, names that went back to the beginning of time in New York, Bedford, Bleecker, Barrow. She would never work the Six again because she lived there and even with the bloody kitchen, she would never move. She was a New Yorker, and what New Yorker would move because of a little blood on the kitchen floor? The crime scene people had dug the bullets out of the table, leaving a deep hole from one of them and a small hole in the top where the second one had just pierced the surface. It was the rarest of mementos.

A cold breeze went right through her coat and chilled her. I have a good life, she thought, and I made it for myself. I saved that life on Friday night without any outside help and I hope I never have to do it again.

She crossed another street, heading toward Sheridan Square. This is my city and these are my streets and I will walk them and not be afraid. How many times in the last twenty years had she thought the same thing after a narrow escape? Too many to count. Walking the streets had always calmed her, pushed the jitters away, made her feel almost whole again.

At her building, she pushed the outer door open, sought her keys in her bag, and pulled them out along with something soft and plastic. She opened the mailbox and emptied it, went inside, leafing through the envelopes. *I had the key in my hand. I rode the elevator up to my floor. I put the key in the lock and pushed open the door.*

Inside, she looked at the plastic bag in her hand. Little beads were inside, Erica Rinzler's beads.

Tomorrow she would return them to the case file.